Dear Reader,

No matter how busy your day, there'll *always* be time for romance. TAKE 5 is a new way to indulge in love, passion and adventure—and still be on time to pick up the kids! Each TAKE 5 volume offers five condensed stories by top Harlequin and Silhouette authors. Now you can have the enjoyment and satisfaction of a full-length novel, but in less time—perfect for those days when it's difficult to squeeze a longer read into your hectic schedule.

This volume of TAKE 5 features five sizzling love stories...five *hot* escapes! A public-relations expert has trouble resisting a new client in *New York Times* bestselling author Barbara Delinsky's *Chances Are*. Bestselling Temptation author Vicki Lewis Thompson turns up the heat in *Mingled Hearts* and *Be Mine, Valentine*. And *USA Today* bestselling author Ann Major spins passionate tales of forbidden love and betrayal in *Married to the Enemy* and *Dazzle*.

Why not indulge in all four volumes of TAKE 5 available now—tender romance, sizzling passion, riveting adventure and heartwarming family love? No matter what mood you're in, you'll have the perfect escape!

Happy reading,

Marsha Zinberg
Senior Editor and

Barbara Delinsky was born and raised in suburban Boston. She worked as a researcher, photographer and reporter before turning to writing full-time in 1980. With more than fifty novels to her credit, she is truly one of the shining stars of contemporary romance fiction. This talented writer has received numerous awards and honors, and her involving stories have made her a *New York Times* bestselling author. There are over 12 million copies of her books in print worldwide—a testament to Barbara's universal appeal.

Vicki Lewis Thompson began her writing career at the age of eleven with a short story in the *Auburn Illinois Weekly*, and quickly became a byline junkie. Then she discovered she could write books—and she's written a lot of them! In the year 2000, Vicki saw her fiftieth book on the shelves. Vicki lives in Tucson, Arizona, and has two grown children and a husband who encourages her to write from the heart.

Ann Major lives in Texas with her husband of many years, and is the mother of three college-age children. She has a master's degree from Texas A&M at Kingsville, Texas, and has taught English both in high school and college. She is a founding board member of the RWA and a frequent speaker at writers' groups. Ann loves to write; she considers her ability to do so a gift. Her hobbies include hiking in the mountains, playing tennis, sailing, reading, playing the piano, but most of all enjoying her family.

TAKE5

Quick Reads. Great Escapes.

NEW YORK TIMES
BESTSELLING AUTHOR

Barbara Delinsky

Vicki Lewis Thompson

Ann Major

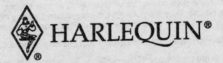

HARLEQUIN®

TORONTO • NEW YORK • LONDON
AMSTERDAM • PARIS • SYDNEY • HAMBURG
STOCKHOLM • ATHENS • TOKYO • MILAN • MADRID
PRAGUE • WARSAW • BUDAPEST • AUCKLAND

ISBN 0-373-83502-7

TAKE 5, VOLUME 6

Copyright © 2002 by Harlequin Books S.A.

The publisher acknowledges the copyright holders of the individual titles as follows:

CHANCES ARE
Copyright © 1985 by Barbara Delinsky

BE MINE, VALENTINE
Copyright © 1989 by Vicki Lewis Thompson

MINGLED HEARTS
Copyright © 1984 by Vicki Lewis Thompson

DAZZLE
Copyright © 1985 by Ann Major

MARRIED TO THE ENEMY
Copyright © 1992 by Ann Major

This edition published by arrangement with Harlequin Books S.A.

® and TM are trademarks of the publisher. Trademarks indicated with ® are registered in the United States Patent and Trademark Office, the Canadian Trade Marks Office and in other countries.

Visit us at www.eHarlequin.com

Printed in U.S.A.

CONTENTS

CHANCES ARE

Barbara Delinsky

"**I** think Veronica should be handling the public relations for the DIG Group," Liz Jerome informed her boss.

Karen Reynolds set down her coffee cup and eyed Liz. "She has her hands full."

Liz began to pace across the plush mauve carpet. "I met with Donovan Grant yesterday. We talked." That was an understatement. While she'd tried to talk strictly business, he'd mixed in more than a little sexual banter. Plus he'd insisted they have lunch together, and they'd ended up, not at the safe little restaurant Liz had imagined, but at his private retreat in the Adirondacks. "I'm the wrong person to work on this case," she added.

"Damn it, Liz. Don't start pacing on me. Sit down and tell me what the problem is."

Liz sent her a frustrated glance. "The problem is Donovan Grant. I don't think I can work with him. He's a tease."

"*Donovan Grant?* Are you sure we're talking about the same man? A tease? No. Charming, maybe." She grinned. "It's been a few years since I've seen him—other than grainy photos in magazines. Has he aged well?"

Liz reluctantly met her gaze. "He looks...good."

Liz recalled the fine sprinkling of dark hair on the backs of his hands, the way his Adam's apple bobbed when he swallowed, the litheness of his walk. But she didn't want to tell Karen about those things. They persisted in haunting her. Even the memory of his voice, warm and soothing, was a balm that grated.

"So, what's the problem?" Karen broke into her

thoughts. "You did discuss the contamination of his fields, didn't you?"

"Oh, yes. According to Donovan, the only sprays used on organically grown products are derived from plants such as garlic and nettle. Someone obviously went out of his way to spray something else."

"Does he have any idea who?"

Liz shook her head. "He's as much in the dark as the authorities are. He makes daily calls to the hospital in Sacramento where patients are being watched. We agreed the best thing would be for him to go public, discussing the problem and the security measures he's taken."

"Security measures?"

"Hired guards and a radar-type detector that can scan his fields and make sure nothing hits them from the air. That's how it was done—a fine-grain poison dusted over one of the fields at night."

"And there are no leads at all as to who it was?"

Liz shook her head.

Karen retrieved her coffee and took a thoughtful sip. "Okay. So you'll go public. What did you have in mind?"

Liz didn't even see herself as stepping into a trap. "There should be letters to stockholders, distributors and retailers. But the most effective thing would be a barrage of television and radio talk shows and news spots—Donovan would be perfect—and large ads in prominent newspapers. If fear leads to a boycott of his entire line of health foods—even though the contaminated items have been removed from the shelves—it could cause irreparable damage to the division. We have to hit soon and hard."

Karen sat forward. "Go to it then. I assume you can get background information at DIG headquarters. Did you arrange something with Donovan?"

Did I arrange something with Donovan? The question brought a jolt. Bounding from her seat, she made it to the window before she turned back. "He said he'd be by later to take me over. I thought you and I could agree on a replacement by then."

"A replacement? This case is tailor-made for you."

"I'm going to have trouble, Karen," Liz countered. Something in her gut stirred. "I just can't relax with him," she ventured at last. "And if I can't do that, I doubt I'll be able to do the kind of job this firm prides itself on. I'd really feel better if you put someone else on his case," she pleaded softly.

"And I think I'd never forgive myself if I did," Karen countered, walking Liz to the door. "Look, Donovan's a special person and I *know* that you're the best one for this job."

Liz sent her a look that said she saw through the flattery, but her position at Reynolds Associates meant too much to her to jeopardize because of one client.

LIZ HAD SECOND thoughts when Donovan appeared at her office door. This time it wasn't his balmy voice that disturbed her, or his smile, which was as brilliant as ever. It was the way he looked. Where were the crew-neck sweater, soft jeans and sneakers he'd sported yesterday?

He glanced down at himself, then sheepishly met her wide-eyed hazel gaze. "I wanted you to be more comfortable today. This was—is more what you expect, isn't it?"

He wore a three-piece suit of the finest beige wool and looked positively gorgeous. "What I expect?" she echoed.

"Formality and all?"

"You look fine," she finally managed, at which point

he grinned and she dropped her gaze to the desk. "Shall we go? We've got a lot of ground to cover." She kept focusing on the paper and pens she was stuffing into her bag.

"I thought we'd stop for lunch before we hit the office."

She ventured a skeptical glance. "You're always hungry."

"At mealtimes, yes." He grinned. "See, I'm trying to watch myself. That comment could have drawn a less innocent response. I just want you to know that I'm trying not to say things that upset you."

She took a deep breath, then let it out. "I'm just supersensitive, but it's my problem, not yours. You've got a job that needs to be done. I have no problems on that score."

"Then if I keep things on a business level we'll be okay?"

"Yes. That's what I was trying to say yesterday." When her phone rang, she excused herself and turned to answer it.

"Elizabeth Jerome here."

"Liz? It's Cheryl. I think we've got a problem."

Cheryl Obermeyer was the chief executive officer of her family's nationwide chain of discount department stores. It was presently having financial worries, and Liz, who'd spearheaded the chain's public relations for the past five years, was intimately aware of them.

"Uh-oh. Not something with the designer contract?" The chain had recently paid dearly for the right to carry the clothing of an internationally known designer.

"No, thank heavens. This time it's Ray. My brother is threatening to leave. It's bad enough that Ray seems to bungle whatever he's given, but now he's asking—no, demanding—more. I can't give him more responsibility if he can't handle what he's got, but if he walks out, he'll take the family image with him.''

"Maybe it's time to rethink the family approach," Liz suggested softly, but Cheryl's resistance was immediate.

"Not yet. There's got to be some way of calming Ray down. If you could speak to him—"

"But I'm in no position—"

"If you were to suggest to Ray that he'd do well to shine with what he's already got, he'd listen.''

"I don't know, Cheryl. It's really not my place.''

"As a friend, Liz? That's how I see you and why I've called.''

This last argument was potent. "Dirty play, Cheryl.''

"I know.''

Replacing the receiver in its cradle, she turned to Donovan. He didn't seem any the worse for his wait. "A client?''

"And friend.'' She rolled her eyes then narrowed her gaze on Donovan. "See? It's a mistake to mix business with pleasure.''

He grinned. "So there's hope for us after all.''

DONOVAN GRANT was interesting and companionable. As for his ability to pierce her soul with a glance, well, that was something she was simply going to have to learn to control.

Sliding his palm down her arm, Donovan took her hand. "You don't mind, do you? Walking, that is?''

His touch imbued her with a sense of protection, one she'd never missed in the past. "I'm used to walking to and from work.''

He looked down at her, catching her gaze. "Don't you ever get worried? New York's not the safest city.''

"No one notices me. I'm perfectly safe."

"You're a pretty woman. I'd say you stand out." When he tipped his head to study her, she tore her gaze away.

At the restaurant the smile he bestowed upon her was heart-stopping. "Would you like me to check your coat?"

"Uh, no, it's okay. I'll keep it with me."

"For protection?" he teased.

"I've been here before," she replied. "Management spares nothing when it comes to air-conditioning, even in October."

He held two fingers up to the hostess and put his hand lightly to Liz's back when they were gestured onward to the small corner table. Dropping into his chair, he leaned forward and grinned.

Discomfited by his attention, Liz scanned the room. "I'm surprised we were seated so quickly. Those others waiting must need bigger tables."

"I, uh, reserved a table."

"But they don't take reservations—"

"Anyone takes reservations with the proper incentive. I wanted you all to myself."

"Donovan, you promised...." But his grin was contagious. "Are you always this way?"

"Nope."

"Then something must be up. Tell me the police have a lead on the mad poison duster."

"If only."

"Oh. By the way, Karen agreed with everything we discussed yesterday."

"You're handling my case, and if you and I agree, that's all that counts. I trust you. Do you trust me?"

She looked him in the eye. "No."

He sighed and sat straighter. "Well, that's something I'll have to work on."

When he continued to look at her, Liz made a ceremony of studying her menu. "Do you know what you want?"

He didn't even glance at the selection printed. "Uh-huh."

She looked up sharply, sure she'd caught a hint of suggestiveness in his drawl. "Donovan...." she warned.

"I like your eyes. Especially when they twinkle. Hey, don't glare. I didn't mean any harm. I *do* like your eyes."

What Liz was thinking was that she liked Donovan's eyes, too—so clear and chocolaty—and she wished she didn't. His eyes could see so much—the beautiful blonde at the next table, the stunning brunette at the table beyond that. And here she sat, with straight brown hair, nondescript features and a figure as plain as the rest of her. Donovan's attentiveness had to be a sham.

The waitress came over to take their order. When they were alone again, he relaxed back in his chair. "So, where do we start this afternoon?"

Liz, too, relaxed. "I'd like to learn as much as possible about the DIG Group. I'd like to meet with your sales and marketing people and look at the media coverage you've had in the past."

"Sure. It's all been pretty straightforward, though, because our products and services have sold themselves. This is the first time we've had to specifically think about PR. When I first spoke with Karen the other day, she mentioned several other crisis cases you've handled. Do you thrive in crises?"

"Actually, noncrisis cases are probably harder to handle. In your case, we're starting with a newsworthy event, so that the media will jump at the opportunity to interview you. In the case of, say, an educational-publishing house that may want to push one of its publications, you have to really *work* to drum up public interest. We can spend weeks brainstorming before we hit on the tack we want.''

''And you're all women at the agency.''

Liz grinned. ''Each and every one of us.''

''Was that a drawing card for you?''

She paused for a minute. She *had* been attracted to Reynolds Associates because it was an all-female firm. Unfortunately, she didn't want to have to explain to Donovan.

''Karen and I hit it off. I admire her for what she's built, and what with the client list she had even then, I couldn't have refused her offer.''

''You haven't answered my question.'' This time it was Donovan's eyes that twinkled.

But Liz wasn't about to answer his question. ''How did *you* know we were all women?''

''I had a hunch, knowing Karen. She was a libber way back.''

''You don't believe in women's lib? You'd like to have a woman at home counting the minutes until you step through the door?'' she teased.

But Donovan was very serious. ''Not at all. I wouldn't respect a woman who did nothing but wait for me.''

''Then what would you want?''

''A woman who had a career but who prized her quiet times with me as much as her hectic ones at the office. A woman willing to share the responsibilities of a home and family.''

Liz felt her throat grow tight. She wondered at the pang of yearning that had momentarily stolen through her iron guard. ''You're an idealist, Donovan. But it's the woman who usually ends up shouldering the larger share.''

''I cook. I do laundry. Okay, so I hire someone to do the cleaning. But I've lived alone long enough to know that I want more from life than a dark and empty house. Maybe I am a dreamer." He sighed. "God knows I haven't been able to find a woman—" his expression grew suddenly softer, more vulnerable, and his gaze fell to her lips "—to share my dark and empty house."

For a minute Liz could scarcely breathe. She could have sworn he was making a proposal. But she knew better. Donovan liked to tease and knew she was susceptible to it.

Corralling her senses, she wrinkled up her nose and played along. "I hate dark and empty houses."

His gaze slid from her lips to her eyes and was every bit as embracing. "It wouldn't be if we were sharing it."

"But I already have a place to live," she countered.

"You could move."

"I don't want to."

"Then...you're not the kind of woman I'm looking for?"

She rolled her eyes. "Ah. I'm finally getting through."

As though a prime hurdle had been cleared, the rest of their lunchtime passed without a hitch. When they finished, he walked her to his office. He didn't hold her hand this time, and one tiny part of her missed the warmth of his strong fingers. He maintained a running commentary on the history of the DIG Group and its installation in the Park Avenue office toward which he guided her.

Donovan was well liked by his staff. Liz could see it in the smiles that lit faces when he appeared. She felt mildly bereft when he deposited her with the head of his sales department and took his leave. From sales she was shuttled to marketing, then to advertising. In the course of the afternoon she learned that, in addition to those endeavors she already knew about, the DIG Group had divisions that sold running and outdoor gear as well as spa equipment. As if that weren't enough to keep one Donovan Grant occupied, she learned that he regularly ran management-training sessions for upper-echelon employees of companies from coast to coast.

As he'd suggested, the publicity the Group had hitherto received had been straightforward, but in no instance had Donovan personally capitalized on the attention. His would be a fresh face, a new voice. And he'd go over famously.

"You're looking very pleased," came that "new" voice.

"I'm impressed." She dropped her gaze to the report she was holding, to buy time to compose herself. "Your reputation's well earned. I hadn't realized you were into sporting gear."

"The motivation for that was selfish. I like sports."

"Do you run?" she asked.

"Several times a week. I also scuba dive when I can. And sky dive."

"Ah-hah. You like to tempt the Fates." She sounded more cocky than she felt.

"That I do. How about dinner?"

She glanced at her watch and gasped. "Oh, Lord, I hadn't realized it was so late. I have to run."

"You run, too?"

"When I'm late, yes." She was about to lift the stack of reports when Donovan's hand caught her wrist. She shrank into herself but couldn't go far because Donovan's free arm was around her waist, drawing her forward. His eyes skimmed each of her features.

"Don't," she whispered, but she couldn't turn her head, couldn't free herself from his grasp, couldn't run.

He said nothing at first, simply continued to explore her

features with a slumberous gaze. "It's inevitable, Elizabeth," he whispered. "Why do you fight it?"

"Nothing's inevitable," she answered painfully. She closed her eyes and moaned, but the sound was barely half out when it was swallowed by Donovan's mouth. With a muted groan of protest, she tried to push him away, but his fingers were suddenly tangled in her hair, holding her head so that she couldn't escape his lips.

Later, Liz was to analyze that kiss, from its first unrelenting claim, through its gradual softening, to its final devastating persuasiveness. She'd remember the way his mouth had slanted over hers, firmly and possessively, then with finesse and a tempered hunger. She'd remember the way his tongue had stroked hers, challenging, calling, tempting. And she'd be shocked that she'd allowed herself this cruel glimpse of paradise.

Now, though, determined only on escaping, Liz broke free and stormed ahead. She didn't look at him once during the wait for the elevator or the purring ride down. Only after she'd somewhat ungraciously flounced into a cab did she hold out her arms for the reports Donovan held in his hands. Not relinquishing them yet, he leaned over to talk to her.

"I'm off to New Orleans tomorrow but I'll be back the next day."

"Fine," she gritted. "I'll pass these reports and my notes on to whomever will be taking over your case."

"You'll be handling it. It's either you or no one."

"You'd actually go to another firm? That's childish."

"See? We're alike that way."

"BUT I JUST CAN'T work with him."

"He said he'd take his case to another firm," Karen stated.

"He's bluffing. He loves games. Listen, Donovan's out of town. The transfer can be a fait accompli by the time he returns, and once he gets a look at either Veronica or Julie or...or Brenda or Sheila, he'll forget me in an instant."

"I doubt that," Karen began, only to be interrupted when her secretary rushed in with a pained look on her face.

"I told him he'd have to wait, but he insisted." She darted nervous glances from Liz to Karen and back, and Liz's eyes widened, expecting Donovan's momentary entrance. But another man stepped into view. He was younger and rather gangly.

Liz was on her feet in an instant. "Jamie!" It had been over six months since Liz had seen her brother Jamie. He lived better than twenty-five hundred miles away.

"Can we go somewhere?" he asked tersely.

Without trying to draw anything further from him, Liz led her brother back to her own office, closing the door quietly when he'd entered and thrown himself into the nearest chair. "Okay, Jamie," she said gently. "Nice and slow. What's brought you to New York?"

"I'm in trouble."

It was nothing new. "What is it?"

"I've been going with this girl—"

"Anne?"

"No. Another one. Her name's Susan. We got into a fight and, well, I guess I hit her."

Liz closed her eyes for a pain-filled minute, then opened them and slowly stepped over Jamie's sprawled legs and made her way to the other chair. She needed to sit down. "You hit her." With a soft moan Liz let her head fall back. "Oh, Jamie," she whispered. "Why?"

"Because she was taunting me. She was making me

feel like a jerk, and I don't have to take that from any-one.'' He gave a grunt. ''She's pressing charges.''

Liz bolted forward.

''I was on a plane before the police could reach me. Susan, dummy that she is, called to tell me they were on their way.''

Liz pressed her fingers to her temple, which had begun to throb. ''Have you spoken with Dr. Branowitz?''

''What good would that do? He's only a shrink, for God's sake, not a miracle worker.'' Then his features seemed to crumble. ''What if I do it again? I didn't mean to hit Susan. I didn't plan it. It just happened. Maybe I'm just like *him!*''

''You're not,'' Liz snapped, then quickly slipped from her chair to kneel beside her brother. ''You're not one bit like dad,'' she vowed. Liz reached for the phone. ''What's Branowitz's number?'' She jotted it down as Jamie recited it, then promptly dialed. Had she been more familiar with psychiatrists, she would have known she'd only reach an answering service. Frustrated, she left her number with a long message for the doctor. Replacing the receiver, she eyed Jamie again. ''How long does he take?''

He shrugged. ''Who knows? You made it sound like a matter of life and death, so my guess is it'll be soon.''

''It *is* a matter of life and death! There's an *assault* charge against you. You could go to prison. And I doubt your employer would take kindly to that.''

''The worst won't happen. That's why I'm here.''

Liz hadn't stopped to wonder why he'd come. She hadn't had to. Jamie had run to her each time he'd dropped out of school, then again when his graduation was threatened at the last minute because of an argument he'd had with one of his professors, then again when he was given his walking papers from the first job he'd had.

It was nearly an hour later that the call came through. Dr. Branowitz agreed to contact the police, as well as a skilled attorney. For her part Liz promised to have Jamie on an evening flight back to San Francisco. After giving the doctor her home phone number, Liz left word with her secretary as to where she'd be, then she and Jamie walked home.

By the time the doctor called again, his news was encouraging. The lawyer, who had agreed to meet with Jamie early the next morning, had already been in touch with the police and felt confident he could help Jamie.

Liz thanked the doctor profusely, then sagged back into the sofa feeling drained. Images of the past rose to haunt her, and she knew she'd get no peace until Jamie was back in San Francisco. Selfish though it might be, she could never live in the same city as her brother. Oh, she'd always take care of him, send him money, bolster him when he ran to her. But she'd always be relieved when he left.

"You committed me to flying back tonight," Jamie said.

"You should have been meeting with the lawyer *today*—"

"You don't want me here," he interrupted. There was a sullenness to him that she'd seen before and was sure she'd see again. "Maybe I cramp your style. Maybe you've got a hot date for the weekend."

"Why are you doing this to me?" Liz asked, feeling hurt. "I don't cut you down. We're brother and sister. Don't you think it would be better to share a little respect?"

"Do you respect me?"

"Of course I do. I know what you can do and be if you put your mind to it."

"I know," he said, his eyes cast downward. "It's just that sometimes I don't believe it myself."

With a sad sigh, Liz put her arm around her brother's waist. "I have faith in you, but it looks like it's the good doctor who's going to have to help you build that faith in yourself."

*

IT WAS NEARLY nine-thirty before she was finally back home after taking Jamie to the airport. Her headache had escalated to migraine proportions. Her only desire was for her dark room and bed, and utter silence.

When the phone rang shortly after ten, she moaned, half expecting to hear Jamie on the other end of the line with a song and dance about missing the takeoff.

It was Donovan. "I just wanted to say hi."

She couldn't seem to lift her head from the pillow.

"Liz, are you all right?"

The genuine worry in his voice prevented her from lying. "I'm not feeling well, that's all. I have an awful headache…if I could only get some sleep."

"I can take a hint."

"No, no, Donovan," she returned in earnest. "I didn't mean it that way." And she didn't. The sound of Donovan's voice was strangely reassuring. "It's just that I feel so tired but I *still* can't sleep."

"Try a little warm milk."

She groaned. "I don't think I could get it down."

"How about a warm bath?"

"I *know* I couldn't drink that."

Only when Donovan chuckled did Liz realize what she'd said. In the darkness she smiled.

"That's better," he said. "I'm going to hang up now so you can rest. Can I take you to dinner tomorrow night?"

"That's a sly move. Trying to take advantage of me when my brain is all muzzied, but it won't work."

"How about Saturday night?"

"I can't. I'm planning to sleep off every bit of the aggravation you've caused me this week." Her annoyance was very much put on. "Sorry about that."

"No, you're not. If you were really sorry, you'd reconsider."

"I feel so lousy, Donovan. Please, not now?"

"Okay. Listen, love, you take care. If you don't feel right in the morning, stay home."

"Yes, Donovan."

"And call a doctor."

"Yes, Donovan."

"And when I get back I'll come over and play nurse."

"No, Donovan."

"Good night, love."

"Night, Donovan. *And thank you for calling.*"

WHEN HER FRONT BUZZER rang early Sunday morning, she had to practically pry her eyes open and drag herself from bed.

The sight she met in her peephole brought her fully awake. "Go away, Donovan! I'm sleeping!"

"Come on, open up. The damn coffee's spilled all over the bag and it's burning my hands!"

She pressed her forehead to the door. Straightening, she slowly opened it.

Without so much as a hello, Donovan dashed past her and headed for the kitchen, which wasn't hard to find since Liz's apartment consisted of a living room, a single bedroom and bath, and the kitchen. "Bagels and cream cheese and lox," he announced. "And coffee that didn't quite make it. Have a seat. I can't eat until my hostess begins."

She put one hand on her hip. "I told you I didn't want to go out with you."

He held up a hand. "Uhh. We're not 'out.' And you said no to dinner. You didn't say anything about breakfast."

"I thought it was understood," she said, but she sat anyway and watched Donovan take a mammoth bite of bagel.

"Mmm." He closed his eyes. "This…good."

"Donovan, you're changing the subject."

His expression grew serious. "You sounded pretty lousy the other night. Are you feeling better now?"

She stared at him for a moment. "Yes," she answered more softly, and bit into a bagel. "You're right," she said at last. "This *is* good. Did everything go well in New Orleans?" she asked.

"Very well. There's a company down there, Ullman, looking for a buyer, a so-called white knight. Company stocks are being bought by some questionable groups and the directors want to be covered."

"If the merger went through, it'd be another division of the DIG Group?"

"A diversifying one. I think it could be a good move." He licked the cream cheese on his finger and grinned. "But it's your turn. Tell me what you've done."

"I drew up some preliminary letters for you to look over. Unfortunately they're at the office. I didn't expect to…see you."

"That's okay. You were right. The weekend isn't for work."

"I'd have thought you'd be champing at the bit to get a campaign rolling."

He shrugged. "I've hired *you* to do the champing. So, what else have you been up to? What brought on the headache the other night?"

If only he hadn't sounded so truly concerned she might not have found herself talking of Jamie. Donovan listened, asking thoughtful questions, expressing sympathy, giving support. Liz told only of the most recent crisis. She wasn't *that* taken with the man's interest that she'd go into a family history. Unfortunately, that was just what Donovan wanted.

"Are your parents still alive?"

She hesitated for an instant. "My father, yes. My mother died years ago. He's still in Baltimore."

"How about Jamie? Barring emergencies like the one this week, do you see him much?"

"He's far away. It's pretty expensive...flying across the country. I do call him once a week." She looked up then and forced a smile. "Why does this feel like an inquisition?"

"I'm just curious. It's strange." He did look puzzled. "I pictured you surrounded by family and friends."

"Coming from you that's a compliment, since you've certainly seen my acid side."

"Nah. Never acid. Maybe nervous or defensive. But you're more comfortable with me now. Just look at you, sitting here in your nightgown and robe having Sunday breakfast with me."

"I'm only doing this so you'll see reason," she retorted defiantly. "I'm perfectly ugly in the morning."

"Are you kidding?" Donovan's voice grew very quiet. "You look that much more desirable coming straight from bed."

Liz jumped from her chair, but he caught her wrist and, tipping her off balance, brought her down on his lap.

"You don't believe me, do you?" he asked.

"Not for a minute. Now let me up."

He didn't bother to answer, but began kissing her, warming her from the inside out. He kissed her again and again, taking but the briefest of breaths between forays. She couldn't pull away because he suddenly seemed her sustenance, more so even than air or light or the blood that pumped so rapidly through her veins. For the moment she was willing to believe that she was different and special and, yes, desirable.

His fingers skimmed her breasts en route to the tiny buttons at her throat when she realized what was happening. He was spreading the vee of her robe apart.

"Don't...oh, no...." Torn apart inside, she begged, "No...please, no...." She was whimpering and close to tears as utter terror filled her. When he looked up in surprise, she clutched the lapels of her robe together.

"I...I don't understand," he began hoarsely.

"You can't do that," she whispered, her head tucked low.

He took a ragged breath. "But...you were...it felt...

She was shaking her head.

"Elizabeth?"

In response she moved awkwardly to her chair, her knuckles white at the neck of her robe. Donovan sat back in his chair and closed his eyes. When he'd opened them, he was in control.

"Why don't you get dressed," he suggested quietly. "We can take a ride up to my place and go for a walk in the woods."

Liz didn't answer for a while, and when she did it was still without raising her eyes. "I don't think...I should."

"I wouldn't try anything, Liz. I swear it. I just want to spend some time with you. Totally innocent. Brother and sister, if you'd like."

It wasn't so much what he'd said as the undercurrent of urgency in his voice that swayed Liz. "Brother and sister," she echoed, eyeing him shyly.

THEY ARRIVED AT THE HOUSE shortly before noon. It was a beautiful day, with the woodlands at their autumnal best.

"Why don't you wander out back? I'll open up the house and then we'll go exploring," Donovan said.

She nodded and headed around the house. The sound of gurgling water lured her on, and she soon found herself by a brook that wound through Donovan's property and into the woods. Donovan found her moments later. "Nice?"

"Mmm. Wonderful. Such a marvelous retreat."

He sank to the ground on a cushion of moss several feet from her. "Early some mornings you can see deer here."

She let him draw her to her feet and toward a path. The crackle of twigs underfoot blended with the sounds of the breeze. In a voice as soft and airy as a whisper of the leaves overhead, he pointed out various animal habitats.

In time they came to an open meadow and sat, side by side, enjoying the serenity in silence. At length Donovan broke it with an indrawn breath, as though he'd been millions of miles away.

"When I was a kid, my parents used to take us off to fancy resorts in the mountains. I thought it was boring. I wanted to be *doing* things. By the time I was fifteen I was arguing that it was a grand waste of money when we could just walk into the nearest park if we wanted fresh air." He chuckled. "I think I was missing the point."

"Which was?"

"To get us all together. To remind us we were a family. I wish I'd understood it sooner."

"Most kids are that way."

"Were you?"

"I suppose. Then again, my situation was different. With my mother dead, we didn't have much of a family life."

"Who took care of Jamie and you?"

"A housekeeper. We'd always had help because my mother wasn't able to do much, but in the later years of her illness dad got harder to live with, so there was a fair turnover."

"He must be a lonely man."

"I wouldn't know," Liz stated simply. She shot him a sad glance. "Loving family I've got, isn't it?"

But he was feeling a sadness of his own. "I could have had all you didn't, and I threw it away for a while. It's pathetic, when you stop to think of it."

"You didn't throw it away. You simply... deferred it."

"Some things you can't gain back. My mother's gone. My father's getting older. My sister and brother have their own families and lives."

Liz put her hand on Donovan's arm and shook it gently. "Donovan? It's not like you to bemoan the fates."

"I know," he said, his eyes meeting hers. "But you bring some things out. You seem to be everyone's confidante. Who's yours?"

She laughed. "I'm the lady of steel. I don't need a confidante...." Her voice trailed off and she looked away.

Frightened of pushing her, Donovan began to talk of other things. They left their tree stump, retracing their route to the house. By the time he'd built a fire, she felt relaxed and surprisingly happy.

True to his word, Donovan was perfectly brotherly, though so much more thoughtful than Jamie had ever been that Liz had to redefine the term.

She and Donovan made dinner together and ate before the fire, talking. Liz was stunned that she and Donovan shared so many views and were able to discuss their differences.

All too soon, the day ended. While Donovan drove back to the city, Liz sat contented in the passenger's seat, dozing at the last. She was groggy when he walked her to her apartment, and she only half heard herself ask him in for coffee before she dozed off again on the sofa.

When she awoke the brother was gone, replaced by the man who'd been tethered all day.

HE WAS KISSING HER, sliding his body over hers, shaping her hip, the inside of her thigh. Donovan's deep groan sparked a warning in the back of her mind, but she had to know where the anticipation that coiled in her belly would lead.

The quivering tendrils that shot to the pit of her stomach had her arching her hips. Everything in her body responded so naturally to Donovan that surely this was meant to be, she reasoned from amid her dream.

But when he raised his body to allow his fingers a hasty release of the snap of her jeans, the sound reverberated in her brain. "Oh, God!" She gulped and grabbed his wrists. "No, Donovan…oh, my God…stop!"

He raised his head and stared at her, dropped his gaze to study the stiff way she lay, then slowly pushed himself up until he sat an arm's length away. "All right, Liz," he said with remarkable calm, "you're going to tell me why. Was there someone in the past who hurt you? A minute ago I saw terror in your eyes."

She quickly shook her head, unable to speak.

"*Was* there someone?" Again she shook her head. "Never?" She shook her head a third time. "Please. I have to know. Is it something about me?"

"It's me," she whispered at last.

"You are a virgin."

Very slowly, she nodded.

He was closing the distance between them then, taking her in his arms. "God, Liz. I wish I'd realized it sooner. It's just that I didn't expect... I mean, you're nearly thirty...I just assumed...." He pressed her head to his chest and stroked her hair. "Do you have any idea how good it makes me feel to know that I'll be the first?"

"You won't be," she stated sharply. "You don't need me. I'm just a...a plaything."

"Like hell you are," he growled. Donovan was turning her around. "Why is it you find it so hard to believe that I want you?"

When she saw that he was staring at her in amazement, she lowered her hands and pleaded, "Look at me, Donovan. I'm nothing. I'm plain and unattractive and—"

"You're wrong. You're a beautiful woman from the inside out."

"Now that," she stated baldly, "is an outright lie."

"I don't lie, Liz. You just refuse to see what I'm saying."

Liz sighed and dropped her chin. "I don't need flattering, Donovan. I'm a realist." She paused. "I think you'd better leave now."

"You'd just forget this whole thing as if it never happened?"

She tipped up her chin and held it firm. "I already have." She simply stared at him until he turned and left. Then she crumpled onto the sofa and cried.

THE DIG GROUP letters went out, and Donovan's media blitz took shape. By the end of the week she was able to present Donovan with a list of a dozen appearances and interviews she'd set up for the next two weeks.

For his part, Donovan was thoroughly accessible. When she called, he came. When she spoke, he listened. She prepped him on ways to most effectively handle the press, posing questions interviewers might ask, then helping him to analyze and strengthen his answers.

He made no mention of what had happened at her apartment. Nor did he try anything further, other than to issue an occasional invitation to dinner that she refused in the same teasing tone in which it was offered. But she always felt an inkling of excitement waking up on a morning when she knew she'd be seeing him, and if there was a method to his madness in giving her space, she was unaware of it.

While he was on the road he called her at least once a day in the office and then again at her apartment at night to discuss his day with her, to hear about what she'd done. And again they lapsed into the sexual bantering she'd thought they'd left behind. She told herself that it was really harmless. But she spent more and more time thinking about it, about *him,* and fearing trouble.

IT BEGAN the following week. He called her at seven to say that he had to make an emergency trip to New Orleans.

"It looks really good for the merger, but there are a couple of things I've still got to iron out. I should be back by tomorrow night. Meet me then?"

"I can't, Donovan. I'll be with a client."

"Damn it, Liz. There's always something. You're avoiding me."

"We could meet in the office the morning after you get back."

"How about at the Park Lane for breakfast? Hell, there's nothing I can do in a public restaurant, Liz."

She clicked her tongue. "You're in a temper this morning."

"Come on, Liz. What with the circles you've had me running in the past few weeks, I've gotten zilch done at the office. It'd save both of us time. Breakfast?"

Feeling unbelievably helpless, Liz nodded. "What time?"

THEY WERE SEATED at a round table by the window overlooking Central Park. It was good to see him—just how much, she tried to ignore.

They ordered breakfast, and Liz looked up to find him staring at her. "Don't look at me that way, Donovan."

"I enjoy looking at you. I feel like I'm finally home." He grinned. "Hey, what's the word on Jamie? Is everything okay?"

"For the time being, yes. The girl decided to drop her complaint. Not that she didn't have a case. But the lawyer told me he was fully apologetic when he saw Susan."

"Did he sound it to you?"

"I haven't spoken with him." She realized how odd that sounded and rushed on. "I'll talk to him next week, when things have died down."

"Next week's Thanksgiving. Have you made plans?"

She brightened. "I'm going for dinner on Long Island with some friends from the office. How about you?"

"Since you're deserting me, I guess I'll have to put in an appearance in St. Louis."

She eyed him boldly. "Don't give me that 'since you're

deserting me' line. You've had reservations for months to get on a plane going anywhere for Thanksgiving.''

''You'd like my family.''

''I'm sure I would, but I can't go. I've already got plans.''

Their breakfast arrived then, and they set to work eating. It was only as they prepared to leave that Donovan reached into his pocket. ''Here. This is for you.''

Liz stared at the box, then Donovan.

''Go on. Open the box.''

She couldn't remember the last time someone had bought her something just for the fun of it. Hands trembling slightly, she slid the ribbon from the box and lifted its lid. ''They're stunning,'' she breathed. ''But…there's one problem.''

''They're for pierced ears. I know. I debated about that for the longest time.'' Actually what he'd spent the longest time thinking about were the *other* earrings he'd buy her in time.

''I don't know, Donovan. They're so beautiful….''

He took her hand then and squeezed it. ''Think about it for a while. I'll take you if you want to have your ears pierced. If not, I'll have a jeweler put on a conventional back.''

She still didn't look up. ''You didn't have to buy me anything.''

''That's what made it fun. Will you…think about it?''

''Yes.'' She looked up then, her eyes suspiciously moist.

LIZ DIDN'T HEAR from Donovan that weekend. She spent time thinking about the Sunday they'd spent at his house north of Troy, spent time thinking about the closeness she felt toward him, spent time looking at the earrings he'd given her.

On Tuesday there was good news. An anonymous tip had led federal authorities to a man suspected of poison-dusting Donovan's fields. He was being booked.

"Today is worth marking," Donovan announced on the phone. "I'll pick you up at the office tonight and we can—"

"I can't, Donovan," Liz broke in. Of the thinking she'd done, a good deal had centered on the ramifications of her accepting his gift.

He breathed an undisguised sigh of frustration. "Then I won't see you before Thanksgiving."

"No," she acknowledged quietly.

It hurt her to hurt him. She thought about him long into the night, and was still thinking about him when she was at her desk, supposedly working.

On Wednesday she had her ears pierced.

*

HE CALLED HER at the office after Thanksgiving, then again at home, when she was in her nightgown getting ready for bed.

"A date. Tomorrow night," he began.

"But we—"

"Have a business relationship? We've *had* that. Now it's time to move on. Or haven't you thought about that?"

"I've thought about it," she whispered. "There's no point."

There was a momentary silence from the other end of the line, then a more gentle, "What're you afraid of, Liz? I won't hurt you. I've told you that before. I've tried to prove it to you by taking things slow. I haven't pushed you lately, have I?''

"No. But you're pushing me now."

"I want you, Liz."

"You don't want me. Not really."

"Christ, we're going in circles. Look, I'm flying in tomorrow and I'll be at your place by seven."

"I won't be here."

"Where *will* you be?"

"That's none of your business." When she heard him grunt she relented. "I'm going to a party." It was a cocktail party at Cheryl Obermeyer's home. Actually she'd been on the fence about going, but it seemed the perfect out now.

AND SO SATURDAY NIGHT found her at the cocktail party she'd rather have skipped.

Liz lifted her glass to her lips and would have taken a healthy swallow of whatever it was the bartender had handed her this time. But Cheryl removed the glass from her fingers and set it on a passing tray.

"Talk to me, Liz. And don't tell me nothing's wrong. Who is he?"

Later Liz would blame her loose tongue on liquor. But for the moment she was beyond anything but sharing her woes with Cheryl. "His name's Donovan Grant."

Cheryl gave a whistle. "Grant. The DIG Group? I've read he mans four very profitable divisions—"

"Six. And about to take over the Ullman conglomerate."

Cheryl's eyes widened, then narrowed on her brother, who had sidled up during the conversation. "We're having a private discussion, Raymond." Tightening her grip on Liz's elbow, she inched her away. "Donovan Grant. Have you two been dating?"

"He wants more and I'm not sure I do." Given her light head, Liz had to struggle to express herself. "He's everything I'm not."

"If you decide you don't want Donovan Grant," Cheryl said grinning slyly, "give him my number."

She felt jealousy when she pictured Cheryl with Donovan. That jealousy shocked and disappointed her so much that when Donovan showed up at her door on Sunday, she was spoiling for a fight.

"Back to your tricks?" she said, standing aside to let him in.

"If the downstairs door's wide open, what can I do?"

"You could have buzzed up anyway."

"And you would have told me to get lost." He was staring at her, then a smile spread over his face. "You had your ears pierced."

Almost shyly, she fingered one earlobe. "I...I decided the earrings were too beautiful to sit in a drawer."

"They look great," he murmured, pushing aside her hair and touching the upper curve of her ear with his lips.

She told herself she'd enjoy this last bit of heaven before she put it behind her. She didn't object when he murmured soft sounds against her cheek or when his hands left her back to skim her ribs, her breasts. He hummed a smile against her cheek, then seized her lips with a force that stole what little breath she had. "This is what I've needed, what I've missed," he growled.

If only he hadn't spoken... thank God he'd spoken! He wanted to make love to her. Unmistakably. Urgently. She began to shake, but not in passion.

He gripped her shoulders as she tried to ease back. "Oh, no. Don't back out on me now, Liz!"

"I never promised you this, Donovan. All along I've been telling you I didn't want it."

"Your body tells me differently. And so does mine, damn it!" But he saw the fear in her eyes. He held up both hands and stepped back. His eyes widened for an instant. "Maybe I'm missing something here. You do like me, don't you?"

"Yes, I like you. As a person, yes."

"And as a man?"

"I... I don't want to think of you that way."

"Because you *do* like me that way and it scares you."

"That's not the point," she countered, eyes flashing. "If I choose not to look at you in sexual terms, it's my right."

"You *do* see me in sexual terms, and you're fighting it. Why?"

"I don't want sex."

Donovan stared at her, absently rubbing his upper lip. "I've given this lots of thought, Liz. Lots. You're open to a relationship, but only to the point of sex. You back off then with pure terror. You say there haven't been any men in your life, but you're terrified, and there's got to be cause. It's my guess that your father abused you."

For a minute Liz couldn't answer, but only for a minute. "You're way out of line, Donovan!" she cried. "You're too bullheaded to believe that I don't want you. I've been saying it, but you've refused to listen. It's all a game to you! All a game!"

"Hold on now," he gritted, rising from his seat and approaching her. "I'm dead serious about my interest in you. Is that what's got you worried? That I'll love you and leave you?"

She squeezed her eyes shut. "I don't *want* you to love me! You're not listening! I don't want any *part* of you!"

"No?" He reached for her, but she twisted to the side and ran to the door, swinging it open with a flourish.

"Get out, Donovan." Her voice shook, though her entire body was stiff. "I don't need you, and I don't want you." When he didn't budge, she was livid. "I *don't* like you!" she yelled. "You're an arrogant bastard who thinks he knows everything. Well, you don't, buster. You don't know what I—" she prodded her chest with her forefinger "—think. You might be the idol of the business world, but in *my* world, you're nothing! *Nothing!*"

It was all she could do to hold her head high until she'd shut the door on him. Then her eyes filled with tears. For the first time in her life she felt truly lonely.

SHE LEFT FOR KANSAS CITY Friday morning and spent a relatively relaxing five days away, getting to know a new client, letting the wounds of the past days heal.

If she assumed that Reynolds Associates had completed its work for the DIG Group, though, she'd been mistaken. It seemed that Donovan had decided to retain the firm to do publicity on the merger with Ullman. At his request Liz had been removed from the account.

*

"GOT A MINUTE, LIZ?"

Liz looked up from her work to find Brenda Nussbaum at her office door. "Sure, Brenda. Come on in." It had been over a week since she'd been back.

"I need your help. And the DIG Group hired *us*...."

"Uh-oh." Liz's easy smile faded. "What's wrong?"

Brenda threw a hand in the air. "It's Donovan Grant.

How a man could come across as being so congenial, so easygoing in the press and turn out to be a—''

Liz felt her heart pound. ''He's coming on to you?''

''Just the opposite. He all but turns me into ice with those eyes of his.'' She was frowning. ''I rack my brain trying to come up with novel ways to present the Ullman merger to the public. And he takes it all in, then quickly ushers me to the door.''

Liz was amazed. Brenda was adorable and available. If Donovan wanted a playmate, she was his for the asking. And now Brenda had come to her for advice. How do you tell a girl that the game was only fun if the object was unadorable, inexperienced and disinterested?

Liz felt a bitter laugh bubbling but squelched it. ''I think he's wrapped up in the Ullman thing and—''

''You can say that again! He put me through the second degree yesterday because some idiot is buying chunks of Ullman stock. Donovan all but accused me of selling inside information to the Obermeyers. Actually, the son, Raymond.''

For a minute Liz couldn't breathe. ''It's a federal crime to pass on inside information,'' she murmured. ''Whoever buys stock just prior to a merger stands to make a bundle as soon as the merger is announced.''

''That's what Donovan said.''

The more Liz thought about it, the more uncomfortable she grew. It could be a coincidence, Ray's buying Ullman stock. On the other hand, there'd been that cocktail party after Thanksgiving…and Liz had had one too many…and she'd talked with Cheryl. What *had* she said…?

LIFTING THE PHONE, she called Cheryl Obermeyer.

''Cheryl, do you remember that night at your party

when we were talking? What all did I tell you about Donovan Grant?''

''Just that he wanted to date you and you didn't want to.''

''Did I say anything about his business interests?''

''I don't remember. Why? What's this all about?''

With a grimace, Liz hung her head. ''I…I think I told you something I shouldn't have. Something about a merger.''

With the prompting Cheryl remembered. ''With the Ullman Distributorship, wasn't it?''

It was all the confirmation Liz needed to support her suspicion.

BY MORNING, Liz knew that she had to do something. She headed for DIG headquarters.

Donovan's surprise was momentary and was quickly checked.

When he'd seen Liz last, she'd hurt him with her words—until he realized that she'd struck out in self-defense. He'd realized then that he had to wait for her to come to him, and he'd reminded himself of that each time he'd lifted the phone to call her.

It was her turn. ''Did you want to see me?'' he asked evenly.

She prayed for as even a tone. ''I've…got a problem. It's about the Ullman merger.'' She saw alertness flicker through his gaze. ''I've made an awful mistake. I didn't mean to, and I didn't even realize it at the time—''

''Sit down, Liz, and spit it out.''

She knew then that he wouldn't make things any easier for her, that she couldn't expect any of the warmth, the gentle understanding that had once seemed such an integral part of his nature. She looked at him and swallowed, then summoned every bit of her inner strength and told him everything.

"Honestly, Donovan," she finished, "I would never have mentioned your name if I'd known he was listening." She focused on her fingers, which were kneading her purse.

A muscle flexed in Donovan's jaw. He was angry that Liz had been the one to betray him, yet he couldn't sustain his anger long. She'd come to him on her own. Perhaps it was the move he needed to force her hand. "That's a federal offense." Germs of an idea were taking shape. "And you're as guilty as he is."

"I didn't do it intentionally—"

"But you did it," he said. "For all I know you may be getting a cut of Obermeyer's profit." He knew it wasn't true, but he was buying time.

"I'm not! I...just wanted you to know the truth."

"You and I seem to have different perceptions of the truth," he countered, and she knew he was thinking of the things she'd said to him when last they'd seen each other.

"I'm sorry," she whispered. "I shouldn't have said those things. I was angry and...and I didn't know what else to do."

"You were terrified. But then, you've been terrified of me ever since we met. The only difference is that now you've got due cause. And now that you need my help, you're apologizing? You've had a good long time to apologize, Liz. Why only now?"

She clutched her hands in her lap. "I couldn't face you before. I...I was afraid that you'd take my apology as a sign that I...that I...."

"Want me? I know you do. But that's where the terror comes in, doesn't it? Now you want my help." He leaned back and laced his fingers together. "Okay, Liz. I'll help you." She looked up at him, only to have the hope in her eyes fade. "But on one condition." ·

"What's…that?"

He hesitated for only an instant. He didn't like what he was about to say, but he had to free her of the shadow that dogged her, even if it meant coming across like a bastard. "You move in with me. Become my lover."

The blood rushed from her head and she clutched the arms of the chair. "You can't be serious."

"I am. I know you prize your freedom, like to make your own choices. Well, the choices are these. Come to me of your own free will, or I'll go to the authorities." He was bluffing as never before.

She was shaking her head, trying to deny the images that crossed her mind. "Why?" she whispered brokenly.

"Because I want you. I always have. I'd pretty much given up on you, but since you've put the tool right in my hands—"

"The weapon, you mean."

Determinedly he held his gaze steady. "Whatever. I still feel the same about you."

Liz stumbled from her chair and made for the door, but she could only clutch its knob and press her forehead to the wood.

"Finally putting terror in perspective?"

She pressed pale fingers to the door. "Please…don't make me…."

"I'm not making you do anything. You've got a choice." He tore the top sheet off a small pad then approached her. "My Manhattan address. Take it, Liz."

THROUGH THE NEXT two days she agonized. She pictured herself being charged, going through the legal processes.

Her job, her reputation in the field, her security would all be gone. And she wouldn't be able to help Jamie.

So she would go to Donovan's apartment at noon on Sunday. He'd see her and taunt her and, in the end, find that the game wasn't as much fun as he'd anticipated.

But a tiny part of her did want to be Donovan's lover. She was stunned by the knowledge.

*

LIZ REACHED THE ADDRESS Donovan had scrawled on the paper. It was an elegant high rise in the East Eighties. Had she been capable of feeling, she would have been proud of the way she walked toward the elevator and stepped inside. That composure barely faltered when Donovan opened the apartment door.

His expression was shuttered as he surveyed her bags. "Is this all you've brought? Not much for a prolonged stay."

"It may not be prolonged."

"That wasn't our arrangement," he gently reminded her as he took the suit bag and overnight case from her hands.

She blotted the sound of the closing door from her mind, much as she'd blotted out everything else all morning.

After setting her things down on a chair by the door, he headed down the hall. She was still by the door when he returned. "You can come in and sit down."

"I'm not sure what I'm supposed to be doing."

"For now you're supposed to be making yourself at home."

She nodded and walked forward, about to descend the

two steps into the living room when Donovan stopped her. "Why don't you come into the kitchen with me?"

As though she'd only been waiting for his command, she turned and followed him.

"You liked my country kitchen. This is its city cousin."

Dutifully she ran her eye around the room. "Very nice."

His grin was weak. "Such enthusiasm. Close your eyes." When she looked puzzled, he repeated himself. "Close your eyes." She did. "Now tell me what you saw."

She hesitated for as long as she dared. "I...can't."

"That's what I thought." He sighed. "Well, I've got no intention of leading you through life."

"I'm sorry. You can always send me home."

"Oh-ho, no. The deal was that we'd be lovers." He was purposely goading her, told himself it was necessary.

Liz felt a stirring of emotion. "What would you have me do—waltz in all smiles when I'd rather be anywhere else?"

"Unnh!" he held up a finger. "The deal was that you'd come to me of your own free will."

"Words. Only words. You gave me two choices. I picked one. That doesn't mean I have to like it."

Donovan remained silent a moment. "I'll clean up here. Wander around. I'll be done in a minute and we can take a walk."

Liz sat in a chair until Donovan joined her.

"Will you be warm enough?" he asked as he held her coat for her. "It's pretty cold out."

"I'll be fine." She buried her hands in her pockets, but Donovan retrieved one and closed his fingers around it.

By the time they'd walked several blocks Liz was shiv-

ering. As they approached the Plaza, the sidewalk traffic
had picked up and she was forced closer to him. Each
time their hips brushed she stiffened.

Rockefeller Center was seasonally cheerful, with
Christmas lights in abundance and a huge tree surveying
all. Then they headed for a coffee shop on Sixth Avenue,
where he ordered hot chocolate for them both.

"There's a party Thursday night we'll be going to,
and—"

"You don't need me along."

In a moment's exasperation Donovan scowled at her.
Then, regaining control, he softened. "I want you with
me because I enjoy your company." He grinned. "Right
now, you're a real challenge. But I've seen you differently. Which is why I said that I enjoy your company."
He tipped his head as he stared at her. "There's something
about you, a warmth, a compassion, that appeals to me.
And besides—" he smiled his thanks at the waitress who
delivered their drinks "—by Thursday night you'll be
feeling very good."

"Thanks to you?"

"Thanks to *you*, Liz. You're your own worst enemy.
You've got yourself convinced that you're unappealing,
that there's no reason I should be attracted to you. You're
wrong. No comment?" he prodded.

"No."

"You usually tell me off when I give you compliments."

"It's not worth the effort."

"You're seething inside, but biting your tongue."

"I'm not seething."

"It'd give me too much satisfaction, right?"

"Something like that."

He laughed. "You are a gem, Liz. And speaking of

gems, I see you're wearing the earrings. I thought you'd have ripped them out." He held up a finger. "*That's* what we can do one night this week. Shop for earrings."

She looked at him sharply. "I may be forced to share your bed, but I'm *not* going to be paid for it."

He grinned and punched the air with his fist. "Atta girl. Fight with me. Tell me where to get off."

"I never should have had them pierced," she muttered.

When she set the cup down, Donovan lifted her coat from the back of the chair. "Shall we go?"

She hesitated for an instant.

"Got cold feet?" he teased, leaning close to her ear.

"They've been cold for three days."

"I'll have to warm them up for you when we get home."

She gave him a quelling stare but said nothing more.

By the time they reached his building, Liz understood why Donovan had walked her so far. She was exhausted, and she cursed the fact, because she needed every bit of her strength to remain composed through what she was sure lay ahead.

Once inside his condominium, he took her hand and she stumbled after him down the hall, fully expecting to find herself in his bedroom. To her amazement she found herself being led to a long leather couch. After depositing her in its richly scented folds, he crossed to a television set, turned it on, switched the channel, then returned.

"There we go. All tied up." He lowered his voice in urging. "Come on, Knicks, come on."

Liz jumped from the sofa, walked to the bookshelves, then walked to the window.

"The waiting's finally getting to you, is it?"

He'd hit the nail on the head. "I don't like basketball, and there's nothing else for me to do."

"I'd say you're impatient. Maybe excited?"

Her outward calm fled, along with the numbness that had protected her earlier. "Don't flatter yourself, Donovan," she gritted. "It's occurring to me, more and more each minute, that I wasn't wrong in what I said to you that day. You *are* arrogant. *And* bullheaded."

As she railed on, the easy indulgence that had dominated Donovan's expression fled. In its place was a certain grimness. "Be careful, Liz," he warned.

She threw up her hands. "I don't care! Drowning would be better than what I'm going through now."

He looked at her for a minute, then finally spoke in a tone of deadly calm. "Is that the way you feel?"

"That's *precisely* the way I feel."

He thought a moment longer, then sat deeper into the sofa. Though he looked confident and relaxed, inside he was a bundle of nerves. "Okay," he said quietly. "Take off your clothes."

Liz stood perfectly still. She couldn't believe what he'd said.

"Take them off now," he said softly, "or I'll make that call to the police."

"This isn't like you," she said, gulping.

He was pushing himself as desperately as he was pushing her. "It's what you've done to me."

"Please, Donovan," she whispered, her eyes wide, "don't do this to me." The tiny part of her that had wanted his lovemaking was stunned into neutrality.

"You can start with the sweater."

Her breath was short. "I can't ...don't make me.... "

"You can and you will. I'll give you ten seconds. Nine...."

Hands trembling, Liz reached for the hem of her sweater and drew it up. It was over her head before she looked at him again. The pleading in her eyes went unheeded.

"Now the jeans."

"Donovan...I'm begging you...."

"You won't do it?" He lifted the receiver, dropping it only when she reached for the snap of her jeans. He watched her bend over, pushing the jeans down her legs.

She didn't straighten all the way. She couldn't. Even if her stomach hadn't been cramped, the humiliation she felt would have prevented it.

"He...he made me...do this, too," she sobbed, unable to stem the words because defeat had robbed her of what little pride she had. She was shaking uncontrollably. "He made me...stand...in front of him...and take my clothes...off...just like this...and then—"

"*What?*" Donovan cut in in a whisper, suddenly before her, his hands on her cold quaking shoulders.

She barely registered his presence. The words just seemed to spill. "My father...he told me how...how ashamed I should be...how disgraceful I was. That I shouldn't...shouldn't ever think that...that someone might want...me....." She broke down completely then, weeping copiously. But Donovan pulled her against him, his trembling hands roaming her back as though he had to warm, to soothe, to protect every inch of her.

"My God," he murmured brokenly. "What have I done?"

He hugged her to him and rocked her gently. Then he slipped an arm beneath her knees, lifted her and hurried from the den. He ran the last few steps to his bedroom, only releasing her legs to snatch his robe from the closet. Quickly he slipped her arms into the sleeves and belted the fabric around her waist. Then he sat down on the edge of the bed and held her tightly.

"I'm sorry, Elizabeth," he whispered against her hair. "So sorry. I didn't know...I'd never have made you do that..... I knew that there had to be something, but you wouldn't tell me and I got so damned impatient with loving you and being blocked out."

She cried for a while longer, her body curled into a ball. Over and over he murmured soft words of apology and love, while he hugged her and rocked her. Then, when her sobs had finally begun to ease, he took her face in his hands and turned it to his.

"Please, sweetheart, look at me. I don't want you to be frightened of me," he said, speaking very, very softly and gently. "I love you, Elizabeth. No, don't shake your head. It's the truth. I would have told you sooner but you seemed threatened, and I didn't know what was bothering you. I didn't think you'd believe me, and you don't, but I'm going to spend the rest of my life proving it to you. Don't shut your eyes again, sweetheart. Please?" Only when she opened them did he go on.

"How old were you when your father did that to you?"

She bit her lip, but he prodded. "Tw-twelve...and thirteen...and on...."

With a groan he pressed her head to his chest and held her. "No wonder you're convinced that you're ugly," he murmured, then held her back so he could look at her again. There was an intensity in his gaze. "Your father must be a very sick man." Again he framed her face with his hands. "Elizabeth, you *are* beautiful. I know you don't believe it, but you *are*. You give so much to people. Look at what you do for Jamie."

When another thought intruded he frowned. "Liz, what did your father do to him?"

"He beat him." Her words spilled quickly, slurring together at times. "I used to stand in another room wanting to go to Jamie's defense, but I was too scared. All I could do was to comfort Jamie afterward and feel so guilty.''

"Oh, God," Donovan murmured, then grew suddenly fierce. "Did he ever touch you?"

"No. He did what I told you…just words…ugly words.''

Donovan took a deep ragged breath. She felt a tension enter him, saw the vulnerability on his face. "I know this may be too much to ask after all I've done." He hesitated, never once taking his eyes from hers. "Do you, uh, could you love me, even just a little?"

He was the old Donovan then, baring himself, speaking sincerely and Liz felt her chill begin to fade. But she couldn't lie.

"I don't know, Donovan," she said softly. "I've pushed the idea of love from my mind for so long. I wanted so badly to please you but knew I'd only disappoint you—"

"You haven't disappointed me, love." His smile was gentle enough to melt another layer of her chill.

"Are you…going to keep me here?"

"By force, no. I only did it before out of desperation. When I think of a future without you it's pretty dismal, and if there's any chance that you could grow to love me…well, I can live with that." He grinned.

"What about…" Her eyes shifted briefly to the bed.

"I still want to make love to you. But I want you to feel better about yourself first, and about me." He hesitated. "Liz, if you stay I won't push you. I mean, there's only this one bed, but it's big and I'll put pillows between us if you want, but what I'd really like is to be able to hold you in the night. We don't have to make love. But I've dreamed of waking up with you there, and… and…you have to take *some* pity on me….."

"I will stay."

On impulse he swooped down and sealed her lips with a kiss. Then, nearly as quickly, he pulled back. "I'm sorry. Would you rather I not do that?"

The smile she gave him was the first honest one she'd manufactured in days. "I kind of liked it," she said shyly.

But rather than repeating the kiss, Donovan put his arms around her and hugged her.

Very slowly she slid her arms up and hugged him back.

*

THE NEXT MORNING when she woke, Donovan was holding her, and she found that she liked it very, very much.

Tuesday morning she was in Donovan's arms again. She took stock of her surroundings, namely his chest, which was solid and fragrant in an utterly manly way. She touched him, timidly skirting one nipple, then lifted her lips for his kiss when his quiet gasp told her he was awake.

By Wednesday morning her legs were entwined with his when she awoke. She felt surprisingly secure, and grew more adventurous with the exploratory hand she ran over his chest and his arms. She set her head down on his chest and dropped her gaze to where his pajamas rode low. Then, without thinking, she slid her palm down the dark, narrowing trail of hair to that point.

Donovan sucked in a sharp breath. "God, sweetheart, you're playing with fire." He drew her hand up to his heart, which beat strong and fast.

HE PICKED HER UP at the office, and they headed for an exclusive department store. Donovan stayed with her until she'd selected a stunning silk burgundy dress to wear to the party they'd been invited to. After settling the account with the salesperson, he ushered her to a jewelry store, where he insisted on buying her a pair of elegant pearl studs.

She blushed. "I think you've lost your marbles."

He simply wiggled his brows, then took her arm and escorted her to a small sandwich shop near her office before he dropped her off.

THURSDAY, AFTER WORK they headed home to change for the party.

Liz had had a hot bath and was dressing when Donovan called from the bedroom.

"Are you decent?"

She looked down and automatically crossed an arm over her breasts, then slowly, determinedly, she lowered her arm. "Yes."

The door swung open and Donovan sauntered in wearing dark dress pants and a fine white shirt. His eyes ran over her breasts which were delicately encased in a new bra, and with a low moan he turned to the wall.

"Oh, God," Liz breathed, distraught. "You don't like it."

"Just the opposite," was his deep groan. Very slowly he straightened, then as slowly turned to her. "The problem is that we might well not make it to that party at all."

Liz felt feminine at that moment. And sexy...almost beautiful.

He gave her a hungry look, then kissed her deeply and thoroughly. She was beginning to think that it wouldn't be so awful if they did miss the party.

THEY DIDN'T EXACTLY fall over her at the party, Liz mused, but the attention she got, the admiring glances did stun her.

"It must be the dress...." she murmured, when Donovan swept her away. "I'm floating on the coattails of your charisma. I've never received compliments like these."

"You probably have, but you've ignored them. I know." He arched a pointed brow. "You ignored most of mine from the start. And don't give me that baloney about *my* charisma."

When they got home that night, Donovan turned her to him. An inkling of unsureness wrinkled his brow. "I want to be with you when you fall asleep tonight."

She gave him a soft smile, then nodded. "I'd like that." She hesitated for an instant. "You can even...if you like..."

He draped an arm around her shoulders and led her down the hall. "What? And let you think I'm easy? No way! Nope. Tonight we'll sleep. Besides," he murmured more naughtily, "it'll take most of the night to do what I'd like, and we've got work tomorrow...."

Left unsaid was that they didn't have to work Saturday.

THE DRIVE TO THE COUNTRY was slow, what with the weekend exodus from the city and the snow that was lightly falling.

After they'd turned on the heat, built a fire and made dinner, they sat together in the loft watching a movie. Curled comfortably against Donovan, Liz tried to concentrate on the movie, but couldn't. She wanted him and marveled at the way he could lie there so unaffected. Tipping her head back so that she could study his face, she found her answer.

"Donovan?" she whispered. "Donovan? Wake up."

"What happened?" he murmured groggily.

She threw back the afghan and reached for his hand. "Come on. To bed with you." She felt a little like a mother as she led him to the bedroom and helped him into bed.

"You're coming, too, aren't you?" he mumbled.

He *was* beautiful, all the more so in the pale blue light. She who hadn't dared once to dream now wanted so much...so much...

He raised the corner of the blanket in silent invitation, then held his breath. He didn't have to hold it long because she was quickly in bed with him and his arms were around her. "Oh, love," he gasped. "Are you sure?"

She nodded.

A shudder went through him as he hugged her. "Slow. We'll...take it slow!" It was almost a command, clearly directed at himself.

The feel of his nearly bare skin against hers was instantly rewarding. Her lips were parted when he caught them, and he took a long while kissing her, letting her adjust to the feel of his warmth against hers. Only when he heard her soft, purring response did he very gently run a hand from her navel to her collarbone and back.

"I can't believe you're actually here," he murmured.

His hands wandered farther down, coasting over her stomach to her thighs, returning over the juncture of her legs. Wherever his fingers delved the fire raged hotter, and she was clutching his waist, instinctively urging him toward her.

"Donovan!" she breathed, unable to cope with the pleasure-pain a minute longer. Yet she did, for another minute, then two and more. Only when Donovan was satisfied that she was fully ready did he slide between her thighs.

Liz cried out softly and arched to escape the sharp pain, but he held himself deeply embedded in her while he murmured soothing words.

"That's it, love. The worst is over. Just relax. It'll ease."

She bit her lip against the shallow panting she couldn't control, but he was right. The pain was easing.

"It'll never be like that again. It only gets better and better. Believe me—" he sealed the vow with a kiss that grew slowly seductive, then he began to touch her again, teasing her, coaxing her, until she was the one to move her hips in demand.

From then on the pleasure spiraled for them both. From time to time he whispered endearments, but soon he was too caught up in her flame to do anything but gasp and drive onward. She held on for dear life when she felt she would shatter into a million star-flung pieces.

"Donovan…?" she cried, frightened at the end.

"Let it come, love. It's there. Let it come. I'll hold you."

He did, but it was for his own sake, as well, for with the first of her spasms his own body erupted, and he could think of nothing but clinging to this woman.

It was a long time before their harsh pants eased and either of them could speak. Donovan kissed the moistness from her brow and the tip of her nose, then drew her to nestle against him. "I love you, Liz." When she tipped back her head and opened her mouth, he put a long finger against it. "Shh. Just let me say the words. If you say anything now, I'll always wonder if it was passion or gratitude or simply exhaustion. When you say those words to me you'd better mean them. Because as soon as I hear them, I'm going to ask you to marry me, and you'd better be prepared to say yes. Understood?"

Liz knew that she loved him, but with a gentle kiss to his fingertip, she nodded, then settled down to enjoy the spanking new happiness of the moment.

*

THE WOMAN WHO RETURNED to Manhattan with him Monday morning glowed. She felt fulfilled in a very feminine way and more self-confident than she'd ever been before.

Little by little she let slip to her friends that she was staying with Donovan. Where she'd half suspected they'd be surprised that Donovan should remain interested in her, they weren't. They were thrilled for her.

As the weeks passed, Donovan made her feel she was the best thing to ever come along in his life. He called her a born seductress, and occasionally, when his body was limp and drained, bemoaned the Pandora's box he'd opened. But his words of love were always soon to follow.

Workwise, their lives meshed as comfortably. Shortly before Christmas the Ullman merger went public. Donovan took the news of Ray Obermeyer's windfall in stride. Indeed, he was almost grateful for what Ray had done, since it had brought Liz and him together.

Christmas came and went, and was the happiest Liz could remember. Then, two weeks into January, shortly after he and Liz had arrived home, the phone rang. Donovan reached it first.

"Hello?" There was a long silence. "Hello!" he repeated, puzzled.

At last a man's voice came through, somewhat irritably. "But this is supposed to be Elizabeth Jerome's number."

Donovan felt a certain premonition. "It is. Hold on. I'll

get her.'' He put the phone against his chest, then held it
out to Liz.

"Hello?"

"Who was that?" a familiar voice asked.

She looked at Donovan. "Jamie. Hi! Is everything
okay?"

"Who *was* that, Liz?"

"That? Uh, that was Donovan Grant. The man I've
been seeing."

Jamie laughed. "That's a new one. What's he doing at
your apartment?" The tone was definitely one of demand.

Liz felt her hackles rising, but she couldn't quite come
out with the truth. Jamie needed time.

"I'm at the airport."

"Here?" She paled, and Donovan put a gently suppor-
tive hand on her shoulder. "*Is* something wrong?"

"Nah. This is vacation time, which my boss is generous
enough to dole out." His sarcasm did nothing for Liz's
peace of mind. "You're not running out of town, are
you?"

"Uh, no."

"Good. I'll be over soon."

"Jamie, maybe— Jamie?" She looked up at Donovan.
"He hung up. He's on his way to my apartment. He
doesn't know we've got the phone on call-forwarding."

Donovan gently kneaded her shoulders. "You don't
owe him elaborate explanations, Liz," he reminded her
quietly. "Listen, put your coat on and I'll take you over.
You can let Jamie in and get him settled."

Liz stood on tiptoe and cinched her arms around his
neck. "Okay. I might as well get this over with."

Within ten minutes they were at her apartment. Jamie
arrived twenty minutes later. Self-consciously Liz intro-

duced Donovan, whom Jamie had been staring at since he'd entered.

At Donovan's suggestion they went out for dinner. Liz was conscious of Jamie glaring at her from time to time, but she made no mention of the fact that she wouldn't be staying with him until they'd returned to her apartment.

"Jamie," she began, knotting her fingers together, "you can have the run of the place for as long as you want. I'll, uh, I'll be staying at Donovan's."

Jamie looked utterly dumbfounded. "Hey, Lizzie. I've never needed the place to myself before. And it wouldn't be much fun for Donovan to be imposed upon that way."

"It's not an imposition," Donovan stated.

"What Donovan means," Liz hurried to explain, "is that I've been staying with him for a while now."

"What's the matter?" His gaze narrowed. "Are you getting crank calls or something?"

"You don't understand. Donovan and I are *living* together."

Jamie stared at her, his eyes wide. "Come on, Lizzie. Do you honestly expect me to believe you've taken a lover—or that he's taken *you?*"

"That's exactly what I expect," Liz ground out. "I also have a *right* to expect that you'll be happy for me."

"Right? What right? Damn it, you heard Dad. You're nothing—"

"That's enough!" Donovan exploded, but Liz kept him from saying more.

"Let me handle this, Donovan." She turned to her brother. "Dad was wrong, Jamie. Dead wrong. I've finally come to see that, thanks to Donovan."

Jamie gave an ugly laugh. "What could he ever see in you?"

"I've asked myself the same question a hundred times.

But Donovan loves me, Jamie, despite every fault I've got!'' When Donovan started to argue, she squeezed his arm.

"You know, you've been putting me down for years. Oh, maybe more subtly than Dad did, but it's always been there. You've held me responsible for everything you've suffered—thinking that I might have somehow spared you Dad's beatings—''

"Damn it, Liz!'' Jamie cut in. "Not in front of him!''

But Liz was livid. "He knows it all, but the point *is* that there *wasn't* anything I could have done to help you. I took my own beatings, Jamie.''

"I was just a kid!''

"*So was I!* We're all grown up now, Jamie, and I need to put the past to rest. Donovan loves me. And you know something? *I love him!*'' Her expression still cross, she looked at Donovan. "The answer is yes!''

Then she turned back to Jamie, but her tone gradually softened. "I love him, and I'm going to marry him, and I'd like you to share some of what Donovan and I have. Our life is going to be wonderful, far different from anything you and I ever knew. I've lived in the dark for too long. And so have you. Think about it, Jamie.''

The pride in Donovan's face was unmistakable.

"He's got you brainwashed,'' Jamie muttered.

"DID YOU MEAN IT?'' Donovan asked, crowding her against the wall just outside her building. "You do love me? You'll marry me?''

"In a minute.'' She laughed and threw her head back. "But if you lean any closer you may have to worry about charges of indecency. I don't think they allow lovemaking on the streets of New York.''

"Mmm. I think you're right. Come on. Let's go home."

"Now that's the best idea you've had all night."

ACTUALLY IT WASN'T, but Liz didn't find out about the other until she got out of her bath and went looking for Donovan.

"Where were you?" she asked softly.

"I just called Jamie. I'm meeting him for lunch tomorrow."

"You don't have to do that, Donovan."

"But I do. You're still angry at him, but by tomorrow you'll be feeling badly. *I* feel badly. All things considered, Jamie must be feeling lost. I'm not sure how much he absorbed tonight, especially the part about his being welcome to spend time with us, but I want to reinforce it. I don't think I'd forgive myself if I didn't try."

She threw her arms around Donovan's neck. "Have I ever told you how wonderful you are?"

"That's not what I need to hear. It's those other words...."

"I love you? I love you...love you...love you...." She was still chanting when he lifted her and carried her to bed.

BE MINE, VALENTINE

Vicki Lewis Thompson

It began with the snow. Years later Roxie would wonder if old Charlie had arranged that, too. After all, if he'd told the truth about himself, then creating a little snowstorm in February wouldn't have taken much effort, even in the middle of the desert. The unusual weather could have been a coincidence, of course. Everything that happened afterward could have been a coincidence.

On that Friday afternoon when the snow hit Tucson, Roxie couldn't believe the fuss over a few drifting flakes. After twenty-seven winters in New Jersey she'd seen enough white stuff to last her forever. Apparently that wasn't true of her co-workers in the county clerk's office. With the first incredulous cry of "It's snowing!" they hurried outside to catch the snow on hands and tongues.

She was the only one who noticed when old Charlie trudged into the waiting area, his battered briefcase in his hand. His home was a bench in a nearby park. Every morning he brought a red rose to the county clerk's office for couples who applied for marriage licenses there.

"So what brings you here this afternoon?" Roxie leaned against the counter and smiled at Charlie.

"The weather." Charlie took off his worn fedora and brushed moisture from the scraggly feather stuck in the hatband. "When I chose to winter in Arizona, who would have imagined that I'd encounter snow?"

Roxie speculated for the hundredth time how a seemingly well-educated man ended up on the streets. "I don't want to embarrass you or anything, but...what will you do if it gets really cold tonight?"

"I haven't the slightest idea," he said, taking out a surprisingly snowy handkerchief to polish the figure-eight-shaped pin he always wore on his lapel. The gold pin and the pewter chess set he carried in his briefcase were probably the only things of value Charlie possessed. He played chess every day, and he wore the pin at all times, sideways, like the symbol for infinity. "I suppose my regular bench will suffice. I'll add another layer of newspapers, perhaps."

Roxie imagined the long night. What if he froze to death? "Charlie, I think you'd better come home with me until the weather improves."

"With you?" His blue eyes twinkled but he shook his head. "Oh, no, I wouldn't think of causing you any inconvenience."

"No, it'll be okay. The Osborns have a small guest house. You'd have complete privacy there." The more Roxie thought of the idea, the better it sounded. She'd been, she might as well face the fact, lonely. Before they left for the Orient, the Osborns had introduced her to the neighbors on either side, but Roxie had hesitated to intrude considering that she'd be house-sitting for only a year.

Of course there was Como, but she was just an animal, after all. Roxie thought of another argument to persuade Charlie, something to make him feel needed. "You could also help me with Como. She's been acting strange lately, and I'd like a second opinion about whether to call the vet. I don't want to waste the Osborns' money unnecessarily, but on the other hand...."

"Discerning an animal's needs can be difficult, all right. But Roxie, my child, aren't you getting ahead of yourself? Perhaps the Osborns would object to a common vagrant living on the premises while they're gone.''

"You're not a common vagrant. You're my friend. I've known you for six months and we've shared our lunch hour for the past two. It's settled."

Charlie's wrinkled face creased into a smile. "Bless you, Roxie Lowell."

"Hey, Roxie." A man with dark hair and eyes left the crowd outside and strolled over to the counter. "Hi, Charlie."

Charlie nodded to the man. "Doug."

"Roxie, everybody's talking about going home early, and I wanted to make sure we were still on for that drink at the Samniego House."

"Gee, Doug, I'm sorry. I forgot about that, with the excitement about the snow and everything."

"A little snow wouldn't stop you, a girl from New Jersey, would it?" He pronounced the name of her home state "New Joisey," as he always did to tease her.

She laughed to humor him, but the joke had become old and she wished he'd find a more clever one. "No, of course the snow won't bother me, but I'm taking Charlie home tonight, because of the bad weather."

Doug's eyebrows shot up. He took her elbow and steered her several feet away from the counter. "Are you crazy? He's a bum, a transient."

"Doug!" Roxie glared at him defiantly. "I'm doing this, so don't try to stop me."

Doug raised both hands in a gesture of helplessness.

She returned to her desk for her coat and purse and soon joined Charlie in the lobby.

"He doesn't approve, does he?" Charlie asked.

"It's none of his business. We're dating, not married."

"Oh, Roxie, I certainly hope you won't consider marriage to Doug Kelly, of all people."

She glanced at him as they walked down the tiled hall of the courts building. "I have considered it, Charlie. I'm twenty-seven. I'm ready to settle down, raise a family." Roxie guided Charlie toward the elevator that led to an underground parking garage.

"There's not enough love in him to inspire you," he said as they rode down. "It may not be entirely his fault, of course, with that name."

"Charlie, what are you talking about?"

"I'm talking about Doug's last name. Kelly means *warrior*. The name doesn't match at all with yours, Roxie," Charlie said as Roxie unlocked the passenger side of her old Volvo. Charlie waited until she was seated behind the wheel. "Lowell means *beloved*," he said.

"And your last name is Hartman." She started the car and drove out of the garage.

"Of course, that's not my real name. But I like the assonance of Charlie Hartman. It will do."

Roxie blinked. *Hartman wasn't his real name?*

They left downtown traffic and climbed northward into the foothills of the Santa Catalina Mountains.

"Isn't the snow delightful? The desert looks rather... surprised, wouldn't you say?"

"Yes, it does, at that. Well, this is the street, Calle de Sueños." Roxie flicked on her left-turn signal.

"Street of dreams. How lovely."

"I should have guessed that you'd know Spanish."

"Ah, you have something under construction on your corner. That's a sturdy-looking chap on the roof. I like the way he holds his shoulders."

Roxie peered through the thickening snow to the man standing on the roof of the skeleton building. Charlie was right, the man created an intriguing picture silhouetted against the gray sky, his yellow hard hat like a beacon.

Roxie studied the large sign at the corner of the lot. "It says Craddock Design and Construction, Hank Craddock."

"Craddock, now there's a name for you."

"Okay, I'll bite. What does Craddock mean?"

Charlie looked at her with a satisfied expression. "Abounding in love."

FOUR DAYS of rain followed the freak snowstorm. Then the sun came out. Roxie made use of Como's absence with Charlie to clean out the stall in the miniature barn the Osborns had constructed for their llama. Then she lined the floor with fresh straw and raked the small corral. As she walked back toward the house, Charlie and Como arrived through the side gate fresh from their walk.

"What a joyous morning," he said, unbuckling Como's halter and closing her in the corral. "This halcyon weather is reminiscent of Southern Italy." Charlie's expression became dreamy. "Of course, Northern Italy is breathtaking, too. I remember how much Romeo and Juliet loved it."

"Romeo and Juliet?"

He glanced up, as if coming out of a trance. "They were...I suppose in today's vernacular, clients. That boy and girl had so much love, but—" He paused and shook his head. "I prefer not to dwell on the sad stories." He opened the French door that led into the kitchen. "I want to tell you about Mr. Craddock."

"Who?" Roxie carried a grapefruit to the sink and rinsed it off.

"Hank Craddock, the chap we saw on the roof the first day I came here." Charlie hung his fedora on a rack beside the door. "Excellent person. We had a nice chat. I told him about you."

Roxie stopped sectioning the grapefruit and looked at him. "What do you mean, about me?"

"I told him you had flame-red hair and eyes the color of the sea. Oh, and I mentioned the freckles, too. He appears to be a man who would appreciate a few freckles."

Roxie put the knife down and turned to face him. "Charlie Hartman, whatever possessed you to do such a thing?"

Charlie smiled at her in that sweet way that had won her heart months ago when she'd first met him. "I could see no other recourse. Tuesday is St. Valentine's Day. Roxie, my dear child, we're running out of time."

Roxie stared at Charlie. "You really scare me when you say things that don't make sense."

"St. Valentine's Day could determine your whole future." Charlie spoke to her with the patient manner of a teacher confronted with a hopelessly slow pupil. "When you are a woman ready to fall in love, the first eligible man you meet on St. Valentine's Day is destined to become your lover and marry you within the year. There have been rare exceptions, of course, but—"

"Charlie, you can't believe such superstitious nonsense."

He sighed and held up one hand. "Now, what worries me is that Tuesday is a work day. The first eligible man you're likely to meet will be that weasel-faced Doug Kelly."

"Weasel-faced? That's a terrible thing to say. Charlie, listen." Roxie put a hand on his arm. "It's sweet of you to take an interest in my love life, and I'm sure this Craddock man is very nice, but if he's like most wonderful men, he's already married, anyway."

"No, he's unattached at the moment."

Roxie gasped. "You asked him?"

"Subtly, of course."

"Charlie, you're about as subtle as a Mack truck. Listen, I don't care what your Mr. Craddock told you. I've learned that men don't always tell the truth in these matters."

"Hank wasn't lying to me. Not with that strong face and those capable hands."

Roxie decided the time had come for some revelations. "Charlie, wake up. I fell for a guy back in New Jersey who had the most trustworthy face you'd ever imagine. For three long years he convinced me that we couldn't get married because he hadn't achieved enough success with his business. Newark's a big city, and he almost got away with it, but one day by a wild coincidence I met his wife."

Charlie accepted the news with a sigh. He reached over and patted her hand. "I suspected that you'd been disappointed in love. So that's why you came here?"

"Yes, and I was lucky to have the chance. When I heard my parents' friends needed a house-sitter, or in this case a llama-sitter while they spent a year in the Orient, I jumped at the opportunity."

"You know, on the way to work Tuesday morning, to humor an old man, you could stop by the construction site, just for a moment."

"Charlie, give it a rest." She searched for another topic to make him forget his daydreaming about her and Hank Craddock. "Do you think anything's wrong with Como? Does she seem listless or is it just my imagination?"

Charlie snapped his fingers. "Yes, Como. I do know what her problem is. She's lovesick."

"Oh, Charlie." Roxie shook her head and poured cereal into a bowl. "You've got love on the brain."

"So does Como. She's a lonely llama."

Roxie chuckled. "Now that I think of it, Fran Osborn did mention that they'd tried to mate Como but nothing happened. She was too young. Maybe I'll get the vet out here, to make sure there isn't something we ought to know about the situation," she said.

She picked up the receiver of the wall phone in the kitchen and dialed the number.

When she'd finished talking, she turned to Charlie with a smile. "Looks like I won't be seeing Doug Kelly on the morning of St. Valentine's Day. Dr. Babcock is free Tuesday morning and then he'll be out of town for two weeks, so I had to grab him when I could. I'll stay home from work that morning and go in at one o'clock."

A look of panic crossed Charlie's face. "What time is he coming over?"

"The appointment's for ten."

"Is this Dr. Babcock married?"

Roxie laughed. "I have no idea. Really, Charlie, aren't we carrying this a bit too far?"

Charlie mumbled as he reached for the coffee. "I'll take care of—that is, everything will be fine, just fine."

*

ON TUESDAY morning Hank pulled into the circular drive. When no one answered the bell, he rang again and finally heard the front lock click. Then the heavy carved door opened and he was face-to-face with flame-red hair and eyes that were, indeed, the blue-green of the sea.

"So he did it," Roxie said. "He got you down here before the vet arrived."

Hank frowned in bewilderment. "Lady, I don't have the faintest idea—"

"Aren't you Hank Craddock?"

"Yes, and I was wondering if—"

"Charlie sent you down here, didn't he?"

"Yes, but I—"

Then she laughed. "You might as well come in, Mr. Craddock," she said, stepping back from the door. "I'm afraid this is bigger than both of us."

"Listen, could I use your phone?" Hank decided to take charge before he found himself in the twilight zone. "The mobile phone in my truck went out and I have to change a window order."

"What a coincidence." Still smiling, she beckoned him into the house. "Sure, you can use the phone. The closest one's in the den."

He followed her down a tiled hallway and noticed that the top of her head came to his chin, making her about five seven. A nice height. The urgency of his business was beginning to wane. He liked the way she wore her hair, brushed back from her forehead on top, and luxurious, touch-me fullness at the sides and back. "You should have heard how Charlie talked about you," he blurted.

She flushed slightly. "You have to excuse Charlie. He means well, but he—"

"Underrated you," Hank shocked himself by saying. A quick glance at her left hand told him what he needed to know, and he began to imagine taking her out to dinner and maybe dancing.

Hank liked dancing although he was a little out of practice. In his dating years before he'd met Sybil, dancing had provided a socially acceptable reason to be close to someone and discover if her body fit with his. Just eyeing the situation Hank thought he and Roxie would dovetail very nicely.

"Have you ever tried country swing?" he asked. At her puzzled look he realized that he'd made a quantum leap forward in the conversation. "I—"

She smiled and laid a hand on his arm. "You don't have to ask me out, you know. Charlie probably begged you to, but don't feel under an obligation to save Roxie from weasel-faced Doug Kelly."

"Who?"

"Charlie didn't mention him and the St. Valentine's Day legend?" she asked.

"Look, all I know is that Charlie happened to be at the site when my mobile phone went out this morning, and he suggested I come down here to make my call."

"Which you haven't made yet," she reminded him gently.

"You're right. Charlie didn't mention my asking you out, but that doesn't mean it isn't an appealing idea." He decided to go for broke. "Would you like to sometime?"

"I—we'll see. Make your call."

"Okay." As he withdrew his wallet from his back pocket, he dropped it, spilling pictures and business cards on the Oriental rug under their feet. "Well, damn." He stooped immediately to retrieve everything.

"Accidents happen," she said, bending to help him.

"I haven't managed a stunt like this in years," Hank said. "Not since the night I was trying to use a fake ID to get a drink at the Wildcat House."

She didn't laugh or respond at all, and he glanced up in surprise. Then he stood and frowned in confusion as she silently handed him the stuff she'd retrieved. The friendly expression had completely vanished from her face and in its place was the blank stare of a woman who could have been in a scene from Madame Tussaud's Wax Museum.

"Is something wrong?" he asked.

"Nothing that I wouldn't have expected, Mr. Craddock. You can lock the front door on your way out." She turned and left the room.

ROXIE WAS alone in the sunny kitchen when Charlie came in, all smiles and winks.

"What did you think of him?" he asked as if certain of the answer.

"He's a handsome devil, all right. He's married."

"He most certainly is not."

"Then how do you explain the picture in his wallet of him with a blond woman and two children that look very much like both of them? He dropped his wallet on the floor and I helped him pick everything up."

Charlie tapped his chin with his forefinger. "I can't believe that I'm wrong about this man, but let's find out for certain." He walked to the shelf under the kitchen telephone and took out the directory.

"What are you going to do?"

"Call his house and ask for Mrs. Craddock."

Roxie put down her mug and stood. "If you're really going to do this let me listen in on the extension."

"Just don't cough or anything, my dear, or the jig's up."

Roxie picked up the telephone receiver in the den and remembered that Hank's lips had been as close to the mouthpiece as hers were now. She'd seldom looked at a man upon first meeting him and wondered what his kiss would be like, but she'd done that today with Hank.

The phone stopped ringing and a woman answered.

Charlie spoke with smooth confidence. "May I speak with Mrs. Hank Craddock, please?"

"There is no Mrs. Craddock," the woman said.

"I beg your pardon?" Charlie responded. "There must be some mistake."

"I think the mistake is yours, sir," the woman said. "You see, Mrs. Craddock passed away two years ago."

Roxie gasped and immediately clapped her hand over the mouthpiece. Then she gently lowered the receiver to its cradle without bothering to listen in on Charlie's apologies to the woman. Died! His blond wife in the picture had died! The thought had never occurred to her that someone so young…

Roxie bit her lip. Those poor children. In the picture they'd looked small and vulnerable—still in elementary school.

"Does that answer your question?" Charlie leaned against the doorway of the den and gazed at her.

"I feel awful. After I'd seen the picture I was really nasty to him. He has to think that I'm a shrew."

"Perhaps I'll meander down there later today and repair the damage."

"No! I mean, that would seem so—oh, I don't know what to do. By now he probably thinks that both you and I are lunatics." She slumped to the leather chair and rummaged in the desk for paper and pen. "If you'll deliver it, I'll write him a note. I'll ask for forgiveness for my rude behavior, and I'll— I know—invite him to bring his children over for supper on Saturday night, to see Como. How's that?"

Charlie walked over to the desk. "You'll be fine with those children."

"Charlie, you're way ahead of yourself, here. But no

doubt about it, some sort of apology is called for and dinner for Hank and his kids seems like the answer.''

Roxie had written four versions of her apology-invitation note before she was satisfied enough to let Charlie take it down the street to Hank Craddock. By the time Charlie returned, carrying what looked like a piece of scrap lumber from the construction site, Roxie was waving goodbye to Dr. Babcock as he pulled out of the circular drive.

She stood by the open front door and waited for Charlie to reach her. He handed her the two-foot length of pine. ''This is your reply from Hank.''

''The guy couldn't find paper?''

''I'd say he did quite well on short notice.''

Roxie read the words out loud. '' 'I'll never be ''board'' with you. Be my Valentine.' What a terrible pun,'' she said with a grin.

Charlie took her elbow in a courtly gesture as they reentered the house. ''It's been a good morning's work.''

Roxie shook her head in amazement. ''Anyone would think you engineered the whole thing.''

Charlie settled into his favorite kitchen chair. ''I certainly try. And while we're on the subject of sweethearts, how's our Como?''

''Well, you were right. Poor Como needs a boyfriend, but I'm afraid she'll have to wait until the Osborns get back. I'm a city girl, and even if the Osborns gave me the go-ahead, I'm not ready to play Cupid for a llama.''

''Do you think the Osborns might approve such a course of action?'' Charlie showed interest in the possibility.

''Charlie, now stop it,'' Roxie said. ''Be satisfied with your human matchmaking, okay? That could get us in enough trouble without adding in llama love.''

"But—"

"No, Charlie." She picked up the scrap of wood on the kitchen counter and waved it at him. "This is enough mischief for one day. End of discussion."

"Just remember that you're holding the most important valentine you'll receive today, perhaps ever. I hope you'll treasure it."

"Shall I sleep with it under my pillow tonight?"

"Perhaps."

"Charlie, I wasn't serious."

"Give yourself time, Roxie, and you will be."

*

THE FAMILY portrait that greeted Roxie when she opened the heavy carved door was incomplete. She could almost see a dotted line drawn around the spot where Hank's wife should have been. Here stood the handsome, square-jawed father holding the hand of a little girl with a blue and lavender scarf tied over her brown hair. Next to them, close enough for security but far enough to establish his growing independence, was the blond, hesitant son. They had arranged themselves as if making room for someone else who had once turned the odd number to even.

Roxie felt the tug, the urge to fill that gaping hole herself, and knew that she couldn't be the only woman to have felt that way. She'd have to be careful, very careful, not to let that emotion influence her attraction to Hank.

"I'm so glad you all made it," she said. "Come in and meet Charlie Hartman, a dear friend of mine."

"These are my children, Ryan and Hilary," Hank said with obvious pride. "Kids, this is Roxie Lowell."

"Well!" Roxie began, rubbing her hands briskly.

"Would you like to go straight out to the patio and see the llama before you take off your coats?"

"I would," Hilary said right away.

"Sure," Ryan added, but more casually. He was in training for adolescence, Roxie could see, and didn't want to appear childishly eager for anything.

Charlie stepped forward as if on cue, taking Hilary's hand in his. "I'll take them, Roxie, while you finish dinner preparations."

"I'll stay and help Roxie," Hank said. "You kids go on out with Charlie."

As simply as that, Roxie thought, as if they were in cahoots, Charlie and Hank had arranged things so that the valentine couple would be alone for a while.

"About the scarf," Hank said. "I hope you don't mind if Hilary eats her dinner with it on. She made me promise that she could. She...well, she had a little disaster with her hair. I swore to her that I wouldn't tell."

Roxie laughed. "Now I'm dying to know what she's done, but you're a nice daddy to keep your word. I won't pester you about it."

"Thanks. She'd be furious if I spilled the beans, and I'd pay the consequences for a long time. Hilary has a memory like an elephant and she doesn't forgive easily."

Roxie nodded in understanding. "I'm kind of like that, myself. That's why when I thought you were married, I— well, never mind."

She hung his jacket in the closet and ran her fingers lightly down the supple suede. "If we have our drinks in the kitchen I can finish my work and you can peek out the window to see how the kids and Charlie are getting along."

"I've never seen Hilary take a stranger's hand that

quickly before. Did Charlie come with the house or something, like the llama?''

Roxie was extremely aware of Hank as he leaned
against the counter. ''I met him my first day at the county
clerk's office.'' She paused to take the ice-cube tray out
of the freezer.

''So Charlie works there?''

''No, but he comes in every day.'' She put ice in
glasses and bourbon and filled the drinks to the top with
water. When she started to hand one glass to Hank she
drew it back abruptly. ''This is stupid,'' she said, shaking
her head. ''I made this without asking you.''

''I like it.'' Hank took the glass and waited for Roxie
to pick up hers. ''Follow your intuition where I'm concerned and you'll probably be right on target.''

Logic hadn't governed anything she'd done concerning
Hank Craddock, yet his presence here felt exactly right.
''My intuition also tells me that I'm going to like you
very much,'' she admitted.

''Mine tells me the same about you.'' He touched the
rim of his glass to hers.

She acknowledged the toast with a nod and sipped her
bourbon.

She made herself busy taking the roast out of the oven
and finding a platter for it. ''How're the kids doing?'' she
said in an effort to appear nonchalant and in control.

''Great. Ryan's leading Como, and Hilary's riding her.
You still haven't told me who Charlie is.''

She couldn't come up with any way to gild the lily.
She turned to him. ''Before I brought him to live in the
guest house the night it snowed, he was living on a park
bench downtown.''

He gazed at her. ''Really?''

''Yep.'' Roxie paused to sip from her drink. ''When

the snow came I was afraid he'd freeze to death on that bench, so I invited him to stay in the Osborns' guest house. He's been here ever since.''

''Well, I'll be damned!''

''He wouldn't hurt a flea, Hank. I've believed in him ever since I met him, which is ironic considering how illogical that is. Maybe I'm not as logical as I think.''

''Maybe not.'' Hank looked pleased with the idea. ''I'll sure never forget the first day *I* met him. There he was, an old English-looking gentleman leading a llama. I thought I had some resident who was ready to burn my behind about the construction. Instead he complimented me on the job and implied that my name had something to do with it.''

''I know. He's very big on names.''

''Then he must have told you what yours means.''

Roxie got out the flour for the gravy without looking at him. ''He said that Lowell means 'beloved,''' she mumbled.

The back of Roxie's neck grew warm. She knew he was staring at her and she was afraid to turn around and catch him at it.

''According to Charlie my name means *abounding in love*. Tell me, what does Charlie think will happen if two people with names like ours meet on St. Valentine's Day?''

From the corner of her eye she could see that he was right beside her now. Summoning her courage, she glanced up at him. ''Oh, he thinks we're destined for each other,'' she murmured, stirring the gravy.

He took a deep breath and put down his drink. ''I wish that I'd known you a little longer, Roxie.''

''Why?'' she whispered.

''Because I'm going to kiss you, and Charlie or no

Charlie, you'll probably think I have no business doing that yet.''

The spoon slipped from her trembling fingers and landed with a plop in the gravy. Gently he turned her toward him and tipped her face up to his.

Heart pounding, Roxie closed her eyes and waited for the first sweet pressure of his lips. She felt the whisper touch of his breath and wound her arms around his neck. Just as his lips grazed hers, a screech from the backyard wedged between them and they reeled away from each other in shock. After one startled glance at each other, they raced for the French doors into the patio and almost collided with Hilary.

''My scarf came off,'' she wailed, pushing past them. ''Don't look!'' She charged down the hall and into the first room she found. Immediately she closed the door.

Charlie and Ryan came through the French doors discussing the incident between them.

''It wasn't my fault,'' Ryan said.

''Of course not,'' Charlie agreed. ''You couldn't have known that Como would try to nibble on that scarf.''

''I know,'' Ryan suggested. ''We'll all pretend we didn't see her spotted hair because she was running so fast.''

Hank gave Ryan an appreciative look. ''That's nice of you to think of Hilary's feelings, but I think she's well aware that her secret's out.''

''What *did* happen?'' Roxie asked. ''Did she try to bleach her hair?''

''I told her it was a dumb idea,'' Ryan said, taking off his jacket.

Roxie looked over her shoulder at Charlie and Ryan. ''How would you guys like to finish setting the table for me?'' she asked. She quickly opened the refrigerator and took out the salad and dressing. "Hank, you can toss this while I talk to Hilary. That is, if it's okay."

"But I can't guarantee she'll be all sweetness and light." His gray gaze swept over her. "Listen, Roxie, there's something you should know. She wants to bleach her hair so she'll be a blond like her mother was."

"Oh." Roxie wondered if she was about to make a tremendous mistake getting involved.

SHE STILL wasn't sure when she exited the room hand in hand with Hilary. She practically ran into Hank.

"I was coming to see if you had fallen asleep," he said.

Hilary gazed up at her father. "We were talking," she said. "Later Roxie's going to talk to you about bleaching my hair." She dashed down the hall, her multicolored hair flying behind her.

Roxie gulped.

ROXIE TRIED to explain when she and Hank went out for the after-dinner video the kids wanted.

"What if you told her she could be blond, but first she had to watch the whole process being done on someone else?" Roxie asked as he started the car. "I can't believe she'd still want to go through with it after about three hours of watching."

He glanced at her and smiled. "Considering that I'm getting this advice from logical, practical Roxie, perhaps I ought to listen. Let me think about it. In fact, I appreciate your sharing the load on this crisis. It's lonely at the top," he said reaching for her hand as they entered the shop.

They toured the aisles quickly, hand in hand. After a few minutes Hank took a family comedy from the shelf. "This'll do," he said, as he led Roxie to the checkout counter.

Hank was silent as he tossed the movie into the back seat and wheeled the Lincoln out of the parking lot.

A short distance later he swerved the car into the vacant cul-de-sac of a new housing development and cut the engine. He drew her slowly into his arms. In the darkness she couldn't see his expression. Was he as solid as he seemed, or was he a rogue under the clean-cut exterior he allowed her to see? She'd been a terrible judge of character three years ago. What made her think she was any better at it now?

His lips slowly merged with hers, with a sureness that made her quiver.

The exhilaration of kissing him wiped away her fear of risk and replaced it with a need she dimly recognized. Was it possible that the passion she'd found so difficult to renounce six months ago had been only a weak forerunner of real desire? Dazed and disbelieving, she looked into his face as he lifted his head and shook it once, as if to clear his vision.

"I guess Charlie knew what the hell he was talking about," he muttered.

It was just a kiss, she told herself. Charlie's predictions have worked you into a fever pitch of anticipation. This will seem different in the light of day. But she didn't really believe any of that.

"I've...just been through a bad experience," she found herself saying. "That was the main reason I moved out here, to...to recover."

He turned to her. "Do you still love him?"

"No."

"Because I'd hate to think you were kissing him instead of me."

"I wasn't," she said, gazing at him. "Who were you kissing, Hank?"

He touched her cheek. "You. Only you. And if we don't start the car I'll do it some more. When can I see you again? Are you free Tuesday night?"

Her pulse raced. "Yes."

ROXIE SPENT Sunday morning on her hands and knees cleaning the kitchen floor. She sat back on her heels and looked at Charlie.

"All in all I'm quite pleased with my work," he said, almost to himself. "Now, if we could solve poor Como's problem."

"Charlie, I've warned you about tampering with Como's love life. She's fine."

"Come and look out the window and tell me she's fine," he said, holding out his hand to help her up.

Roxie peered out the window. "She's looking over the corral fence. That's all she's doing."

"She stands like that for hours. She wants a sweetheart," Charlie insisted. "You said the Osborns took her somewhere once, the time she wasn't old enough to breed. Was that the direction they went, do you suppose?"

"Charlie, we are not getting involved in this. I promised to feed and brush and talk kindly to this llama. I agreed to clean her stall and put down fresh straw. I never said I'd play Cupid."

"Wouldn't it be lovely to do that, though?"

"No."

*

ON TUESDAY night Roxie discovered that the destination for their date was The Last Territory Steakhouse. The hostess led them past a barrel filled with unshelled peanuts and over to their table. The red-and-white-checked table-cloth was anchored in the middle by a knobby red glass container with a candle inside.

The waitress appeared and they both decided beer was the appropriate drink for a night among the cowboys.

"To broken telephones," Hank said, raising his glass to hers. "Without those we might never have met."

"To broken telephones," Roxie repeated, tapping her glass against Hank's and raising it to her lips.

Hank took a large swallow and put down the glass. "Let's dance," he said, holding out his hand to her. The band was playing a ballad about love gone wrong, but Hank refused to be superstitious. The song didn't matter as much as the chance to hold Roxie again.

As they reached the dance floor she snuggled against him as if they'd been dancing this way for years.

He cradled her head against his chest and laid his cheek on the pillow of her bright hair while they slowly circled the floor with the other dancers. He rubbed the small of her back and heard her sigh of pleasure. How he wished that everyone else in the room would disappear.

The music ended, and he reluctantly eased away from her. The beat picked up and several dancers began the shuffling step used in country swing.

Roxie watched several couples glide by before shaking her head. "I can't do that," she said.

"I'll teach you," Hank said, catching her around the waist and bringing her close.

He guided her through the simple steps and gloried in the way her eyes shone and her cheeks flushed.

ROXIE GAZED into the intense gray of his eyes and knew that she was falling in love.

They were standing outside in the cool air. Hank put his arm around her shoulders. "Feel like taking a drive?"

She looked at him and wondered how to say that she longed to cuddle in his arms in a secluded spot away from the rest of the world. "We could take a drive," she said hesitantly. "Whatever you like."

He turned to face her. "Listen, I don't know how you'll react to this, but I...reserved us a room. Here. It was only a thought." He frowned. "Forget it."

Her mind swirled. "No," she whispered, running her fingertips along his jaw. She began to tremble. "Oh, Hank, please don't think of me as less than a lady for wanting you, too, so soon."

His kiss was sweet and lingering, a promise of what was in store when they were alone.

"There is...one thing," she said. "I didn't seriously consider that we'd—I'm not prepared for this. I don't take birth control pills anymore," she finished in an embarrassed rush.

He smiled. "No problem."

Roxie sighed with relief as he guided her to the room.

"ROXIE, my God, Roxie," he mumbled, pressing his lips against her throat and running his hands with firm pressure over every part of her body. "I want to memorize you. I want to learn you the way a blind man learns Braille. I want to know everything there is to know about you, Roxie."

She moaned as he cupped her breast and brought it to his mouth. The rhythmic suction of his tongue and lips transmitted a pulse beat through her until she throbbed with longing. With sure hands he caressed her belly, her thighs, and at last the moist center where her need for him had become an unbearable ache.

He settled his lips against hers, absorbing her whimpering cries. She writhed against him, and as her movements grew more frenzied he slowly withdrew and moved over her.

The velvet strength of him entering her at last was all she needed to propel her over the edge. Her hips lifted and she gasped for breath as the undulations rippling inside shook her whole body. A roaring filled her ears, almost blocking out his tender murmured words.

She entwined her legs with his and held on tight as he buried himself in her again and again. At last, with a cry, he surged forward one last time and shuddered in her arms.

Something about him made her crazy with desire, so crazy that she could think of nothing but this wild surging together, this celebration of physical love. Something, however, wasn't quite what she'd expected. And then she realized what it was. Where in their passionate exchange had he taken care of birth control, as he'd assured her he would?

Hank stirred and lifted his head to look down at her. "Fantastic," he said. "You're wonderful."

"So are you," she replied, tracing his lower lip with her fingertip. "Um, I do have one tiny question, though. You promised to take care of the uh, protection."

He chuckled. "I didn't explain all that very thoroughly, did I?" he said, kissing her gently. "I'm out of the baby business."

She stared at him and tried to assimilate what he was saying. He couldn't have children anymore?

"Sybil and I decided after Hilary was born that two

kids were enough, and the operation was far simpler for me than for her. Roxie, is something wrong?''

"No, of course not." She managed a smile.

"Something's changed, though, Roxie." His gaze roved over her face. "I can feel it."

She swallowed. "All right," she said, taking a deep breath. "The thing is, Hank, I love children and always expected to have some of my own." She blinked back tears.

"Roxie," he said, cupping her face in his hands, "Hilary and Ryan are still children, you know."

"I know." *But they're not mine,* she wanted to add. Hadn't she warned herself about becoming the person who filled in the missing space in this little family?

Gently he stroked her back, and they were both quiet for a long time. When he finally spoke, it was with a sense of wonder in his voice. "I love you, Roxie," he said. "Lord help me, I already love you."

Roxie closed her eyes. Loving Hank meant dealing with two half-grown children and apparently giving up hope of having her own. This wasn't the way she'd planned her life at all, and yet...

AT HOME the next morning Roxie quieted the voices that reminded her that she'd never teach a toddler to walk, or record a child's first word, or rock her baby to sleep. Life was full of choices, and she couldn't expect to have everything, she reminded herself as Charlie joined her in the kitchen.

Charlie winked at her knowingly.

"Charlie, you're impossible." Roxie's face grew warm as she remembered being in Hank's arms only hours ago. "I have a couple of favors to ask of you."

"Anything at all."

"Hank has asked me out on Thursday, and I wondered if you'd look after Como for me?"

"It would be my pleasure. What was the other favor you wanted?"

She wondered if she could ask him, when the question would reveal the exact nature of her relationship with Hank. Maybe he would object to the responsibility.

"Don't be shy, Roxie. What is it?"

"Um, it's about the weekend." She glanced at him furtively. "Hank's children will be away at their grandparents', and he wondered if I—"

"Certainly," Charlie interrupted, sparing her further explanation. "Young lovers need more than a stolen moment. I'll take care of everything here." His lined face creased in a smile. "Don't worry about a thing."

ON THURSDAY night Hank arrived in jeans.

"Let's go," he murmured. "The past couple of days have seemed like an eternity. I have a picnic hamper in the back with some wine and some goodies from the deli."

A thrill of anticipation traveled through her as they drove toward an expensive housing development. He then turned down a dirt road that ended at a house half-hidden in a grove of mesquite trees.

"Where are we?"

"A good friend of mine is building this house and hopes to sell it for a lot of money. But Ed trusts me and also owes me a few favors, so he said the house was mine for the evening."

"Your friend knows why you wanted the key?" In the darkness Roxie flushed.

"He's a good guy, Roxie. When I told him I'd met a lady, he slapped me on the back and said, 'It's about time.' He said that giving me the key made him feel like Cupid."

She turned in her seat to look at him. "He hasn't been talking to Charlie, has he?"

He smiled. "Not that I know of."

Hank opened the door and helped Roxie out of the car and into the house. Their steps echoed as they walked through a tiled foyer.

Hank led the way down three carpeted steps to the sunken living room and over to a beehive fireplace. He set the wicker hamper on the raised hearth and turned to her. "What do you think?"

She gazed up at the beamed ceilings. "I like it. This house has an atmosphere of caring in it."

"That's right." Hank spread a blanket in the square of moonlight coming through the floor-to-ceiling picture window. Then he took her hand and pulled her down beside him. "The perfect atmosphere for loving you," he said gently, easing Roxie back on the blanket.

She cried out and writhed against the blanket as he loved her. Again and again they came together, each time more explosive than the last.

He lost count of how many times he told her he loved her until at last he tightened his arms around her and rolled them both to their sides, facing each other. "I love you," he said again. "I can't think of anything more important to say than that."

"And I love you." Her voice was husky. "There isn't anything more important to say."

He gazed at her for a long time. "There might be one thing more to add."

"What?" she asked softly.

"Marry me."

She didn't answer him.

"Maybe…maybe you're not ready for that question."

"Hank, I—"

"No. Never mind." He placed a finger across her lips. "You love me. That's enough for now. Don't think about the other yet."

ROXIE DID THINK of it, though. She thought of his proposal almost constantly the next day, because she'd almost said yes.

Hank was everything she wanted in a husband and lover. But for Roxie the word *marriage* had always been paired with the word *family*. Hank's family came ready-made, with no additions allowed. She'd have to become an instant mother to Ryan and Hilary and give up the notion of her own baby, or more exactly, hers and Hank's baby. That idea was tough to relinquish, because Roxie believed that having a baby together was an important way for two people to express their love.

*

HANK BROUGHT his daughter to Roxie's house by eight Saturday morning and turned Hilary over with such confidence that Roxie was touched. He'd agreed to let Hilary watch the bleaching process and make up her own mind.

"How long will I have to watch this other lady get her hair bleached?" Hilary asked as she and Roxie drove the short distance to the beauty shop.

"Georgia, my hairdresser, said it could take two and

half or three hours." Roxie glanced at Hilary belted in beside her. The blue and lavender scarf, its original beauty obscured by days of playground dust, was knotted under her chin. She was a determined little girl, but Georgia had assured Roxie that the process was sufficiently obnoxious to discourage Hilary from having it done.

And it was. Part way through the process Hilary gazed at Georgia with wide eyes. "Phew, it stinks!" Hilary said, holding her nose.

"That's ammonia," Georgia explained. "We need something this strong to take all the color out."

"I didn't know it would stink so bad." Hilary covered her mouth and nose with cupped hands and breathed into them while she watched Georgia work with growing anxiety. "How much longer?" Hilary asked.

"At least another hour," Georgia said.

Roxie tossed Hilary the next piece of bait. "How long does the semipermanent hair color take to apply, Georgia?"

"If someone sits very still, I can have that person out the door in thirty minutes."

"Yes!" Hilary said, jumping up from the chair. "It stinks too bad in here!"

Under cover of Georgia's amused chuckle, Roxie sighed with relief. The plan had worked.

A SHORT TIME later she heard giggles from Hilary and exclamations of pride and wonder from Georgia.

"I'm ready to go now," Hilary declared and paused dramatically beside the cash register counter.

"My goodness, how beautiful you are," Roxie said. Georgia had not only returned Hilary to her original color but given her a shorter cut that emphasized her large gray eyes. The longer hair, in a style similar to her mother's, had been wrong for the shape of Hilary's face.

"And I'm not even blond," Hilary responded proudly. "I can hardly wait to show Dad and Ryan!" Hilary lost her regal poise and jumped up and down. "They won't believe I look so good. Then I get to show my grandma and grandpa."

On the ride home Roxie kept glancing at Hilary, who really didn't look like the same child. When they reached her house Hilary raced across the gravel driveway toward her father. "Daddy, Daddy, see how beautiful I am now!"

Hank swung Hilary up in his arms and smiled at her. "You've always been beautiful."

"You sure look different, Hil," Ryan said as he joined them.

"But good, huh, Ryan? Don't I look good?"

"Yeah, I guess so. You look good with short hair."

"I know." Hilary beamed at everyone.

Hank lowered his daughter to the ground and Charlie escorted the children around to the side patio gate to where Como was penned.

When they were gone, Hank walked over to Roxie and rested his hands on her shoulders. "Thanks." He looked deep into her eyes. "You did a hell of a job with this mess."

"I—thanks." She flushed with pleasure.

His grip tightened. "And now that the hair business is over, I can hardly wait to drop these kids off at their grandparents' house."

HANK USHERED her in through a door that led to a spotless kitchen in a blue-and-white country decor. It was tasteful and welcoming, but Roxie had the urge to pull down the curtains patterned with cows and geese and replace them with Mexican serapes.

"What do you think?"

She turned to find Hank watching her. "Honestly?"

"Honestly." He set her overnight bag on a kitchen stool.

She met the assessing look in his clear gray eyes and knew that she couldn't fool him into believing that she felt at home here. She was in another woman's house, confronted with another woman's tastes. He must have seen that as quickly as she had.

But as she studied his face and wondered how to answer his question, the importance of the decorating scheme faded. Who cared what a room looked like when it contained this man? Slowly she took off her coat and walked over to him. "I think," she said, "that it's been a very long time since you kissed me."

"An eternity," he agreed, wrapping his arms around her, his mouth moving hungrily over hers.

Finally he lifted his head, and when he spoke his voice was rough with desire. "I've never loved you in the daylight."

"No."

"I think I'll like it very much."

He led her to the master bedroom.

Loving him completely, every bit of him, was the most natural thing in the world. Her body soon sang in tune with his. When they were joined she moved without thought, as effortlessly as breathing, as sure of his body as she was of her own.

Their climax was sure and swift, the end to a dance with no missteps. It left her weeping with joy.

"Hush," he crooned, kissing her salty tears. "It's all right. Hush now, love."

"So beautiful," she sobbed. "We're so beautiful together."

"Yes." He kissed her trembling lips.

"I don't want to waste that beauty," she said, tears still wet on her cheeks. She took a ragged breath. "I want to have your baby."

He became completely still. After a moment he gazed down at her. "I can't give you that."

"The operation...could be reversed."

His silence pushed between them, a gray intrusion upon their joy. "There are no guarantees with that, Roxie," he said with careful emphasis.

"At least we'd have a chance," she said, her gaze pleading.

He closed his eyes and leaned his forehead against hers. "Oh, Roxie, don't ask this of me."

Despair crept through Roxie. "You don't want to try reversing the operation?"

"No, I don't." Hank rolled onto his back and stared up at the ceiling. "I have two children, and that's plenty in this day and age, with the cost of everything from orthodontia to college. Besides that, I've been through diapers and 2:00 a.m. feedings, and colic and chicken pox."

"Not even—" She paused to swallow the lump in her throat. "Not even if you knew how much it would mean to me?"

"Roxie, listen." He raised himself up and turned onto his side, propping his head on his hand. "If you marry me, and I hope to God you do, you'll have your hands full with Hilary and Ryan. We'll spend more time together, the four of us. You'll see how complete a life we'll already have. We don't need a baby.''

"*We* don't? How can you speak for me?'' Her despair curdled into anger. "You've had your chance to hold a newborn child. You've seen their first tooth and heard their first word. Don't you understand? I want the chance, too,'' Roxie said, moving away and leaving his bed. "Obviously I misjudged the situation. I thought the only thing standing in the way of our having a baby was an operation that you had before you knew me.'' She reached for her clothes.

"Roxie!'' He swung his legs out of bed and stood beside her, magnificent in his nakedness. "Making the adjustment with Hilary and Ryan will drain us enough without adding the complication of a baby.''

"I have a feeling,'' she began, fighting back tears, "that no adjustments will be necessary.''

"Roxie, don't crucify us on this issue.''

"Why not?'' Tears leaked from the corners of her eyes. "The problem won't go away, Hank. I want a baby.''

"More than me?''

His image blurred as tears flooded her eyes. "I don't know. Maybe—maybe I do,'' she choked out.

"I can't believe—'' Hank's sentence was interrupted by the ringing of the bedside phone.

"Answer it, please,'' Roxie said, buttoning her blouse with shaking fingers. "This discussion is over, anyway.''

He glanced at her before walking over to the telephone and picking up the receiver. He spoke to the person briefly and then turned to Roxie. "It's Charlie. He sounds upset.''

Join the group, Roxie thought. Reluctantly she took the receiver from Hank. "Charlie? Is something wrong?''

"Oh, Roxie, my child, I feel dreadful about this, just dreadful. You were right; I should have rested on my laurels once I brought you and Hank together."

"Charlie, what is it?" Alarm swept through her like a brush fire.

"It's Como. She's...gone."

AT HOME Roxie found an old book of addresses and telephone numbers in the study. She asked Charlie to try them all and find out if any of the Osborns' friends knew where they'd taken Como to be bred. And the vet. Maybe he had information about it.

Charlie's lined face looked older than ever before. They left him with the number of the truck's mobile telephone in case he discovered through his calls where Como might be, and they also promised to call Charlie immediately if they found the llama.

"According to Charlie, the last time he saw her she was headed west on Sunrise Drive, right?" Hank asked Roxie as they drove away from the house.

"Yes. I hope she didn't stay on it, though. The traffic is—" She couldn't finish the sentence as a picture of Como dodging Saturday-afternoon traffic flashed into her mind.

Hank said, "We'll assume she turned off on a side street and continued west that way."

Hank shifted down so they could take the drive at a slow enough pace to look for any signs of Como. Roxie examined the street.

"Wait, Hank, there!" she said at last. "The entrance to that exclusive development, with all the flowers and the waterfall. She might have been attracted by the waterfall, don't you think? She could be thirsty."

"It's an idea. Maybe the guard at the gate has seen something."

The guard became very excited when they mentioned a white llama. "So that's what it was? I saw this animal come trotting in here as if it owned the place. When it stopped to drink at the waterfall I tried to catch it, but it took off across the golf course."

Roxie clutched the dashboard of the truck as Hank stepped on the gas, calling a quick thanks to the guard.

"Hank! I see a flash of white!" Roxie cried a few minutes later.

"Get a bead on her. Aren't there some houses over there where she's headed?"

"Yes, there are. Could one of those places be her destination?"

"Let's hope."

They started in the direction of the houses. When the mobile phone rang, Hank picked it up and spoke briefly with Charlie.

"We're on the right track," he said to Roxie after he hung up. "Charlie's located the people with the male llama, and from the address I'd say they live somewhere in that cluster of houses."

By the time they arrived at the address Charlie had given them, a Mrs. Griffith was standing next to a well-tied Como and stroking her neck. Como seemed oblivious, however, as she touched noses with a handsome black llama on the opposite side of the tall rail fence.

"Will you look at that," Roxie said. "Charlie was absolutely right."

"So, are you going to let the lovers share the same pen tonight?" Hank raised an eyebrow in her direction.

"No, I'm certainly not. I don't want the responsibility of a pregnant llama. Too many things could go wrong."

He stopped the truck and turned to her. "I feel much the same way about you having a baby."

Roxie opened the door of the truck. "It's all right, Hank. You've stated your case. But I don't have to agree with you. I appreciate your help in finding Como, but after we get home, we won't be seeing each other again."

THE TASK of returning Como to her corral and retrieving Roxie's car took very little time. Within an hour everything was accomplished and Hank had left. Roxie had tears in her eyes.

Charlie hurried to her side. "Roxie, my child, please tell me what's wrong," he said, putting a hand on her arm.

Determined not to cry, she began brushing Como vigorously. "I guess Hank won't be my valentine, after all," she said.

"Why ever not? You two were getting on so famously."

Roxie tried to clear the lump from her throat. "Charlie," she said tremulously, "do you consider having a baby an expression of love between two people?"

"Why, I suppose it can be, Roxie."

"What do you think of a man who refuses that experience, even when...he knows that the woman he loves wants a b-baby very much?" With a sob Roxie put her arms around Como.

"Oh, my dear." Charlie patted her shoulder awkwardly. "Maybe Hank needs time to get used to the idea."

She lifted her damp face and turned to him. "I never

want to see him again!'' Once more she buried her face against Como's neck, and the llama nuzzled her shoulder as if to comfort her.

''Oh, dear—oh, dear.'' Charlie sighed. ''Maybe I'm through. Maybe I've lost the old touch, the savoir faire to do this job. Retirement's been suggested, but I've been stubbornly clinging to my motto that Love Conquers All, but now I just don't know.''

Roxie lifted her head and wiped her eyes. ''Charlie, what on earth are you talking about? Retire from what?''

''My job, of course.'' He took out his handkerchief and polished the gold pin on his lapel. ''I was so certain of you and Hank. The two of you had restored my faith in the wonder of true love. But now....'' He shook his head sadly. ''I hate to end my career with a failure.''

Roxie faced Charlie. ''End what career? Who are you?''

He swept off his hat and gave her a courtly bow. ''St. Valentine, in person and at your service.''

Roxie stared at him incredulously. ''My God, you *are* crazy,'' she whispered.

''That's possible, after all the centuries I've been handling this assignment. I've been thinking of training a younger assistant.'' He gazed morosely at the flagstone pattern beneath his feet. ''Now that may not be necessary.''

''An assistant,'' Roxie marveled. ''I'd love to be there when you ask someone to take that position.''

''There are those who have already asked,'' Charlie said with great dignity. ''Geoff Chaucer for one. He was perceptive enough to notice that birds pair off on February fourteenth. However, I rather favor Charles, the Duke of Orleans. What a fellow. When he sent his wife a love letter from the Tower of London on St. Valentine's Day, he started a whole new trend.''

''A real trendsetter,'' Roxie said, deciding to play along with this amazing fantasy. He was absolutely, totally crazy. Yet she still loved him.

Charlie shifted. ''I may just have to consider retirement.''

''And then what?''

''I don't know.'' Charlie stared at his hands.

''You could stay with me. You know that.''

He glanced at her. ''As if I really were Charlie Hartman, you mean?''

''Yes.'' She nodded solemnly. ''As if you really were Charlie Hartman.''

''I'll give it some thought.'' Charlie held out his lapel and peered down at the gold pin. ''If I retire, I could sell this.''

''I've always meant to ask you about that pin, Charlie.''

''It comes with the job. It's a love knot. When I successfully complete a project, I give this pin to the lucky couple and get another. There's an endless supply of pins as long as I'm successful, but—'' He paused and shrugged.

Roxie wondered why she was asking questions, as if it mattered what he said. But participating in Charlie's craziness took some of the ache from her heart.

AS IT TURNED OUT, the Osborns called and announced they were flying home early. They told Roxie that she was welcome to stay in the guest house as long as she liked, at least until she had enough saved to work out a deal on a condo or town house.

''I am moving back to the park tomorrow,'' Charlie

announced when Roxie told him that the Osborns would return on a flight the next evening. ''The weather is delightful now, Roxie. The bench won't be a bad place at all.''

''Oh, Charlie.'' Roxie sighed, knowing that his decision was final. She tried to ignore the depression that was settling over her and growing more dismal with every passing minute. First she had pushed Hank away, and now Charlie was leaving.

Roxie felt drenched in sadness. Charlie had been living in a dream world, and for a short time, so had she. In the real world love was not enough to overcome life's problems.

*

THE RETURN of the Osborns gave Roxie something she hadn't enjoyed since leaving Newark—a trusted woman friend in whom to confide.

Fran and Roxie had planned to spend the afternoon fertilizing and pruning the citrus trees. The fragrant air hung still and silent, except for the hum of bees gathering nectar from the orange and grapefruit blossoms. Even Como was gone, transferred for the week to her sweetheart's corral. Roxie had told Charlie about Como's changed status, and he was happy for the llama, but nothing, Roxie knew, could ease his disappointment concerning Hank.

As she and Fran worked, Roxie searched for a way to begin a discussion of what was bothering her. ''You and Dave seem so happy, so in love,'' she said. Roxie pulled out a weed from the tree well and tossed it aside. ''Fran, tell me if this is too personal, but did you ever consider…having children?''

Fran answered at once. ''I couldn't have them, although we went through a truckload of doctors before that conclusion was finally drawn.''

''What about adoption?''

''We moved around too much,'' Fran said, clipping branches as she talked. ''And in the end we decided to give up the whole desperate game of baby-makes-three.'' She stopped pruning and looked at Roxie. ''Kids are nice, but they seldom stay around, you know. It's the person you'll be married to for the next fifty years who counts.'' She studied Roxie for a moment. ''And now I get to ask you a personal question. Who is he?''

Roxie's mouth opened in surprise.

''Just as I thought. Are you going to tell Aunt Fran about it?''

Roxie leaned on her shovel. ''Yes,'' she said, gazing at Fran. ''I've been wanting to for days.''

The story rushed out like water into a dry irrigation ditch. Roxie told Fran everything, including the parts about Charlie and his claim about being St. Valentine, and Como's escape.

''Whew!'' Fran said when Roxie had finished. ''China wasn't nearly that exciting.'' Fran put down her clippers and walked over to hug Roxie. She eyed her shrewdly. ''I suppose the only way to keep Charlie in business is for you to patch it up with your Mr. Craddock.''

''Even if it means giving up my dream of having a baby?''

''But what sort of dreams are you giving up now?''

Roxie was silent for a long time. The drone of the bees was the only sound in the sunny patio as Roxie thought about her choice. "I'd rather have Hank and no baby than no Hank at all. I love him, Fran. More than anything or anyone else." She took a deep breath. "And I'm not going to let this baby business come between us."

"That's my girl. Go get him, Roxie."

"I believe I will."

And Roxie tried, but no one answered the telephone at Hank's house. She called again every half hour until ten o'clock that night.

She debated whether to call again and finally decided to dial the number once more at ten-thirty. Hank answered the phone.

"Roxie?" he said as soon as she spoke. "Is anything wrong?"

"No," she said, trembling at the sound of his voice. "I need to talk to you. In person. I wondered if maybe we could…get together sometime. Sometime tomorrow." She swallowed hard.

His reply was swift. "I'll pick you up at ten." There was a pause. "You know I'd walk on hot coals for a chance to be with you again, Roxie."

THE NEXT morning Hank arrived exactly at ten. To cover her bad case of the jitters at seeing him again, Roxie dragged him immediately into the kitchen and introduced him to Fran and Dave, who looked up from their Sunday paper with a bemused expression.

"It's wonderful to meet you," Fran said. "Would you like some coffee?"

"Thanks," Hank said, glancing at Roxie, "but we'd better be going."

"Uh, yes, we'd better," Roxie said. She rushed out the front door before she made a blubbering fool of herself by falling into his arms and begging him to marry her within hearing distance of Dave and Fran.

As they drove she noticed little things that she'd missed before. The shape of his earlobe, the small mole on the curve of his cheekbone, the breadth of his hands—all were precious to her now. She hoped that he still loved her enough to forget her harsh words of two weeks ago.

"We're going to the house, aren't we?" She recognized the route to the house his contractor friend was building, even though they'd traveled it at night before.

"Yes."

When they turned down the winding drive, she quelled the unbidden feeling of homecoming.

Roxie's appreciative gaze roamed over the graceful lines of the Santa Fe-style house. Everything about it enchanted her, from the huge carved double entry doors to the round log beams that protruded from the stuccoed exterior. New leaves sprouting on the mesquite trees would soon shield the house from the sun and create a cool haven in the desert.

Engrossed in her thoughts, she didn't realize that Hank had left his seat until he opened her door and helped her out.

He stood silently beside her, surveying the house. "Like it?" he finally asked.

"Yes," she said, afraid to admit to more.

"I put a deposit on it this morning."

Her gaze flew to his and her eyes widened.

"And if you like this house, I mean really like it, I want us to live here—you, me, Ryan, Hilary—I told the kids I want to marry you—and of course, Charlie." He paused. "And the baby."

Disoriented, she shook her head and tried to assimilate

all that he'd said. "The what?" she whispered, putting her hand over her heart.

"I went to see the surgeon last week, and he's ready to try reversing the operation whenever I say."

She struggled with a light-headed feeling of unreality, of moving through a dream. "I have my little speech all ready about how I've discovered that you are more important than having a baby, and now you're telling me—"

"That I was wrong," he said, stepping forward and taking her into his arms.

"Wait a minute." This might be a dream, she thought, but she'd say her piece anyway. "I've thought this through and spending my life with you is far more important than whether I ever have a baby."

He smiled and stroked her cheek. "I got out the old albums, the ones we put together when Ryan and Hilary were small. Looking through them, I realized those were special times. You deserve that experience, and I deserve to have it with you."

Slowly she began to believe in the moment, in what he was saying. "You really have changed your mind," she said in wonder.

"Yes. I wasn't around nearly enough for the other two. I want full participation with this one. Let's schedule the baby during the slow season in construction, okay?"

Her joy overflowed and she smiled at his earnest, impractical request. "I don't think it's quite that simple."

"Sure it is. I'll get Charlie to work some of his St. Valentine's magic."

"Oh, Hank, Charlie will be thrilled with this news. He won't have to retire, after all. We have to tell him tomorrow."

Hank pulled her close. "We'll take him to lunch when

I come downtown for the license. In the meantime, I have other plans. Some old man once told me that I was abounding in love, and it's been frustrating keeping that bottled up the past two weeks.''

"I wouldn't want you to be frustrated, Mr. Craddock.''

"Good,'' he murmured, finding her lips and claiming the kiss that was undeniably his.

ROXIE COULD hardly wait for Charlie to arrive at the county clerk's office with his red rose Monday morning. When he walked in, his smile a ghost of the jaunty grin he'd once had, her heart ached for him.

She hurried toward the counter as he arranged the single rose in the vase. "Hello, Charlie.''

"My, but you look wonderful this morning,'' he said, taking off his hat and laying it on the counter.

"I should,'' she replied, anticipating his delight. "Hank and I are applying for a marriage license today.''

Disbelief transformed itself into ecstasy on Charlie's lined face, and Roxie accepted his hug of congratulations with breathless laughter.

"A more delightful surprise I've never had. I thought all was lost.''

"Just when I had decided that Hank was more important than having a baby, he was deciding that we should have a baby, after all.''

"How delightful. Each of you willing to sacrifice for the other. Will you have the baby or not?''

"Hank insists that we'll try,'' Roxie said, lowering her voice as she became aware that others were listening. "But even if we can't have one, I don't mind anymore. I'll have Hank.''

"And because you don't need this child so much, you'll have one," Charlie predicted.

"Perhaps." Roxie smiled. "We're buying a new house, Charlie, and we'll all live there, even you."

Charlie's blue eyes twinkled. "You're too kind, Roxie. I don't know what to say."

"Just say yes. The wedding's in two weeks. Oh, and we're taking you to lunch today, right after we settle the license business. We'll meet you at your bench."

Charlie reached for her hand. "I wish you and Hank all the happiness in the world, Roxie."

Roxie squeezed his hand. "I know you do."

At the door he tipped his hat in her direction. "It's been a pleasure, my dear."

"See you at twelve-thirty," Roxie called, waving. Then she forced herself to tackle the paperwork that seemed so unimportant today.

Hank arrived at noon, and by twelve twenty-five he and Roxie were walking hand in hand toward the park.

Hank looked around as they reached the park. "I don't see him. I thought he'd be here with bells on."

Across the park, a city maintenance man stopped emptying trash cans and looked at Roxie and Hank. Then he left his job and walked toward them. "You Charlie's friends?" he asked when he was within calling distance.

"Yes." Roxie hurried forward.

"He asked me to give you this." He took a crumpled envelope from his back pocket. "Said he was moving on. Well, excuse me, but I have work to do." The man left.

Roxie glanced pleadingly at Hank, who was standing quietly beside her. "He wouldn't just leave, without saying goodbye, would he?"

With trembling fingers Roxie tore open the envelope

and almost dropped the figure-eight gold pin that fell out of it. "Oh, Charlie," she murmured, holding the pin. "You did say that you gave the love knot away at the end."

"At the end of what?" Hank asked.

"At the end of each job as St. Valentine."

"Roxie, are you saying that you think he's really—"

"I really don't know what to think. Let's read what his letter says."

Together they scanned the brief note.

Dear Ones,

My work here is finished and I must prepare for my next adventure in love. I leave you knowing that your future together is bright, for you have been blessed by the special magic of St. Valentine's Day. For a brief while I feared that the spell no longer worked, but now my faith is restored and I must continue my journey. Give my love to Como.

My fondest regards,
St. Valentine (Charlie Hartman)

Slowly Roxie folded the letter and tucked it back in the envelope. "I don't know what to believe," she said, gazing up at Hank.

"I do." His gray eyes were warm with affection. "I believe that Charlie Hartman, whoever he is, gave me the chance to love a wonderful woman, and thank God I didn't blow the chance. Whether Charlie is really St. Valentine doesn't matter anymore. Our love is real, and that's all that counts."

He put his arm around her and led her away from the park.

*

"MUST BE NICE," the driver of the eighteen-wheeler said, "to pick up and go whenever you want. Not a bad life, old man."

"No, it isn't a bad life," Charlie agreed. "But you're mistaken about the schedule. I do have one. By September I have to create a base of operations, locate and find suitable people."

"What you got, some sort of con game going on?"

"Heavens no, young man. My purposes are purely philanthropic. But everything must proceed on schedule. I can't afford to miss my all-important deadline."

"What deadline?"

"Why February fourteenth, of course. It's the most important day of the year for lovers." Charlie leaned back against the seat and smiled. "Still."

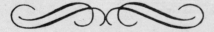

MINGLED HEARTS

Vicki Lewis Thompson

"**Y**ou're backing out on me!" Stephanie scrambled to her feet. "You're sticking me with a double mortgage payment!"

"You won't be stuck, I promise." Valerie's dark eyes pleaded for understanding.

"You expect me to share this apartment with some stranger?" Twin flames of anger lit Stephanie's blue eyes. She slid her hands into the back pockets of her cutoffs and surveyed the living room cluttered with cardboard boxes and crumpled newspaper. "Do you know *anything* about this person?"

"A little. Marge just referred to her as Dr. Barclay. I think she's a marine biologist at Scripps." Valerie walked to the large sliding doors that opened on their fourth-story balcony. "That should be a selling point, you know. The institute's right over there." She waved her hand toward the curved shoreline north of La Jolla Cove.

Stephanie joined her friend at the open door. Her eyes moved over the half-moon beach and sculptured sand-stone cliffs of the cove, then traveled down the line of surf to the buildings of Scripps Institute of Ocean-ography. Damn. Val's decision to marry Jim was ruining everything.

Valerie pulled her attention from the turquoise sweep of water. Covertly she eyed her friend. "Forgive me?"

Stephanie glanced up in surprise and read the guilt in her friend's face. "Sure I do," she said quickly, hugging the taller woman.

"Thanks." The strain eased from Valerie's delicate

face, but the sound of the doorbell brought a new look of apprehension. "I guess they're here."

Stephanie swallowed nervously. "Might as well get this thing over with." She took a deep breath and opened the door.

"Oh, you're not—" She looked into eyes the color of ripe wheat and felt an illogical tremor of recognition. Yet she knew she'd never met the man whose broad shoulders filled the doorway. "Excuse me, I was expecting...." Her apology died on her lips as she glimpsed Marge bustling up behind the stranger. Her green eyes were watchful, wary as she made a rapid introduction.

"Dr. Barclay, I'd like you to meet Dr. Collier."

Silence stretched between them like a taut rubber band.

"You're—" they began in unison, then stopped, staring at each other in disbelief.

Marge held up manicured hands. "All right, I admit I practiced a slight deception."

"*Slight* deception?" The man raked a shock of dark hair from his forehead.

Marge sighed. "If either of you had known the truth, you would have rejected the idea without meeting each other. So I took a chance." The real-estate woman's natural optimism bubbled forth. "Of course! I know how you must feel, Lloyd, but wait until you see the view from your bedroom. Stephanie's taken the one on the right....." Her voice trailed off as she walked into the other bedroom. Lloyd followed, stoic tolerance in his bearing.

"Valerie, so help me, if you knew this before—" Stephanie whirled to face her friend.

"I didn't! I swear I thought she was bringing a woman," Valerie protested.

Stephanie crossed her arms and stood stiffly until Lloyd and Marge reentered the living room.

"And of course you get the same spectacular view of the cove from the living room, which also opens on the balcony through these sliding doors," Marge explained, pushing the door aside and silently inviting Lloyd to step onto the balcony. As if to get away from her constant chatter, he walked over to the wrought-iron railing and scanned the expanse of sparkling water.

Marge tiptoed over to Stephanie. "I wouldn't be so quick to throw away your chance to live here, if I were you," she warned. "The market's tight, and I can't guarantee someone else, much less a woman, will come along."

Stephanie felt a sinking sensation in the pit of her stomach. She glanced furtively at the broad-shouldered figure on the balcony. Something about the set of the man's shoulders disturbed her. Except for Gary, she'd always been able to handle the men in her life, to keep them in safe compartments where they didn't interfere with her goals. Something told her Lloyd Barclay would defy that kind of control. As if sensing her scrutiny, he turned, his golden eyes trained directly on her. For a moment their eyes locked, then each looked away as he strode back into the room.

"It's hard to argue with that wonderful view."

Stephanie saw a difference in his face. The resistance was still there, but a gleam of anticipation shone through. Unexpectedly her heart hammered against her ribs.

"Okay, Marge, I like the place, but what about Stephanie's objections? Suppose she has a boyfriend who might not appreciate having her live with another man?"

"As a matter of fact, there is someone," Stephanie babbled, deciding on the spur of the moment that Jeremy might be good protection from her rampant thoughts.

"Jeremy and I are practically engaged." Deliberately she avoided Valerie's amused glance.

"Wouldn't he have a fit about this?"

Stephanie shivered. The conversation was becoming far too personal. "I don't know." *He won't give a damn, if the truth be known,* she amended to herself.

"Then he's a fool," Lloyd muttered.

Crazily, the words warmed a place in her heart that had been cold for a long, long time.

Slowly Lloyd's golden eyes evaluated her, traveling lazily from tousled head to grubby sneakers. "I think you and I need to go to lunch and talk this over. And that's the perfect outfit for riding on the back of my motorcycle."

"Motorcycle?"

"I think that's a terrific idea," chortled Marge. "Well, I'll just mosey back to the office."

"And I have a date with Jim for lunch," Valerie added. "Something about picking out a ring." Excitement shone in her dark eyes, and Stephanie gave her arm a quick squeeze.

"I *am* glad for you, Val." She grabbed the key ring from the kitchen counter before following the others out the door.

Forlornly she stood beside the polished ebony cycle, watching Marge follow Valerie's Camaro out of the parking lot.

"You'll need this." Lloyd thrust a white helmet in her direction, and she noticed he had already strapped a similar one over his dark hair. Strong fingers grasped the strap and snapped it deftly in place, and Stephanie's face tingled where his knuckles had brushed her cheek.

Awkwardly she swung up her bare leg and managed to straddle the shiny machine.

"Put your arms around my waist," he said. "Try to feel the direction of my shifting weight and shift yours accordingly."

She tensed when he flipped up the kickstand and gunned the engine, but managed to lean in the proper direction as they veered out of the parking lot.

With each turn, her breasts became more sensitive to the shifting muscles of his back and her thighs tingled where they brushed his. At last they swerved into the parking lot of a fast-food restaurant.

He grinned at her as she climbed unsteadily from the back of the cycle. "No atmosphere. No ocean view. Let's see how we feel about this proposed arrangement when the glittering waves aren't seducing us."

She unsnapped the strap of her helmet. His even teeth flashed again, revealing a boyish warmth she found charming. Charming? Gary had once charmed her, too. She would have to be careful. She could not risk another heartbreak. Not when all her plans were at stake.

"Is that a perm or the real thing?" His eyes roved appraisingly over her short blond curls.

"The frizz is real, I'm afraid."

"It suits you." He turned and headed for the chrome-and-glass doors of the restaurant before Stephanie could react to his unexpected compliment.

Within minutes they sat facing each other over a Formica-topped table, munching cheeseburgers and sipping milk shakes.

His golden eyes held hers. "What got you into this mingle business, Stephanie?"

"Money," she said simply. "I couldn't see any way on my teacher's salary to save enough to open my own psych clinic. This co-op condominium is an investment. I plan to sell in a year or two and make enough profit to get me through the first six months of running my own business.''

"Why the big push to open your own clinic? Don't you enjoy teaching?"

"It's not bad." Slowly she stirred her milk shake with her straw. "But I got into psychology to help people with problems, not teach others to do that."

"Impatient, are you?" His golden eyes twinkled.

"Perhaps. What about you, Lloyd? A single man in your position should be able to afford a place all to himself.''

"True. However, I made the mistake of getting married several years ago, and I'm still paying for it, literally." Bitterness invaded his eyes. He picked up a French fry. "How come your friend is backing out? Did she suddenly remember you snore?" His grin was disarming, and she chuckled.

"No, I have Cupid to thank for this mess. A former love returned and proposed. I can't blame her. If I'd been in her shoes, I probably would have done the same thing."

"Any lost loves in your background?" The question came softly. "What if I'm suddenly stuck with two mortgage payments? I warn you, I'd have a lawyer filing suit before you took that first step down the aisle."

"I give you my word you don't have to worry about that." Gary would never come back and beg her to marry him. An "anachronistic custom," he had called marriage the night she had made such a fool of herself.

"What about Jeremy?" Lloyd insisted. "The words I believe I heard were 'practically engaged.' Wouldn't you rather get him to buy Valerie's half?"

Stephanie twisted the paper from her straw around one finger. She had to explain this carefully to keep Jeremy as a buffer between her and this charming stranger. "He doesn't believe in getting his money tied up in property. He owns some bonds, and someday, when we open a clinic together, I'll use the equity from the mingle and he'll cash in his bonds.''

''And in the meantime, he won't mind if you live with another man?''

''You make it sound as if we'd be doing something illicit!'' She forced a laugh. ''I don't know about you, but I'm very busy. We'll probably never see each other.''

''Unless we choose to.'' Lloyd's tawny eyes seemed to evaluate what her bulky sweatshirt concealed.

She gulped and dropped her eyes.

''The last thing in the world I wanted was a woman as a living partner. I had enough of that when I was married.''

''Then perhaps we should forget it.''

''Not necessarily.'' His words brought up her head with a jerk. ''If I had never stood on that balcony, I could kiss this idea good-bye without a single regret.'' His eyes lingered on her face for a moment. ''Well, perhaps with one regret.''

Stephanie watched him silently, afraid his thoughts had taken the same direction as hers. But without Lloyd, her plans were doomed.

''I'm probably a damn fool for even considering this.'' He raked his fingers through his dark hair. ''What do you think, Stephanie?''

She thought it was the riskiest, most foolhardy thing she'd ever considered.

''I think we should give it a try,'' she said.

''Me, too.'' His eyes held hers and she felt suddenly short of breath. What was she doing? What would she tell her parents, whose middle-class attitude surely would not accept their daughter living in a co-op with a man? And there was Sigmund. She had forgotten him completely until this moment.

A KEY TURNED in the lock arrested her attention. "He's here." She wiped her suddenly moist palms against her jeans.

"Anybody home?"

Before she could answer, an ear-splitting shriek shattered the silence.

"Stephanie? My God, are you all right? What—" Lloyd burst into her bedroom and spun in the direction of the awful noise.

"It's my scarlet macaw," she said wearily. Unconsciously she moved between Lloyd and the bird in a protective gesture.

Sigmund tilted his crimson head, regarding them with yellow eyes. "Study the ego," he croaked happily.

"Oh, no," Lloyd groaned. "He talks, too."

"Of course," Stephanie snapped. "Sigmund's very intelligent, and quite tame. Until he gets used to his new surroundings, I'll keep him penned up."

Lloyd brightened slightly. "Does he try to fly out the front door when you open it?" he asked hopefully.

"Don't try it," she warned.

He stared balefully at the crimson-headed bird. "You should have told me about this bird last week."

"I was afraid if I tried to explain a forty-inch talking macaw, you'd back out." She dropped her gaze.

"After that motorcycle ride, even a talking macaw wouldn't have driven me away, Stephanie."

"What?" Startled, she glanced up and met his gaze. What she saw there sent a paralyzing numbness through her system.

"Oh, Stephanie." His words came out as a sigh.

"Don't you know I'm as afraid of this attraction between us as you are?" His hand moved up and smoothed the slight crease in her forehead. His touch. She had been waiting for it all week without realizing it.

"Don't fight it. You feel it, too." Her protests fluttered ineffectively against the pressure of his mouth. She squirmed to free herself, but he held her firmly.

With an anguished groan, she wrenched free. "Lloyd! I don't want this," she wailed.

He dropped his arms to his sides, but she saw the clenched fists. "Okay, Stephanie. Maybe I was wrong about your reaction to me."

"Wrong!" squawked Sigmund.

"He'd better keep his comments to himself if he doesn't want to end up in barbecue sauce!" Lloyd stalked from the room, leaving Stephanie a quivering mass of confusion.

She didn't even know Lloyd Barclay! Yet she feared him, feared the ache he inspired.

The doorbell chimed, shaking her away from her thoughts. Jeremy would arrive after the heavy work was done. She hurried to the entryway and yanked open the door.

He held up a bottle of wine. "Housewarming present. It's the best wine $5.98 can buy."

"Jeremy," she said, "I still have some unpacking to do, and a couple of glasses of that might make me decide to give up for the day."

"What're you trying to do, impress your new roommate?"

Stephanie colored. "Not on your life!"

"Hmm." Jeremy rubbed his rounded chin. "Had an altercation with the marine biologist already?"

"You might say that." She rubbed the back of her

neck. "Sigmund gave a couple of his famous screeches, and Lloyd came unglued."

"Good old Sigmund." Jeremy grinned appreciatively. "I knew I could count on him."

Sigmund let out another eardrum-piercing cry, and Stephanie cringed.

"Is there some way we can keep that bird quiet?" Lloyd tore out of his bedroom, then stopped when he saw Jeremy. "Oh. Sorry if I sounded rude." He looked anything but apologetic.

"He'll grow on you," remarked Jeremy, his pale eyes evaluating Lloyd, then shifting with a worried expression to Stephanie.

He knows, thought Stephanie frantically. *He can tell something's gone on between Lloyd and me.* "Lloyd, this is Jeremy Hammond," she said a little breathlessly. "Jeremy, Lloyd Barclay."

"Glad to meet you," said Jeremy, shaking hands unenthusiastically. Anger pinched his face, but he managed a smile. "I'll just leave the wine here for another time, and the two of you can work yourselves to death." He plopped the bottle on the counter and left, closing the door with a loud thud behind him.

"I don't think your boyfriend cares for me," Lloyd offered. "But then I didn't take an instant liking to him, either." Golden eyes penetrated the depths of her blue ones for a moment before he turned and walked to his bedroom.

Stephanie stood stock-still for several seconds, then shook her head as if to clear it. "Damn," she said softly, then wandered back to her room to tackle the rest of the unpacking.

By ten o'clock, she lay propped in her own bed studying lecture notes for the next day's classes. It wasn't long before she reached to switch off her bedside lamp. She *had* to get some sleep. Had to....

An intense white light, followed closely by an explosive crash and Sigmund's blood-curdling shriek, jolted Stephanie from sleep. A deafening peal of thunder and the glare of lightning sent her bounding under the covers in terror as Sigmund screeched.

"Stephanie?" Lloyd's large frame loomed in the doorway.

Thunder shook the glass door to the balcony, and instinctively Stephanie catapulted into Lloyd's arms, burying her head against the reassuring warmth of his chest. She felt his arms tighten around her, and a sense of safety began to replace her fright.

"This kind of storm is really something for a midwestern girl," she mumbled against his chest.

He looked at her then, the kindness in his face barely discernible in the darkness. "Only fools wouldn't have a great respect for that kind of power, Stephanie. Don't be ashamed by your fear."

"I'm a psychologist who helps other people overcome their fears, yet I'm not ready to overcome mine."

He chuckled, a warm sound in the chill of the room.

"Well, I feel much better, Lloyd. Thanks." It was a cue, a signal for him to leave her room, and he sensed it. He dropped his arms to his side. "It must be late."

A sudden flash of lightning bathed them both in white light. "Well, good night and sleep tight." He bent his head and aimed a kiss at her cheek, but an irresistible urge made her turn her head and his lips landed directly on hers.

She felt his sharp intake of breath before he gathered her with a groan into his arms. The sheer nylon of her gown shielded little of the impact as her breasts flattened against the hard wall of his chest.

Already his tongue sought the warm recesses of her mouth and one large hand molded her hips against the soft silk of his robe, where she could easily feel his arousal.

Stephanie fought the urge to arch against him. "Lloyd, I'm sorry. I don't know what made me do that. I didn't mean—"

"Oh, I think you did, Stephanie." He traced the lacy scallop of her neckline to the hollow between her breasts. "Can't you tell how natural this feels, how right?"

"But I hardly know you!" she protested.

"Does Jeremy make you react like this?" His thumb flicked against her nipple and she gasped. "Or this...." Pushing the material away, he bent his head to take the stiffened tip in his teeth. "Beautiful." The word fell around her like a cloak as she stood swaying slightly in front of him. "You're beautiful, Stephanie."

"Lloyd, I think we're making a mistake...."

"Loving is never a mistake, Stephanie. We need each other tonight." His voice drew her magically.

"Good morning, Stephanie!" The voice sounded clearly in the darkness.

"What the h—" Lloyd jumped back.

Suddenly the room felt cold. "Lloyd, I think you'd better go," she said miserably. The spell was broken.

"I may murder that bird," said Lloyd in amazement. "I think Sigmund just ruined what could have been a beautiful moment in our lives, Stephanie."

"I'm sorry, Lloyd, but I'm not willing to trade my future for a moment, no matter how beautiful."

"Is that right?"

Stephanie hugged the sheet around her quaking body, trying to ignore the hurt in his voice.

After she heard the bedroom door shut behind him, she sat up in bed for several minutes, stunned by the sudden turn of events. How had things progressed so far?

STEPHANIE SNAPPED awake to the aroma of freshly perked coffee. How could she face Lloyd after what happened the night before? She wanted to live in this co-op on her own timetable, selling when the market was right instead of when a love affair soured. She had watched office romances, seen the pain when two people were forced to work side by side after a relationship ended. How much worse to have to live with a former lover!

Somehow she had to convince Lloyd of her indifference to his charms. She had to develop the strength to refuse him! Spending more time with Jeremy would help, and Sigmund could be a continuing barrier, just as he inadvertently had been the night before.

Having showered and dressed she smoothed the antique quilt over her bed and strode purposefully out of the bedroom, feeling brave and confident.

"You finally decided to get up." Lloyd lounged casually on a bar stool.

"My first class isn't until ten."

He looked as if he hadn't slept the night before, and she longed to smooth the lines of fatigue around his eyes.

"You must realize that all your thoughts show on your face." He folded his arms across his chest and regarded her calmly. Then his fingers closed on the soft silk of her sleeve, and her heart tripped into high gear. She noticed the sudden gleam in his golden eyes.

"You were in that shower more then ten minutes. Twelve, to be exact. I shower in less than five."

"Henceforth I will take my alarm clock into the bathroom with me," she flung at him, "unless of course you want to sound a gong outside my door when you think I've used up my quota of hot water."

"We could save even more money if we showered together," he offered. She gaped, her eyes wide, as he struggled to suppress a smile.

"Not on your life!" she exclaimed, and watched helplessly as he broke into laughter, the rich sound filling the apartment.

"If you don't mind, I'll get some fruit for Sigmund's breakfast and be on my way." She lifted her chin, determined to salvage a shred of pride.

"Stephanie." His tone softened. "About last night—"

"Let's just forget it, shall we?"

"I can guarantee that you won't forget it, and neither will I."

She glared up at him defiantly, meeting the challenge in his eyes with all the strength she could muster, but the longer she tried, the more she seemed to drown in the topaz depths.

"I have to get going or I'll be late for class," she said at last. She turned and walked from the room, certain that his eyes followed her until she disappeared from his sight.

*

"OKAY, SIGMUND, hop onto my shoulder," Stephanie coaxed several days later as she considered what to have for supper. From the doorway of her bedroom she could see Lloyd, sprawled in his shiny black chair reading a new scuba magazine.

"Supper," croaked Sigmund, fluttering gently onto the

towel she draped over one shoulder to protect her winter-white eyelet dress.

Lloyd's eyes lifted from the pages of the magazine. He shook his head.

"You know, that dress makes you look like a sacrificial virgin. I find it difficult to think of anything but making love to you."

"So! We're back to that, are we?" Her fingers shook as she sectioned the orange and began feeding it to Sigmund.

"We never left it, Stephanie. You may think your little ploy of keeping Sigmund around will separate us, but it can't work forever. That bird is getting more used to me every day, and soon it won't matter whether he's in the room or not."

"If you imagine I need Sigmund to keep you at arm's length, you underestimate me, Lloyd," she said. "Now if you'll excuse me, I need to heat up this casserole and eat before Jeremy gets here."

"Ah yes, Jeremy. The other decoy. What have you cooked up to bring him on the scene this time?"

He knows what I'm doing, she thought frantically.

"I didn't 'cook up' anything. We're co-leaders of a group therapy session tonight."

"In that dress? I thought group therapy involved punching pillows and venting your anger."

"It's obvious you have lots to learn about psychology," she said icily.

"I learned everything I needed to learn when Jewel and I went through marriage counseling. God, but it was pointless!"

"You may have gotten a poor counselor."

"This one seemed to have trouble with the English language. I told him repeatedly that I didn't love my wife, but he refused to accept it.''

"How could you be so certain you didn't love her?"

"I was sure." His tone was cold. "Would you know whether or not you loved someone?"

Why did the question have such an effect on her? She took a deep breath. "Yes, I suppose I would."

"Good." He picked up his magazine once again. "I rest my case."

DESPITE HIS THREAT to circumvent her evasive tactics, Lloyd avoided Stephanie for the next few days. As she drove home from the last day of class before Christmas vacation, she wished herself past the upcoming two weeks. Classes were over until January, and all she had to occupy her were the term papers stacked beside her on the car seat. She couldn't afford to go home this Christmas.

She pulled into her parking space. As she expected, the black motorcycle was gone. She could spend the afternoon with her term papers.

She plowed through three of them before lifting her eyes with a sigh to gaze at the dripping gray sky. The peal of her doorbell promised a reprieve from the gloom.

"This is the perfect day to curl up with a gorgeous blonde in front of a blazing fire. Look what I brought you." Proudly Jeremy produced two pressed-wood logs wrapped in red-and-black paper.

Stephanie smiled as he followed her into the living room. His happy-go-lucky personality was just what she needed.

"I presume Lloyd's not here?" Jeremy set the logs on the circle of slate under the fireplace.

"No, he works in the lab during the afternoon."

"Good." After coaxing a flame from the two logs, he pulled her next to him on the beige carpet. Stephanie detected a glitter in his pale blue eyes when they traveled from her face to the smooth skin visible above her carelessly buttoned shirt.

"My stocks just went up yesterday," he said.

"That's good." Suddenly the air seemed to go out of her. When she pictured the office space with two consulting rooms, she had trouble imagining Jeremy using one of them. A soft sigh escaped her.

"Don't be discouraged, sweet Stephanie," Jeremy cajoled, his lips just inches from her ear. "The time will pass sooner than you think." He began to nibble past her shirt collar to the sensitive hollow of her throat.

"Jeremy," she pleaded, reaching to intercept his other hand, which was creeping across her thigh.

"Come on, Steph," he murmured against her skin, capturing her hand and holding it down by her side.

"Let me go, Jeremy."

"Hey, we are long overdue for this." His wet lips felt hot against her skin. "How long d'you 'spect me to wait?" Jeremy's voice slurred with passion as he began tugging at the snap of her jeans. She tried to pry his fingers away.

The resounding slam of a door accomplished her goal as Jeremy stiffened apprehensively. Stephanie managed to push him off her and stand up. Lloyd was glowering at the two of them. "I want you to go," she said.

"But—" Jeremy scrambled from the floor, adjusting his belt "—I thought—"

"You'd better leave, Jeremy. Now."

"Hey, if that's the way it is, fine with me." Jeremy edged toward the door, giving Lloyd a conspiratorial glance. "Never can tell about these females, can you? One minute they're ripping your clothes off, the next, they play the role of the soiled virgin.''

"Your clothes look intact to me." Lloyd's jaw clenched. "Now I think you'd better go."

"Sure, sure." Jeremy backed toward the door, fumbling for the knob. "Maybe you'll have better luck than I did, pal." His eyes narrowed bitterly as he left.

Suddenly exhausted, Stephanie sank into the smooth coolness of her pine rocker. She felt the beginning surge of tears.

"Did he hurt you?" In an instant he was beside her, crouching next to the rocker. "Stephanie?"

"No," she murmured. "Oh, Lloyd, it was probably all my fault! I've been seeing more of him, and he just naturally thought that—"

"That he could force himself on you?" Lloyd grabbed her shoulders. "Stephanie, no man has the right to do that, no matter what he thinks!" He stood up. "I can't really figure it, Stephanie. You claim to be so involved with him, but you don't want him laying a hand on you. If you were my fiancée, I'd expect a little more than a good-night peck on the cheek."

The idea of an engagement to Lloyd Barclay sent shivers down her spine. "We'll never have a chance to test that one, will we?"

"Marriage isn't one of my favorite institutions."

"So you're content with one casual affair after another, is that it?" Her heart ached with the knowledge that Lloyd rejected marriage so completely.

His eyes held her transfixed. "My affairs are never casual."

*

STEPHANIE slumped dejectedly in her rocker, convinced this would be the worst Christmas of her life. When the entire stack of term papers was graded, she had nothing to erect between herself and her morbid thoughts. She could no longer consider Jeremy as a business partner for her clinic. Without a partner, it would take twice as much in savings before she could begin the project, which meant living in this mingle and building up equity for twice as long. She groaned aloud. She was having trouble holding out against her attraction to Lloyd now—if they lived together twice as long she'd never be able to resist.

Feeling very sorry for herself, she decided to pour a glass of Jeremy's white wine, which she had been hoarding in the refrigerator for a special occasion. Between sips she fed Sigmund M&M candies as she reviewed her impossible situation. She was very afraid she was falling in love with the man she lived with.

Suddenly the door swung open and the pungent scent of pine needles filled the room.

"Ho, ho, ho. Merry Christmas!"

Lloyd managed to shove the tree all the way through the door in a shower of needles. Her eyes lingered on his dark hair tousled by the wind. He looked wonderful. His golden eyes sparkled in fun, and she realized she had never seen him like this.

"You look like you were expecting a tree-trimming contest." An assessing gaze took in her gaily colored outfit. "With only two days until Christmas, the lot was practically giving them away."

"It's very beautiful," she said.

Standing there in her red outfit looking at the Christmas tree he had bought—*their* Christmas tree—she felt a happy warmth building inside her. Maybe she was finally getting the Christmas spirit.

"I have some wassail for after we finish trimming the tree." She nodded toward her empty glass next to the rocker.

Lloyd carried a bundle of wood to the hearth. "But first we'll start a fire," he said, peeling off his corduroy coat. He surveyed the half-burned commercial logs Jeremy had supplied. "Never did like these darn things," he mumbled.

"Christmas carols!" Lloyd said suddenly, snapping his fingers and jumping to his feet. He disappeared into his bedroom, returning with a portable stereo. Soon Bing Crosby's "White Christmas" chased the last bit of gloom from the apartment.

As they worked to unwind the two strands of lights, Stephanie caught a flurry of red, blue and gold wings from the corner of her eye. "Sigmund!" she cried in sudden apprehension. But it was too late. The large bird landed on the topmost branches like a giant decoration. The flimsy metal stand offered little support for the weight of a forty-inch macaw. The tree toppled as an indignant Sigmund flew screeching back to his perch.

"Lloyd, I'm so sorry," she wailed.

"I'd say that was a perfectly natural reaction on his part," said Lloyd, and Stephanie heard with surprise the friendly understanding in his voice. He brushed her lips gently with his fingertips. She half closed her eyes, expecting his kiss, but it never came.

Side by side they worked in a room lit only by the multicolored glow of the tree lights and the orange blaze of the fire.

"I'm almost done," announced Stephanie, carefully

draping another icicle over the tip of a feathery green branch. "Time counts, you know."

"It does?" Lloyd responded in mock anguish. He began flinging handfuls of icicles on his half of the tree.

Laughing, she rushed around the tree and caught his arm. "That looks terrible," she scolded, taking the icicles out of his grasp. "I think you just forfeited."

"What about the penalty you get for holding?" He looked significantly at her, his golden eyes sparkling.

"What is it?"

"Just a kiss."

"Oh, is that all?" Standing on tiptoe, she pecked him on the cheek with pursed lips. "There."

"Not quite," he said softly, just before his lips crushed hers. His assault was quick, demanding, and Stephanie felt the floodgates of her pent-up need burst open, filling her with desire. She squirmed against him, wanting him, loving him, impatient at the fabric that separated their yearning bodies.

Gasping, Lloyd wrenched his mouth free and covered her face and throat with tiny nipping kisses. "God, Stephanie, how I want you, have wanted you, ever since I first saw you standing there in that disreputable sweatshirt, belligerent as hell about the prospect of living with me."

"I was afraid, Lloyd," she murmured against his cheek. "I still am."

"Don't be. I won't hurt you." His breath was hot against the hollow of her throat. "Feel what's happening between us, Stephanie."

He placed his hand gently over her breast, his fingers playing tenderly with the hard peak of her nipple. "Tell me you want me, Stephanie." He smiled into her love-glazed eyes.

"I want you, Lloyd," she whispered, "but—"

''No, no more words.'' He laid a finger lightly over her lips. ''No more soul-searching, Stephanie. No promises, no commitments. Just tonight.''

His mouth covered hers and he lowered her gently to the carpet. Slowly he undressed her, exposing her body to his burning gaze.

His sharp intake of breath was the only sound in the stillness as she watched his eyes move over her flushed skin. ''This is how I've longed to see you.''

He bent his mouth to her breast, nipping playfully at the soft flesh. As he continued to tease the sensitive tip, his hand moved in ever-tightening circles toward the source of her pleasure, and she instinctively arched her hips in invitation.

''Yes,'' he whispered, his mouth covering hers as his hand sent waves of pleasure through her heated body. Groaning, she fumbled with the buttons of his shirt.

''Lloyd, I want you so,'' she confessed, helping him slip out of his shirt and trousers.

He smiled down at her as her eyes devoured his strong chest, the tight muscles of his belly, and his jutting manhood, blatantly announcing his desire.

She reached to stroke him, relishing his soft moan of pleasure as he sank beside her. She felt his invasion and rose joyfully to meet it. Moving under him, she grasped his firm buttocks and urged him on. He plunged against her again and again, and she called to him as the pressure building within her finally burst, the sensation carrying her away just as he fell trembling against her, gasping her name.

STEPHANIE AWOKE to the clunk of wood against metal. She sat up and watched Lloyd using one of the unburned logs to rearrange the dying coals in the fireplace. He came toward her on all fours. "I feel like getting some fresh air. Let's go for a walk along the cliffs."

"Now? It must be three o'clock in the morning."

"Two-thirty, to be exact. Come on. Let's get going before the moon sets!"

"Okay." Impulsively she agreed and ran into her bedroom to don jeans and a warm flannel shirt. She walked back to the living room where Lloyd stood, corduroy jacket in hand.

He held her hand, his fingers laced comfortably through hers as they went down the stairs. Running like children, they crossed the park, pausing at the low rock wall separating the park from the cliffs of the cove. Waves smashed against the cliffs at their feet.

"It must be exciting to scuba dive."

"Yes." His voice surrounded her, rich and warm.

"You've always wanted to be a marine biologist?" she asked.

"I've always wanted to have some kind of career in oceanography."

She pushed on, wanting to know the details of his life. "So you got a scholarship after high school and went right through to your doctorate, never dissuaded from your goal, right?" She pictured a one-track approach to life.

"Not quite." The warm weight of his arm dropped from her shoulder. "I'm a little late in asking, but are you by any chance on the pill?"

"Y-yes, I am," she stammered.

"At least one of us was responsible, then." His words battered her heart. "I guess a fool never learns." His bitterness stopped her in midstride, and she whirled to face him.

Tenderly his thumbs traced and retraced her cheekbones, and she felt her anger ebb.

"Lloyd…you said that…that 'a fool never learns.'"

She felt him go still, knew when he lifted his head and stared out toward the rolling waves.

"It was a long time ago, Stephanie."

"Please tell me, Lloyd."

"All right." His shoulders sagged a little. She felt his pain, but also something more important—trust.

His words came slowly at first. "It was my senior year in high school. I had big plans for college. I told Jewel all that. I asked her to go on the pill, paid for the doctor visit and the prescription. She even *showed* me the darn things!"

"But she didn't take them?"

"Not even one. She wanted to get married—that's what she told me after she announced she was pregnant. We got married in June."

"And the child?"

He laughed shortly. "She miscarried in July. I should have filed for divorce immediately, but I stayed, kept my job as a low-level manager for a department store, and gave up plans to register for school in the fall. When the second semester came around, she seemed to be in better shape, so I announced I was leaving and going back to school. That's when she really turned on the waterworks, and even offered to go to work herself so I could take a full load of classes."

"Sounds pretty unselfish," Stephanie said.

"I thought so, too. We had a long talk that night, and I told her that after I finished school I wanted to start a family. She agreed."

"Lloyd…." She touched his sleeve and felt him tremble. "Were there children?" She had to know.

"No." Her heart lurched at the regret in his voice. "After I earned my doctorate, she always had a reason why we shouldn't begin a family yet. First we needed a house, then a swimming pool, then a new car. Finally, after she'd had one too many ounces of gin, she admitted she didn't want babies, had never wanted them. The only reason she tried to get pregnant the first time was to land me. She vowed she'd take me to the cleaners financially if I walked out on her. I did, and she did, and the rest you know." He kept his back to her.

"Lloyd, I'm so sorry." Stephanie slipped her arms around his waist. Slowly the tension seeped out of him, and at last he turned in her arms and reached to cup her face in his hands.

"I'm sorry, too, Stephanie. I let that memory invade our happiness tonight." The tangy salt breeze filled her nostrils and lifted the lock of hair from his forehead. Joy surged through her as he traced the line of her upturned nose.

With a throaty chuckle, he captured her smiling mouth with his own, and she answered with an explosion of passion that startled her.

"Slow down a little, huh?" He laughed against her cheek. "How can I take you home with me if I can't even walk?"

Smiling provocatively, she backed away, and they crossed the damp asphalt together.

"Upstairs, you wench!"

The Christmas tree filled the room with its forest scent, and Stephanie breathed deeply as she walked past the door Lloyd swung open for her.

"I can certainly tell which side of the tree you *threw* your icicles on," she commented dryly.

He stood watching her, hands on hips, his face creased in a deep grin. "This is the same argument my mother and dad had every year. I just realized how much fun they were having all that time.''

Stephanie smiled, too, then sobered. ''You did say 'had,' not 'have'?''

''Yeah, I'm afraid so. Dad died of a heart attack. Mom lasted about two years after that. Why aren't you seeing your parents for Christmas, Stephanie?''

''I couldn't afford to go back.'' She shrugged. ''And they couldn't make it out this year.''

''Couldn't or wouldn't?'' He paused, his eyes questioning her. ''They don't approve of this arrangement, do they?''

''No,'' she answered unhappily. ''They still believe when I live under the same roof with a man I should be married to him.'' She looked up in shock. ''Lloyd, I didn't mean—''

''I know. It's hard to ignore your parents' moral standards. That's one of the reasons I stayed married as long as I did.'' He walked toward her. ''Very seldom do we do things just because we want to do them. That's what makes tonight so special.'' He drew her into his arms. ''We are only pleasing ourselves.''

Rising on tiptoe, she curved her fingers around the beard-roughened ridge of his jaw and pulled him toward her, parting her lips as her tongue flicked out to follow the bow of his upper lip. Her desire grew as she heard him moan softly; then he swept her up in his arms and started for his bedroom, dropping her with a loud plop in the center of the undulating water bed mattress.

''Lloyd!'' she shrieked as the warm waves rocked her up and down.

Lloyd toppled next to her on the bed, and she forgot about the movement of the bed as the now-familiar ache spread through her lower body. The mattress swayed gently as Lloyd removed her jeans and her delicate lace briefs.

"I need you," he growled, rolling on top of her and parting her thighs.

When the slow tender rocking began, she was surrounded by shifting warmth, yet anchored by the man she loved. Together they swirled in a vortex of sensation until both uttered a blended cry of triumph.

MORNING LIGHT filtered through pale lashes. Sleepily she rolled over. Her eyes flew open as the bed rolled with her. The water bed! Instantly she remembered, and just as quickly she realized she was alone on the quivering mattress. Awkwardly she climbed over the side of the bed and padded into the living room. Something on the Christmas tree caught her attention, and she walked over to pull a piece of paper from its branches.

"Stephanie," the hastily scrawled note began. "I've gone diving with Sharon. Back this afternoon. See you then, Lloyd."

*

SHE SHOULD have known, she scolded herself bitterly. He *had* said, "No promises; no commitments." Now he was showing her exactly what he meant. He had no intention of tying himself to someone as he had with Jewel. Hugging her arms tight around her, as if to squeeze the hurt away, she plodded into her bedroom.

"Those tawny eyes!" croaked Sigmund, jumping happily on his perch as she entered the room.

"Oh, Sigmund, how could you," she cried, giving way to tears.

"Pretty Stephanie," the bird squawked hopefully, cocking his head in confusion at his mistress's distress.

She drew a shaky breath and battled the wave of nausea that swept over her.

"You know what I'm going to do, Sigmund?" she announced to the yellow-eyed bird. "I'm going to take the longest, hottest shower in history!"

Shoving her head under the drumming water, she doused her curls before reaching for the bottle of shampoo. Ferociously she worked to remove every trace of his presence, scrubbing his scent from the curve of her throat, cleaning every inch where he had touched her so intimately, so lovingly....

A sob escaped her lips as tears mingled with the steamy water cascading over her body. Damn it! Why did she have to love him? She wished she could be like him, willing to grab the moment, happy to move on to other things when the moment was over. Stephanie stood under the hot spray until her skin glowed pink and the tips of her fingers began to crinkle, but the torment inside her would not dissolve.

"Anybody home?" His cheery greeting froze her hand in the act of turning off the tap. He was back. "Stephanie?" He pounded on her bedroom door. "Can I come in?"

No, her soul screamed. *Not into my room, not into my life, not into my heart.* "Just a minute, Lloyd. Sigmund's loose in here." Her voice sounded reasonably normal, masked by the still-running water.

"Okay." She could almost see the broad shoulders shrug and turn away. "Have you had lunch?"

"No," she called. Did he expect to come back to her, after spending the morning with Sharon, and take up where he left off? The thought appalled her. Dressing quickly, she ran her fingers through her damp curls before opening the door.

He was lounging against the kitchen counter, munching from a box of crackers. The sight of him there, smiling at her, nearly undid her resolve to put him in his place. Oh, God, she still wanted him. She leaned against the doorjamb, suddenly weak.

His golden eyes slid possessively over her. "You look cute like that, all fresh and damp." He took a step toward her. "I think I'll have you for lunch."

"No!" She backed toward her bedroom.

"What's the matter, Stephanie?" The question came softly.

"Nothing."

"Are you upset because I went scuba diving this morning instead of staying here with you?"

"You have a right to do whatever you want with your time," she replied haughtily. "I wouldn't dream of interfering in whatever you have going with...with Sharon!" she rasped.

He frowned. "Sharon and I have worked together for years," Lloyd said. "We share the same lab space. She's practically my best friend."

"How marvelous," she flung at him sarcastically. "How is it that you conveniently neglected to tell me about her until after you lured me into your bed?"

"Lured you?"

"And now I suppose you think I won't be able to resist a repeat performance," she interrupted, needing to hurt him. "Well, I'm afraid I wasn't that impressed, so you'll have to make do with Sharon. You probably switch women as quickly as you change clothes."

"I don't think you have any room to talk," he countered, the muscles of his jaw working. "How do I know you don't have a date with Jeremy tonight? As far as I know, you're still 'practically engaged'—'' he mimicked her tone ''—to the guy.''

''Come to think of it,'' she raged, ''going out with Jeremy tonight is a good idea. A very good idea.''

''Fine. As long as I can count on you being gone, I'll invite someone for dinner.''

She sucked in her breath. He would bring Sharon here? ''Don't worry,'' she whispered hoarsely. ''I'll stay out very late.''

''Then it's settled. I'm going to buy a couple of steaks and a bottle of wine.'' In an instant he was gone.

She had no intention of calling Jeremy. He usually spent Christmas in the mountains and wouldn't be in town even if she wanted to see him, which she didn't.

She wondered if Lloyd would build Sharon a fire—and if they'd lie before it, enjoying the cozy warmth of the lighted Christmas tree, the tree she and Lloyd had decorated so happily together. Would he then take her to his water bed? Would he…? She shoved her fists into her eyes as if to blot out the picture of Lloyd and Sharon together on the rolling bed.

She had to get out of there, figure out somewhere to go for the night. Running to her bedroom, she flipped open the telephone book and thumbed through the motel listings. There. A budget-priced establishment far from ocean views and creamy stretches of beach. Shakily she dialed the number of the motel and made a reservation for a single room.

A GLANCE in her car's rearview mirror next morning revealed a tousle-headed young woman wearing a rumpled yellow-and-white shirt. *I look like hell*, she admitted.

Lloyd might well wonder what she had been up to the night before. *Well, let him,* she thought bitterly.

The aroma of grilled tenderloin still hung in the air as Stephanie pushed open the apartment door. She hurried toward her bedroom.

"And just where have you been all night?"

She whirled to find him leaning against the frame of his bedroom door, his rugged face unshaven, his white dress shirt looking as if he had slept in it. The lock of dark hair fell over his forehead, and the lines in his face made him look older than she ever remembered seeing him.

"I don't believe it's any of your business," she replied coolly.

"I considered calling the police, in case something had happened to you." Something—was it pain?—etched itself briefly in his face.

"Your concern is touching."

With an angry growl, he lurched forward, then stopped himself. "Are you, or are you not going to tell me where you were all night?"

She faced him, challenging him with her eyes. "Why should I have to account to you like some—some teenager?" Her voice rose a notch. "How would you like to describe your evening to me? Whatever you are involved in is nobody's business, because you can handle it, right? Well, I can handle my situation, too!"

"That's not the impression I got the other afternoon," he said softly.

Was that concern she heard? She stared at him mutely, wanting to believe he cared, yet distrusting the tiny hope growing in her heart. "I...I was safe last night, Lloyd. I'm sorry if I worried you." Tears stemmed by indignant anger threatened to break through at this first sign of tenderness. She spun on her heel. "I'm going to check on Sigmund."

"He's fine." From the corner of her eye she saw him shrug uncomfortably. "I've given him some fruit and changed his water. He...he was calling for you, and I thought he might be hungry."

"Th-thank you." She stumbled over the words, thoroughly confused.

He eyed her. "Could...could we talk?" He ran nervous fingers through his dark hair.

She sank into her rocker as he paced back and forth in front of the sliding door, feigning great interest in the pounding surf.

"Tomorrow's Christmas," he began, and she realized with a shock he was right. This was Christmas Eve. "Do you think we could declare a truce for tonight and tomorrow? It seems a shame to be at each other's throats like this, especially since—"

"Since what?" she broke in, irrational hope surging within her.

"I'm leaving on a four-week research trip day after tomorrow."

"What?" It was the last thing in the world she expected him to say, and grief welled in her like hot lava.

He turned toward her, a masked expression on his unshaven face. "I'm heading the team going down to Baja, California. I thought you should know we only have to put up with each other for another day and a half before we get a four-week vacation." He gave her a taut smile.

She avoided his eyes, focusing instead on a point just behind his head. She had to ask, "Will...will...Sharon be going?"

"Yes."

His answer hit her like a blow to her midsection.

"I guess the separation will give us each some time to think about something else."

She tried not to imagine what he was leading up to, tried not to let him see her anguish. "Think about what, Lloyd?"

"Renting my half of the mingle to Sharon."

SHE SLEPT fitfully. Next morning she wrapped her terry robe around her and stumbled out of her bedroom.

"Merry Christmas."

She blinked at Lloyd. A picture of past Christmases, the gay litter of wrapping paper, the hugs from her parents, the smell of turkey roasting, brought a rush of tears to Stephanie's eyes.

Gently he cupped her fingers. "I believe Santa paid us a visit last night."

Stephanie's gaze flew to the Christmas tree, and she noticed a box wrapped in red foil. "Oh, Lloyd…I don't have…"

"It's not for you. It's for Sigmund." His golden eyes twinkled. "You know the one. Kind of short, loud dresser, big mouth." Lloyd disappeared into her bedroom and returned a moment later with Sigmund perched casually on his shoulder. Stephanie had a strange feeling it wasn't the first time the bird had sat there.

Her fingers flew over the taped flaps of the red package. Her gasp mingled with Sigmund's screech as she unveiled package upon package of M&M Peanuts.

Sigmund plummeted from Lloyd's shoulder directly to the box, almost knocking Stephanie over in the process.

Stephanie lifted merry blue eyes to Lloyd's face, but her smile slowly faded as she met the intensity of his gaze.

"Lloyd, I…." She stopped.

A sad smile tipped the corners of his mouth. "Merry

Christmas, Stephanie,'' he said softly. His eyes seemed to memorize her features. The silence between them trembled like fragile tissue paper.

"What time will you be leaving tomorrow?'' she asked.

"Early. Before you're up.'' His eyes searched her face, as if seeking the real question behind the polite one she was asking.

"Oh.'' She stood awkwardly. "Is there…is there anything you need me to take care of while you're gone?''

His eyes seemed to melt into hers for an instant. "Just yourself.''

*

FOUR WEEKS of sleepless nights, of endless soul-searching, had brought Stephanie to the conclusion that she must swallow her pride and try to win his love. She might not get marriage—not after Lloyd's experience with Jewel—but he could learn to love again.

Fresh from her shower and clad in lacy bikini briefs and her new bra, she stood in front of the open closet, pondering what to wear. She wanted to strike the right note, something between indifference and outright provocation.

A sudden screech from Sigmund caused her to whirl. If she had not known better, she would have sworn Sigmund missed Lloyd, too.

Selecting an outfit at last, she slipped it on. The pink color was reflected in her cheeks, she noted with satisfaction as she stood before the mirror.

She loved Lloyd, and somehow she would make him realize that she was right for him, that a commitment to love was not a prison sentence.

Her heart fluttered as she realized he would surely be home soon. In a flash of inspiration, she remembered the firewood. Several sheets of crumpled newspaper later, she finally fanned a wavering flame from one of the smaller logs.

As she started for the kitchen sink to wash her hands, she heard the click of a key, and then Lloyd was standing in the doorway.

"You're home," she choked out.

Something leaped in his golden eyes. "Yes," he said with a small sigh.

"I...I was starting a fire."

The tiny flame she had nursed so patiently had died. So much for atmosphere.

"Want me to do it?" he offered.

"No, thanks," she answered, smiling grimly. "I like to finish what I start."

"So do I," he said softly, watching her. Stephanie continued to stuff paper under the grate. Before long even the good-size logs crackled merrily.

"That makes a nice picture."

She tried to keep her voice light. "How about some coffee?"

"Sounds good. We can drink it by the fire."

In a few moments they sat cross-legged in front of the leaping flames, each holding a mug of steaming coffee.

Lloyd leaned back to gaze at Stephanie. "It's good to be home," he said quietly. "I've missed you, Stephanie."

"I've missed you, too, Lloyd," she replied honestly, not daring to look at him.

"May I kiss you hello?" His question came softly, hesitantly, yet his eyes smoldered with an emotion that turned her answer into a tiny gasp of surprise. The pressure of his lips was quick, a teasing warmth. He watched her with bright eyes, taunting, daring her to take the next step.

Sliding one hand slowly under the green knit collar of his shirt, she drew him toward her, parting her lips. Her fingers tracing small patterns across the nape of his neck.

Suddenly his arms closed around her. He peppered her face with kisses as he choked out her name again and again. Joyously she pressed against him.

"Stephanie, these weeks without you have been hell." His hoarse whisper warmed her ear. "I know what we said, but I—"

Stephanie pressed her fingers against his lips. "Shh! You don't have to explain to me now."

"But, Stephanie, what about—"

Again she stopped him. She did not want difficult questions now. Not now. Slowly her fingers crept up under the front of his shirt. She watched his eyes darken with passion as her nails scratched lightly across his chest.

With a groan he swept her into his arms. "Are you sure?" His eyes searched her face.

"I'm sure," she answered with a radiant smile, and he squeezed her tightly to his chest as he carried her into the bedroom.

This time there was no long exquisite exploration of each other; their urgency was too great.

"Stephanie, I want you so much," he rasped as she opened her thighs to receive him.

She watched his face as he thrust into her, watching his eyes shimmer as if with unshed tears. "Oh, Lloyd," she choked, clutching his strong back with her fingers, and feeling him surge deeper.

When he collapsed, shuddering, on top of her, Stephanie wrapped both arms tightly around him. It was going to be all right. And she knew, for the first time in four weeks, that she would be able to sleep all night long.

THE BED was empty when she awoke, and for one terrible moment she feared he had left again. Relief flooded through her as she heard the clang of a frying pan against the stove burner.

She eased her way out of bed. Lloyd's bathrobe, black silk with red piping down the front, was draped casually over the end of the bed, almost as if he had left it for her. Impulsively she slipped it on.

"Breakfast!" Lloyd called.

"Coming," she called back.

The Sunday paper rested next to her plate. And one of their neighbors was minus two marigold blossoms, judging from the flowers springing jauntily from the neck of a wine bottle filled with water.

They began splitting up the sections of the paper, each of them surprised when they both reached for the gardening pages.

"And we don't even have a place to garden in," said Stephanie.

"I know. I'd like to have a yard one day," Lloyd admitted, and Stephanie allowed herself to dream of planting it with him, spending time together on their hands and knees, up to their elbows in the damp richness of peat moss.

This was how a Sunday morning was supposed to begin, she thought.

*

INSIDE THE grocery store, Lloyd pushed the shopping cart. Stephanie scanned the rows of canned soup for tomato. She glanced over her shoulder, can of soup in hand, and discovered him leaning on the front handle of his cart, studying her intently.

"Can you tell me why I'm running away from the most wonderful woman I've ever known?"

She met his gaze, astonished. He wasn't kidding. His topaz eyes impaled her with fierce intensity.

"You just escaped a very suffocating relationship," she said slowly. "Your fears are perfectly natural."

"And they're hurting you, aren't they?"

"Yes." She dropped her eyes.

"I'm sorry, Stephanie. I promised once I wouldn't do that." He shoved his cart forward impatiently, then stopped, rapping the handle thoughtfully with his knuckles. "Damn," he said softly, keeping his back to her.

LLOYD GREW more quiet the closer they got to the apartment. When he made no attempt at conversation while they put away the groceries, Stephanie knew something was wrong.

"I'm going diving with Sharon this afternoon," he said at last. "I made the arrangements yesterday. Do you want me to cancel them?"

Of course, you fool! But then I'll confirm your fears that I'll suffocate you. "No, that's silly, Lloyd. Go ahead."

"Would you like to go along? Sharon and I could teach you the fundamentals."

"No thanks." Her voice sounded strangled to her own

ears, but she prayed it had a degree of normalcy. "I doubt if I'd be very good at it, anyway."

"Well…if you're sure…." He sounded genuinely disappointed.

When he left, she was in her room. She opened the cage door and the large bird climbed out. "Oh, Sigmund, what am I going to do? Just when I thought everything was going so well, he runs off to go scuba diving with her. How can I—" She paused as an idea slowly formed. She gazed out her sliding door to the cove. Somewhere, under its turquoise surface, Lloyd and Sharon were together. She had to enter that world, too, if she expected to capture Lloyd's heart.

THROUGH CAREFUL planning, Stephanie managed to keep Lloyd at a distance for a few days. She scheduled her lessons in the evening, mumbling something to Lloyd about counseling sessions with clients. When she got home late each night, she had no trouble sounding tired, and Lloyd seemed to accept her lack of interest in love-making.

One day soon she would surprise Lloyd with her new knowledge. Until that day came, she wanted to avoid his bed.

The week flew past, and she awoke to a sunny Saturday morning. Lloyd clanked through the door just before noon, his dripping diving gear under his arm.

"Hi!" His broad grin registered pleasure at seeing her.

"Have a good time in the cove?" She hated herself for asking.

"Sure did. I wish you'd change your mind and try it with us sometime, Stephanie." His chiseled features took on a boyish eagerness. "Sharon is such a pro at it, and I'm sure she could teach you in no time. You'd really like her, and I'm anxious for you two to get to know each oth—''

''Well, I'm not!'' She stood up abruptly, amazed that he would suggest that she become buddies with Sharon. ''I'm not sure what kind of person you think I am, but I have absolutely no intention of letting Sharon teach me to scuba dive. I think it's wonderful that you're so casual about all this—'' her voice began to quiver in spite of her efforts to control it ''—but I'm just not that loose, I guess!''

''I'm not ready to be tied down again, Stephanie. I thought you understood.''

''Intellectually, perhaps. But emotionally, I've got big problems when it comes to Sharon. Sometimes I don't want to have anything more to do with you, Lloyd Barclay! Now, if you'll pardon me, Sigmund needs me.'' She turned away from him, but he caught her arm before she stepped out of his reach.

''So do I,'' he said, his voice low and menacing. ''And I've been very patient all week with a woman who had no time for me. I've asked no questions about the fact you've been out every night. I told myself to wait until this weekend. Now you behave as if I were the lowest thing on earth. What's gotten into you, Stephanie? Where's the warm passionate woman who melted into my arms last weekend?''

She was livid with rage. ''All you require of me is my presence in your bed. I satisfy some of your needs, and Sharon satisfies others, is that it? And you use us both, without making any commitments to either one. I used to think I hated Sharon, but I've changed my mind. I feel sorry for her.'' She spit the words at him, wanting to hurt him.

''All right, Stephanie.'' His voice chilled her with its

cold impersonal tone. "I've kidded myself that you could give me time to work this out. I told myself your psychology training might even help. But we can't live together, gouging at each other until there's nothing left. I'll talk to Sharon, see if she's ready to move in."

"And I'm supposed to accept that with no complaint? Maybe I don't want to live with your girlfriend, Lloyd."

"Do you have a better alternative?" he challenged quietly.

"I guess I don't." She sighed. Slowly she walked into her bedroom and closed the door.

THE TELEPHONE was ringing the next day as she entered the apartment. She jerked the receiver from its resting place.

"Hello?"

"Stephanie?"

She frowned in confusion, not recognizing the well-modulated tone of the woman on the other end. "Yes, this is Stephanie."

"This is Sharon. Lloyd said I could come over tonight and meet you, if it's okay."

*

HATING HERSELF for even caring about her appearance, Stephanie stood before her full-length mirror. The pale blue knit dress clung softly to the gentle curves of her small-boned figure. She slipped her stocking feet into the gray suede pumps she saved for those times when she wanted to radiate elegance. This was one of those times.

"Stephanie?" Lloyd's voice sounded through the door.

"Yes?"

"Are you about ready? Sharon should be here any minute."

She opened the door. "I'm ready."

She felt her cheeks flush under his frankly admiring stare. "All this for Sharon?" he questioned softly.

"Oh, no," she said airily. "I'm meeting someone later."

The light in his golden eyes faded. "Jeremy, no doubt," he said.

"I don't think that's any of your business."

She saw a brief flash of pain. "No, I guess—"

The urgent peal of the doorbell sliced through his sentence, and Stephanie took a deep breath.

He held her eyes for a moment, then turned toward the entryway. Stephanie braced herself to face her rival.

"Stephanie, this is Sharon McNeil." Lloyd introduced them smoothly, as if they were meeting at a cocktail party. "Sharon, this is Stephanie Collier."

Stephanie mumbled something polite as she held out her hand to the tall slender blonde standing uncomfortably before her. *She doesn't want to be here any more than I want her to be,* she saw with sudden clarity. All at once Stephanie knew what she had to do.

"Why don't we sit in the living room?" She felt astoundingly calm. "We could all have a drink, and—" She paused, snapping her fingers as if remembering something. "Lloyd, I forgot to make a new tray of ice, and we don't have much left. Would you consider running to 7 Eleven and picking up a bag so we can have a drink?"

He shot her a questioning look, then shrugged. "I'll get my helmet and keys." At the door he paused. "I'll be right back," he said, concern in his golden eyes. He slowly closed the door.

"You wanted to get rid of him." Sharon eyed her with curiosity. "Why?"

"Because I just figured out who the fly in the ointment is here, and it's not you, it's me."

"What in the world are you talking about?"

"Wouldn't it make more sense if you rented my half of the mingle, Sharon?" Stephanie asked gently.

"Why?" Sharon frowned, perplexed.

"Oh, come on, Sharon." Stephanie became slightly ir-ritated. "I've known for quite a while that you and Lloyd have a thing going. So why don't you just rent from me? It would solve everything."

"Not quite."

"Why not?"

Sharon paused. "Because it's not me Lloyd wants. He's in love with you." Stephanie opened her mouth to protest, but Sharon waved her to silence. "After Lloyd's divorce, we dated for about a year. I was head over heels—I won't deny it—but something didn't click with Lloyd. He told me it wasn't going to work. Fortunately, we've been able to remain friends. I've started dating other people. I hope someday to find someone as terrific as Lloyd who will happen to think I'm terrific, too."

Stephanie felt a rush of sympathy for this suddenly very fragile-looking woman. "If that's the case," she ventured, "then what is going on with this renting business?"

"Lloyd's been attracted to you from the beginning, but he's had to battle his old suspicions about women every step of the way. You were the most important thing in the world to him, he said, and you'd told him you didn't want anything more to do with him."

"That true. I said that," Stephanie confirmed softly.

"Well, he wants to change your mind, without the ten-sion of living together. Sort of an old-fashioned courtship is what he has in mind. I'm also supposed to find out how involved you are with this Jeremy fellow. He's worried about that a lot.'' She stopped speaking, but it took Stephanie several seconds to recover from the impact of Sharon's words and close her mouth, which hung open in astonishment through the recitation.

"I haven't been seeing Jeremy for some time. He's no longer in the picture.''

"And how do you feel about Lloyd?''

"I'm afraid I love him, Sharon.''

"Thank God for that.'' Sharon sighed. "I think you two can make it, but you'd better have a good long talk, maybe several long talks.''

"About what?'' Lloyd's overly cheerful voice cut into their conversation as he came through the door and dropped the bag of ice cubes with a noisy rattle into the sink.

"Everything,'' answered Sharon, standing up. "And I'm going to leave you two alone so you can get started.''

"You're not leaving?'' Panic seemed to grip Lloyd for a moment.

"Lloyd, it's up to you, now.'' She left quickly.

As soon as the door closed, Stephanie leaped indignantly from her chair. "You were going to have her spy on me!'' The sheepish look on his face melted her anger like sun on a snowbank. She glanced at him shyly. "Jeremy and I are finished. Have been for some time. We never were a very hot item in the first place, actually.''

Concern clouded his brow. "Then if you weren't out with Jeremy all night just before Christmas, then who?''

She laughed. "I rented a budget motel room that night, Lloyd. I stayed by myself.''

"You crazy—'' His soft voice reached for her, even

before his arms closed around her. "And I paced the floor, waiting for you to get home."

"Good morning, Stephanie," Sigmund croaked.

"I can't imagine life without that bird." Lloyd's golden eyes smiled down at Stephanie. "Or without his curly-headed owner."

She searched his face, needing to reassure herself of his feelings. "Lloyd, I have been possessive about you, but I can't change that. I have to know there's no one else."

"There's no one else, Stephanie." His eyes looked directly into hers. "Sharon is only a friend, nothing more."

"I offered to rent her my half of the mingle." Stephanie stirred inside the circle of his arms. "I thought that would make you happy."

He threw back his head as he rocked her in his arms. "I love you, Stephanie Collier, and I want to marry you."

"You do?" She stared at him in wonder.

He laughed, a joyful sound. "That's not the proper response," he said, kissing her eyes closed. "You're supposed to say, 'I love you, too, and I accept your proposal.'"

"Of course I love you, but—"

"No 'buts' are allowed after that statement." He bent his head to nibble one earlobe.

"Lloyd," she persisted, trying to maintain her train of thought as his tongue explored the inner curve of her ear. "You're still making payments to one wife. Are you sure you want a second one? We can live together, like before. You don't have to—"

"Let me clear up a few things," he said, tilting her chin with one finger to look deeply into her eyes. "First, I understand Jewel is getting married again, so the payments should be ending. But even if they weren't, I still would want to marry you. All this time I've been fighting a commitment which already existed. Oh, Stephanie," he murmured against her cheek. "I want us to be married, to have children, to build our careers together. I want a lifetime, Stephanie. Can you give me that?"

She leaned back against his arms, wanting him to see the love in her eyes when she answered.

"Yes."

They closed the distance between them, their lips touching, sealing the promise they each made. She heard him moan softly against her mouth before pulling away to nuzzle her ear.

"All those little buttons on your dress are driving me crazy." He ran a finger down the row of tiny fastenings.

With maddening slowness he unfastened button after button, his lips following the trail blazed by his fingers.

"Lloyd?" She traced the outline of his beard-stubbled jaw.

"Mmm?" His dark lashes fluttered.

"Let's sell the mingle."

"Sell it? After all this?"

"I've just had the most marvelous idea." Her voice sparkled with eagerness. "If we bought a house, why couldn't I start my clinic in a part of it? Then I wouldn't need a partner to help pay rent, and I could have flexible office hours, and…" She looked anxiously at Lloyd. "Would you mind something like that?"

He smiled at her, his eyes golden with love. "I think it's a super idea, Stephanie. And with the sale and the prospect of Jewel getting married, we might be able to afford a place by the ocean."

"And a yard. Don't forget the yard."

"And a yard," Lloyd agreed, lightly teasing the tip of her breast to arousal. "Although for the life of me I don't know when I'll have time to work in the yard, with all the distractions in the master bedroom.'' He lowered his dark head to nibble gently at the taut peak. "I think I want to postpone this discussion until later," he crooned.

"Me, too," she whispered, lost to any reality but his touch.

"Good morning," croaked a familiar voice.

Lloyd's head jerked up.

"That bird has incredible timing," muttered Lloyd, burrowing against Stephanie's breast. "I'll tell you another thing our house is going to have."

"What's that?" questioned Stephanie languidly.

"A separate bedroom for Sigmund."

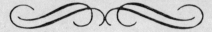

DAZZLE
Ann Major

He did not see the fat brown package beneath the *Times,* hidden as cozily as a time bomb in his mail.

Sipping a tart, fizzling drink, he reached for a section of the *Times* and began to read with the fascination of a man who'd long been married to the business world. He frowned as he noted Dazzle's stock had fallen a point while Radiance's had risen.

On first glance, he did not appear the entrepreneur at all. Prince Mikhail Alexander Vorzenski had the look of a pirate about him. He was tough and lean, a tall man who was powerfully built. Despite his charisma and his easy smiles, he was a difficult man to know. Only one woman had glimpsed beneath his surface hardness. Only she had discovered the lovelessness of his childhood, the parents who had had no time for him—his father a titled playboy, his mother a workaholic.

For the briefest time Liz had shown Alexander a world where love could be had without the need of conquests. After her, he was harder and lonelier, his victories in the business world more ruthless than before.

His strength served him well. If it were not for his sheer ruthlessness and drive, he would have long ago lost the presidency of Dazzle, Ltd., the vast family-owned international company he controlled. There were those who wanted to take it from him. Others still blamed him for what his wife, Liz, had done seven years ago.

His enemies were watchful, resentful. Dazzle, a leading manufacturer of perfume in England and Europe, had been sailing through rough seas for the past few years.

The worst and most recent disaster had occurred only ten days before—the explosion in one of Dazzle's top-security chemical labs in the Alps.

Alexander lay back, watching the pages of the *Financial Times* ruffle when he tossed it aside. The article in the *Times* about Dazzle and the explosion had not improved his mood.

Alexander tried to relax. The quiet, familiar sounds of the Mediterranean came to him; the gentle lapping of wavelets against the snowy fiberglass hull of his yacht, the distant purr of the incessant summer traffic of Monte Carlo.

The papers beside him began to flap. A brisk westerly gust would have sent newsprint flying had Alexander not seized them. He felt the lumpy brown mailer beneath them. Curious, he secured the *Times* beneath two magazines and examined the bulky envelope. In bold black letters Henson's unmistakable scrawl flowed across stiff, brown paper: "Raymond Henson and Sons, Private Investigation, Ltd."

Alexander's pulse thudded with startling violence. Seven years ago he had hired Raymond Henson to find his wife when she'd run away. He was accustomed to Henson's monthly reports. The slim white envelopes, which invariably contained a single carefully typed page that informed him there was still no trace of Liz's whereabouts, had arrived with unfaltering regularity—until now. Three glossy photographs lay before him. Two were of Liz.

The third photograph was of a boy uncannily like the boy he'd been himself at the age of six. Alexander drew a quick, sharp breath. He was inexorably drawn to the child. He scarcely understood his feelings; he didn't realize that all his life he'd yearned for someone to love, that what he'd once sought from his father and his older brother, he would now seek from his son. Alexander knew only that he had no choice but to go after him.

At last Alexander read the report. Henson had located Liz because he'd received an anonymous tip that Jock Rocheaux was traveling from Paris to Mexico City nearly once a month, and the reason for his trips was to visit Liz Vorzenski.

Alexander bristled at the thought of Jock having anything to do with his son. Damn Liz!

Jock was Alexander's own first cousin. They'd been boyhood friends and the most promising junior executives at Dazzle. The first break in their relationship had occurred because of an unfortunate incident involving a young woman they had both been dating.

The severe rupture had happened on a hairpin curve at a speed of over two hundred kilometers an hour. Jock decided winning a certain Grand Prix tour on the French Riviera was worth any price. Unfortunately the price had been Sasha. Jock had sent Alexander's younger brother, who was driving the car beside him, hurtling through a barricade and over a cliff in a ball of crystal flame. Alexander had used all his stature in the company to have Jock thrust out of it. In the end Jock resigned in a rage and went to Radiance, Dazzle's rival.....

Alexander set the report aside. Liz had come back into his life. Burning deep in his soul was the torture of a memory that was still too vivid—his unforgettable, his blazingly bold, his terribly defiant Liz. How he had loved her in those twelve brief weeks he had had with her.

He'd spent a fortune trying to find her. He wanted to try to understand why she had betrayed him.

Once she had told him laughingly, ''Money won't buy everything, my darling. But it can buy freedoms most people can't begin to imagine.'' She had smiled enigmatically. ''You can escape so completely when you're as rich as we are.''

He'd thought she was speaking of *his* fortune. He hadn't known then who she really was and that she was incredibly rich herself, and that she was an expert at escaping, that she'd lost herself in countries, in cultures, in out-of-the-way niches in the world for months on end during the rebellious years of her youth when she'd defied her family. There had been so many secrets she had kept from him. Once he had wanted to know everything about her. That time was past. All he wanted now was his child.

Alexander made two telephone calls. One to Paris and the other to London. He refused to listen when his older brother, Paul, told him that it was impossible for him to postpone his return to Paris, that important decisions he alone could handle had to be made. Alexander overrode every protest and gave orders for his Lear 55 to be flown at once to his private airport on his estate in Grasse.

*

IT WAS the rainy season, and the air was crisply cool and damp. Liz wrapped her rebozo more tightly about her shoulders and sipped her first cup of coffee that morning. An unopened letter from Jock lay on the table beside photographs of her beloved Cornwall. The letter would contain the inevitable demands. ''Marry me. Leave Mexico and come to France. Forgive your father. Forget Alexander.''

The coffee cup clattered as she set it in its saucer. Divorce Alexander?

The haunting vision of Alexander's burnished maleness, his jet dark hair, his golden eyes, rose in her mind's eye. She saw him again as she'd seen him the night they'd met, at a beach party in Deauville after a sailing regatta he'd won. It was ironic that it was Mimi, her father's mistress, who had suggested the holiday on the coast of France.

Mimi had said, "A few days together…away from your father…will give us the opportunity to get to know each other other."

Liz had wondered if Mimi sensed that she felt uneasy in her presence. Mimi had always been friendly, and yet from the first Liz had felt a reticence toward her. Even her father had noted it. He had said, "It is not easy for a man like me to live alone, Liz. I know Mimi is…different, but that is often the case with famous actresses. There is this ego problem."

Perhaps he was right, or perhaps it was only the normal jealousy a daughter might feel toward her father's mistress who was years younger than he.

They'd come late to the grand old château, which was aglitter and alive with laughter and music and dancing. Liz noticed Alexander at once. She was deeply conscious of his eyes following her. She had whispered excitedly in Mimi's ear, "Who is that man? The conceited one with the black hair."

Mimi's throaty voice didn't sound like her own. "You were buried too long in Cornwall before your father found you. That's Mikki Vorzenski. He's the new president of his family's fragrance company, Dazzle. They say he is a despoiler of women. Roger told me that his own family has exiled him to London. You must stay away from him."

"Mikki Vorzenski!" Liz murmured. "Oh, no." A terrifying hollowness in her stomach made Liz feel sick.

Her father had warned her and had made her promise to avoid him.

"Mikki Vorzenski and I are old, old enemies, my child. He is a ruthless thief in the perfume world. He would like nothing better than to hurt me through you."

In the short time she'd known Jock Rocheaux, her father had made it clear that he wanted her to marry him.

Mimi drifted away, and Liz hurried blindly across the ancient cobblestones of the darkened garden. Heavy footsteps thudded behind her.

That night of their first awareness—one for the other— would be forever frozen in Liz's memory. She had never been so immediately drawn to another human being as she was to this striking man, her father's enemy.

He had stared at the mad pulsebeat at her throat and the faint tremor in her hands. His eyes slid over her. Everywhere his gaze touched her, her skin flushed as if singed by a tongue of flame.

Before she could escape him, he seized her hand and drew her to him.

His heady masculine scent enveloped her. A powerful, unconquerable force bound them one to the other in a spell of electric enchantment.

With a half-smothered groan, he crushed her slim body against the awesomely lean power of his.

They'd both come so far, traveling through two lifetimes of loneliness to find each other. He lowered his mouth to possess hers, but she reached up and brushed his lips with her fingers. "No," she said breathlessly.

"Why are you so afraid of me?" he asked. "Why did you run away?"

"Because we cannot be."

"But we are," he said forcefully.

"Yes," she murmured. "And that is more frightening

than anything." In agonized passion she nuzzled her face against the warmth of his throat, and his hands moved caressingly through her hair, pressing her head even more tightly against him to reassure her.

"What should I call you?" she asked after prolonged silence.

"Everyone calls me Mikki," he said.

That name jarred; it was the name her father had taught her to hate and fear.

"I don't want to call you what everyone calls you."

"My mother calls me Mikhail."

She frowned, and he saw that she didn't like that either.

"No one calls me Alexander...."

"Alexander." She said his name softly, sexily, possessively, and then she smiled. "It's a shame to have a name that no one uses. I will call you Alexander."

"What will I call you?"

"Why, Liz, of course."

"No choice?" he asked. "No last name even?"

Her expression was momentarily shadowed, her fleeting smile enigmatic. *Tell him,* a tiny voice sounded in the back of her mind. "Killigen," she said in a strange, tight voice. It was the truth, and yet it was a lie. It was the name of the place she'd called home and of the man she'd called father.

After Alexander conquered her reluctance, there had been no stopping their soaring passion. She had known from the moment his name was whispered to her in Deauville that their love could never be, and yet she soon married him without telling him who she really was.

Now, seven years later, she was in Mexico alone with her twins. How blindly stupid she had been. Crumpling Jock's letter, she threw it in the trash. She would have to keep putting him off, at least for now.

From the balcony, Liz could see the peasants walking up the winding road from their village to open the doll factory—her factory. They dressed as they had for centuries, the women with dark-colored skirts and high-necked blouses, the men in their white cotton jackets and trousers, straw sombreros, leather huaraches, and serapes. The factory they worked in every day was one of Liz's few solaces. It was the one thing she could truly count on.

LIZ SURVEYED the destruction. Her entire factory was floating in three feet of water.

Juan, the foreman, shushed the others to silence so that he could speak. "*Señora*, the water tower on the roof broke and flooded the factory." His low, Spanish voice held both anxiety and defeat.

Liz thought of New York, where she'd found a vast new outlet for her dolls. Now this.

She waded through the water. She felt the stinging fire of tears behind her eyelids, but she fought them back.

"I will not give up. *We* will not give up," she said.

Her Spanish was awkward. But the people who worked for her loved the soft sound of her voice despite her confusing conjugations and hopelessly jumbled pronouns. They heard strength and hope.

Long ago, when Liz had first come to the deserted hacienda, the people had regarded her with suspicion. They gave her their sympathy when they learned she was pregnant and alone, their respect when she'd begun her factory.

Liz beckoned Juan and gave him specific orders. Then she telephoned Manuel Rodriguez, her partner, and told him they had to have more machines at once.

Liz worked long into the afternoon, racing between her

office and the factory, making uncounted decisions as to
what could be salvaged and what should be thrown out.
It was a painful process. An entire shipment of fifteen-
inch dolls resembling miniature princesses from imperial
Russia, all lavishly costumed to attend a dance in the
tsar's Winter Palace, were soaked. The research that had
gone into the creation of these dolls had been monumen-
tal, the labor in their gem-studded diadems, gossamer
veils and rich ball gowns awesome. Now they were
ruined.

She forgot about lunch and the siesta hour until Esmeralda, her baby-sitter, tiptoed into her office. Then Liz's
stomach growled ferociously as she realized it was long
past the hour she usually had lunch with the children.

When Esmeralda said nothing, Liz glanced up and saw
the misery contorting her face. Liz knew that a new ca-
tastrophe had struck.

"What have the little rascals done this time, Emmie?"
she asked lightly.

"Nothing, *señora*," Esmeralda wailed. "The little an-
gels are gone!"

Panic rose like a hot wave in Liz's throat.

"Gone?" Liz's tired mind refused to accept this new
crisis.

"Even the burro Pablo. I left them in the meadow to
ride Pablo, but he was being so stubborn he wouldn't
move. When I came back they were gone."

"ALEX. Samantha. *Queridos*. Oh, my darlings. Where are
you?"

Liz sagged wearily against a tree and listened to the
silence. Her teeth began to chatter.

Just when she thought she must return to get flashlights

and warmer clothing, Liz heard the sounds of childish laughter.

"Come on, Pablo. This way." Samantha was coaxing her pet, who was renowned for his stubbornness.

Liz was about to call to Samantha when the velvet warmth of an all-too-familiar male voice came to her.

"You're sure this is the way back, Samantha?"

"No, Daddy, I'm not sure," Samantha admitted. "Maybe Pablo is right."

It couldn't be. He couldn't be! Not here!

She saw him then, walking in the moonlight, and she stopped as though a witch had frozen her with a spell. Liz felt his intense, devouring gaze. There was a look of astonishment scrawled on his handsome face. His hair was as black as the deepest shadows; his golden eyes were molten with hot, unfathomable emotions.

All the feelings that she'd told herself were dead came alive like the searing, raw pain of an open wound, and she knew how terribly she had missed him, how terribly she still loved him.

"Mommy! Mommy!"

The spell of enchantment that bound Liz and Alexander was broken. The children tumbled headlong into her arms, breathless in their excitement.

"Pablo ran away, and Daddy came! We got lost in the woods chasing Pablo, but we weren't scared because Daddy was with us."

Liz hugged them closely, silently, frantically, before they darted back to Alexander. How had he won their affection so quickly? It was an ominous sign.

"Daddy said you might not let him stay with us," Alex said. "We want him to." There was a mutinous note in his voice.

Samantha cried passionately, "Mommy, please!"

Alexander's silence was no help. Why didn't he tell them it was impossible for him to stay?

"It's getting dark, and the children are cold," Alexander said curtly as she stood up. "It might be best if we went back to the hacienda before we tried to talk."

It was a rational remark, but his tone of command sparked anger in Liz. "After seven years, you and I have nothing to talk about," she lashed out, speaking in French so the children wouldn't understand.

He responded in French that was as rapid and deadly as gunfire. "The hell we don't! I've come because of my children." A muscle spasmed in his jawline.

Fear made her reckless. "You have no rights where they're concerned. You threw me out when I was pregnant."

All of his careful control disintegrated, and as he moved nearer, she realized how stupid she was to provoke him. There was danger in his hard look. It was as if she were facing a stranger instead of the husband she'd slept with, the husband whose children she'd borne.

"Let's get something straight," he said hoarsely. "I wouldn't have thrown you out if I had had the slightest idea you were pregnant. You deliberately left without telling me you were expecting, and now I find there are twins."

"I came to your office that morning to tell you," she replied quietly, "but you were already out of your mind with rage. There seemed no point then."

"Of course I was angry. You'd wrecked Dazzle and me in one staggering blow by stealing Paul's formula and giving it to Jock!"

His brown face appeared contorted through her blinding tears. "I had nothing to do with that," she whispered. "I tried to explain. I couldn't have done that to you."

"No?" There was a jeering note in his hard voice. His fingers tightened cruelly on her shoulder blades. "Then how did Radiance steal and launch the perfume my brother, Paul, had been perfecting for more than three years? Explain why Jock named that particular essence, Liz. And while you're at it, tell me those photographs used in that launch aren't of you, my darling wife. Tell me you weren't the model for Radiance in that stinking, crooked deal! Tell me you aren't Roger Chartres's daughter! Liz, why the hell did you try to destroy me?" The anger in his voice was fierce and frightening. "Tell me, Liz, was Jock your lover?"

"No!" The single word was explosive. "How could you even think that?" she cried. "There's never been anyone except...except...you." Suddenly that angered her more than anything. What right did he have to answers from her now? Her thoughts clouded as a terrible dizziness swept her.

The brutal disappointment of the flood, the hard work, her terrifying search for the children, and Alexander's fierce anger had all taken their toll. She felt curiously weightless. His grave face blurred in a nauseating whirl. Even his strong arms could not keep her from sliding into a void that brought swift, black oblivion.

Alexander lifted her into his arms. He stared into her still face. Her flaming hair fell across his shoulders.

"Why, Liz?" he drawled in a voice that was strangled by torture, repeating the question that had haunted him for seven years. "Why did you do it, when I loved you so?"

*

ALEXANDER strode with Liz in his arms. The hacienda was brilliantly lit against the deeper blackness of the mountains, and as Alexander climbed the path leading to the front gates, Esmeralda, Juan and several others walked out of the house. Curious, worried black eyes accosted him with a thousand half-formed suspicions.

"My wife fainted in the forest," Alexander drawled in his heavily accented Spanish, emphasizing his relationship to her. They nodded in swift understanding and immediate acceptance of him.

Alexander commanded Liz's servants with the ease of a man used to giving orders. "Take me to my wife's room."

Maria scurried to the kitchen while Esmeralda took the children. Juan led Alexander up winding tiled stairs to the *señora*'s spacious bedroom.

Alexander kicked the door open, stalked inside and gently laid Liz upon her great, hand-carved Mexican bed. Juan lit an oil lamp before shutting the door, leaving the couple alone in semidarkness.

"Alexander." Her voice was a soft whisper that stirred long-forgotten intimate memories. "Alexander, is it really you?" she murmured. Her voice held an aching tenderness. She lifted her hands to his cheek and caressed him wonderingly, inflaming him with her touch. Her softly glowing eyes held his.

Alexander groaned inwardly and brought his own hand up to remove hers. Curiously, instead of removing it, his warm fingers wrapped hers. His blood throbbed as with a fever.

Her eyes were closed, and her dreamy expression gave her the look of an angel. He remembered her wildness in his bed, her total lack of inhibitions. He remembered the way she had made love to him with her lips.

He inhaled deeply, thrusting the memories to the recesses of his mind. He had to get out of there. He was rising to make a swift exit when her hands circled his neck. She fingered the inky tendrils that fell over his collar.

A bolt of desire shuddered through him as she lowered her hands and moved them across his shoulders, drawing him down to her.

"Liz, don't do this!" he groaned, but he didn't prevent her trembling fingers from unbuttoning his shirt.

A strip of bronzed male flesh was exposed, and she leaned forward and slid her tongue across his warm skin, trailing a blazing, liquid path from his throat to his navel.

"How I want you, Liz. Damn you," he muttered. "I tried to forget you, but when you're here, holding me, I can remember only how it always was between us."

He stared into her smoldering black eyes and was lost. He seized her and pulled her roughly against his chest, hating her, loving her, wanting her, despising her. His arms were ruthless iron bands binding her against his tough male body. "You wanted this, Liz, remember that."

He touched her everywhere but without even a trace of the infinite tenderness he'd once so lovingly shown her.

His hands moved over her bare arms, her waist, down her thighs, savoring every lush curve.

Their desire built into a wild crescendo of spiraling needs. For a timeless moment their hatred fell away, and they were lovers again, each glorying in the taste and the sensation of the other.

He took her with the swift blind need of a man who'd been too long without the one woman he wanted. For a fleeting moment he glimpsed heights he'd thought he would never see again. Then desire overcame him in a shattering burst of glory. In that final moment he crushed her beneath him as she whispered his name in complete surrender. Afterward they lay in the hushed darkness without touching. He should never have let this happen. There could be no closeness with her. Nothing between them was changed. Still, a new, unnamed unease lingered.

He remembered suddenly the long, languid lovemaking sessions of their past. He remembered the loving hours afterward, when they'd clung to each other after their wild excesses. Alexander rose abruptly, turning his back on the silent woman on the bed. He did not want to think of the past.

LIZ SAT UP, shading her eyes with curled fingers. The leaden weight of anguish lay upon her heart. With her fingertips she felt the crusted residue upon her cheeks from the tears she'd wept during the long night. She'd scarcely slept.

When he'd left her lying in the chill darkness, she'd felt the most profound emptiness, because she realized how deeply she still loved him, just as she realized how hopeless her feelings were.

Liz opened the drapes and looked out on the purple mountains and the broad valley. But this morning, the peaceful landscape did not bring harmony to her troubled mind. At the sound of the door, she spun around, her heart jumping chaotically. Determined not to be intimidated, she tilted her chin defiantly. "They've all been clamoring to wake you for hours, but I wouldn't allow it," Alexander said.

Startled by this unexpected thoughtfulness toward her, she glanced at him. His cutting gaze slashed her. Whatever softness had motivated him was scarcely apparent.

"There seems to be a bit of confusion downstairs,"
Alexander said, "that only you can resolve."

"That's putting it mildly, I'm sure. You see, Alexander,
the water tank on the roof flooded my doll factory yesterday, before you came. But enough of my problems.
What do you want from me?"

He shot her a dark look. "Specifically—divorce and
custody rights. I'm willing to make a generous settlement
if you agree. The children will have stability. I will give
them the best schools. They can spend their summers in
my villa in Sardinia or one of Maman's châteaus in
France."

Her voice was dangerously low. "Did it ever occur to
you that it might do them irreparable damage to be separated from me? You cannot manage children the way you
manage employees in your factories, Alexander. You say
you will give them the best schools. Children need much
more than that. Your mother—" she sprang to her feet,
her hot temper flaring "—all she gave you were the best
schools, those glorious villas you're throwing up at me,
châteaus, and money. That's why you're hard, Alexander.
I won't let you ruin my children the way your mother
ruined you!"

Alexander crossed the room. He towered over her.
"Are you through?"

"No. Yesterday I saw that it was a grave error on my
part to take the children so far away from you despite the
hostile circumstances of our separation. I was sorry for
that."

"And now?"

"I wish you'd never come here." She whirled away
from him, her fists clenched against her stomach as she
stalked toward the windows.

From behind her his voice came, husky, gentler.
"Liz—"

This new softness from him was more than the disturbed state of her nerves could handle. Liz turned around.
His amber gaze startled her, compelled her. His hand
reached toward her, not in anger this time, but in—

She was never to know what would have happened had
they not been interrupted.

There was an embarrassed cough from behind the half-
opened door. Juan stepped inside.

"*Señora*, you must come at once to the doll factory.
We need your help, and that of the *señor* too, if he is
willing."

"I don't think the *señor* is particularly anxious to help
me," Liz said hastily. "He came here to—" She felt Alexander's fingers on her skin.

"Of course I'll help!"

Liz stared at both men in helpless confusion.

"I WON'T HAVE YOU turning my factory over to Manuel
Rodriguez!" Liz said heatedly.

Alexander endured her temper with the infuriating calm
he'd shown all week. There had been many tantrums since
he'd started trying to avert the disaster her factory was
headed for.

"Why not? He's the best man for the job."

She crossed her arms across her chest and glared at him,
detesting his smug attitude. "Well, I don't like it. You're
destroying everything. First you ruin morale by firing
Juan."

"You should never have hired him in the first place.
He's all wrong for this job. He drinks. Besides, I'm nearly
positive he's been stealing."

She was trembling violently now. "And then you started paying overtime, which I can't afford."

"Yes, you can, once we get things organized. You have a good product. I can start Manuel on the road to straightening all this out. The guy's really talented at getting the maximum out of your employees. He knows when to be hard, and you don't. Liz, don't you see, without the factory to manage you'll be free to do more research and create more dolls. That's where you should focus your energy."

"My employees, even Manuel, now look to you as the boss. The *señor* can do no wrong. They think I should be pleased," Liz said grumpily.

She would not have minded his taking over her world had he genuinely wanted to make a place for her in it.

*

THE SOUND of his wife's laughter floating up from the courtyard came to Alexander as he poured over Liz's account books. Liz and the children were playing games in the courtyard. He could not afford to make a mistake where his children were concerned. The last thing he wanted was to drag them through a lengthy court battle and the inevitable publicity such a trial would bring. So for one hellish week he had lived with his wife in order to spend time with his children. He had thought he could ignore Liz by concentrating on the problems of her doll factory, the impending crisis at Dazzle and the children; but she had haunted his thoughts night and day.

How many nights had he sprung from his bed aroused by the vision of her soft, scented loveliness, consumed with the mad intention of going to her room and taking her by force. Instead he would pace the balcony bare-chested in the cold night air, pausing to stare at the moon-light slanting across the jagged black mountain peaks, waiting until his sanity returned. To the children, Liz was warm and loving and patient. No matter what she was doing, she allowed the children to interrupt her. To his amazement, he had discovered a framed picture of himself in each of their rooms, and he'd learned that she had taught them to love him. That was why they had instantly accepted him.

Never having known the joys of family life before, Alexander found that this need in himself to be part of a family gave his wife an even deeper power over him. He was beginning to see that it would not be possible for him to separate Liz from the children. He loved them too much to deprive them of their mother. Much to his surprise, he had discovered that Liz hadn't seen or spoken to her father since she'd run away. If she had stolen the formula for Roger Chartres, why were they now estranged? Roger had come to him once in London after Liz had run away, and begged him to tell him where Liz was. At the time Alexander had not trusted Roger enough to believe he did not know where his daughter was.

Alexander saw no easy solution to the problem of custody. A sacrifice or a compromise would have to be made.

The phone began to ring. It was Paul. The news from Paris was devastating. Alexander was suspected of having caused the fire in Dazzle's lab himself, but when Paul demanded that Alexander return, he refused. Before, it had been uncharacteristic of him to put anything before Dazzle. Now it was suicidal.

NEXT EVENING

Alexander took the children into Mexico City without her.

After watching the last curl of dust behind her red Fiat, Liz sank down in her favorite chair and stared out at the darkening sky. She switched on the television, and Mimi Camille's husky purr filled the room. It was one of Mimi's early French films, with subtitles. Mimi played the part of a demonic woman with the face of an angel. Liz turned the set off abruptly, as always the mere sight of Mimi affecting her negatively. The last thing Liz needed was to think of Roger.

Later it began to rain gently. She went to bed, but she was still awake when the Fiat chugged into the drive.

Alexander and the children came upstairs. The children's voices were sleepy, his gentle and reassuring. At last the children were quiet and Liz heard the sound of Alexander as he walked to his room, the shutting of his door, his movements from within, the creak of his bed when he lay upon it. She wanted to go to him, but she did not.

It was hours later that Samantha's cry jolted Liz awake.

Liz jumped out of bed and ran outside. Alexander's door opened, and he stepped outside wearing only a pair of jeans.

"It's Samantha," Liz said, unconsciously reaching for his hand, and he ran with her to their child's room.

Samantha was sitting up stiffly in her bed. Alexander swept her into his arms.

"What is it, Samantha?"

Samantha's black eyes were wide in her white face. "Juan came into my room. I bit him on his hand when he put it on top of my mouth. He dropped me back onto the bed and ran out."

In a voice of steel, Alexander said, "Liz, hold Samantha while I check on Alex."

He left them, returning almost instantly, his face dark
with alarm.

"Alex is gone. I think Juan took him."

"Oh, no! Juan wouldn't—" Liz bit back her cry of
anguish. She remembered Juan's terrible anger when Alexander fired him.

THE MOON was hidden by the black mountains. They
headed up the twisting mountain road, so overgrown it
was scarcely more than a path etched between fields and
forest. "I smell smoke." Liz peered into the darkness.
"Alexander!" She gripped his sleeve frantically. "Juan's
jacal is on fire!" Then they were running toward the billowing glow, Alexander quickly outdistancing Liz.

Liz reached the little cornstalk hut in time to see Alexander push a drunken Juan to the ground and dash inside the inferno.

It seemed an eternity before Alexander reemerged, carrying the limp child in his arms. Liz screamed in horror.
The back of Alexander's shirt was on fire.

Ripping off her poncho, Liz began beating Alexander
on the back. When the flames were out she flung her
ruined poncho onto the ground.

"Alexander, are you all right?"

He stared at her, the lines of his face grim, his mouth
a grimace because of his pain. "It's Alex," he muttered,
"that you should worry about."

Feeling more helpless than she ever had in her life, she
stroked the brow of her unconscious son. "Alex, can you
hear me? Darling, Mother's here."

From behind her came Juan's drunken voice, muttering

brokenly, "Fire no on purpose, *señora*. The cigarillo, I dropped him. I never hurt the *niño*. I only want to scare the *señor*."

*

THE DOCTOR worked slowly, slicing Alexander's shirt from his back. As the scissors flashed, Dr. Gomez spoke of Alex's injuries. "The boy's received a concussion. The burn on his arm is serious. He suffered smoke inhalation, but he will recover."

Liz exhaled in relief. Then she looked at Alexander. Her husband's dark face was pale. Gently she took his hand in hers as she gazed at the blackened welts and blistered flesh. The doctor gave him a shot for pain and began to cleanse the wound. Alexander went whiter, and the pressure of his grip increased.

"You are going to have to change your husband's dressing every day, *señora*. He needs to take it easy for four or five days. By then I should be able to release your son from the hospital."

When the physician left the room, Alexander said, with a weak smile, "Well, I guess it won't be so easy for you to get rid of me after all."

"I don't want to get rid of you," she admitted softly.

THE HOUR was late that night when Liz and Alexander returned to the hacienda. She helped him get ready for bed. She knelt and poured him a glass of bottled water, and her eyes lifted to the golden brilliance of his. The room was charged with sexual tension.

His brown hand cupped her chin, and he tilted her face.

Slowly and tenderly he lifted her lips to his, which were blazing hot with desire.

"Alexander, you're hardly in the condition for this sort of thing."

A hot, pulsing fire hardened in his loins. "I think I'm, er, a better judge of my condition than you, love," he said on a vibrant chuckle.

His mouth moved to each corner of her lips in turn. Then he explored her eyelids, the lush curl of her closed lashes, the winged arch of her brows.

They clung to each other, their bodies hot and shaking. She could feel his pulse thundering at the same mad tempo as her own. Silently they held each other. It was their first moment of mutual tenderness in seven years. At last Alexander put her from him. "Sleep with me tonight, Liz. More than anything I want to fall asleep in your arms."

"All right," she murmured uncertainly.

Hot golden eyes watched her every movement as she stripped and moved into his arms.

Before she could protest, his mouth closed over hers, and he moved his body erotically over hers, crushing her in a tight embrace and thrusting deeply inside her until their passion built to shattering ecstasy.

THE NEXT morning Liz awoke buried beneath the warmth of Alexander's body. Maria was tapping lightly on the door.

Carefully she disentangled her body from Alexander's and rose, dressing hurriedly.

Liz opened the door and slipped outside.

"*Señora*, Señor Rocheaux is here."

Liz felt a wave of alarm and rushed downstairs.

At the sight of her at the door, Jock rose and crossed the room to join her. His blue eyes slid over Liz. "You're looking—" He paused. "There's a radiance about you that I thought you'd lost forever when Mikki threw you out. He is here now, isn't he?"

Her still face told everything.

"Dazzle is in a state of absolute chaos, and for three weeks the president has been out of the country. There is only one thing in the world that could make him shirk his mammoth responsibilities. You, Liz. Does he want you back?"

"He still believes that I'm guilty of stealing Paul's formula and giving it to you seven years ago."

"I can see you're determined to change his mind."

"Yes."

"That may be more difficult than you realize. Mikki is stubborn. This whole thing is as crazy as that time he accused me of having something to do with Sasha's death. Hell, the guy was trying to force *me* over the cliff."

"Why?"

"I never knew. Sasha had always resented my closeness to Mikki. Mikki and I were once the best of friends. Until we made the mistake of falling in love with the same girl. Rochelle. We both courted her, but when it came time for her to choose between us, neither of us could bear the thought of losing to the other. Egotistical fools. We dropped her, each of us loving her, neither of us thinking how she might react."

"What happened?"

"Rochelle was found dead one morning, having swallowed a handful of sleeping pills. The guilt was the first wedge in our relationship. Then there was Sasha. Now we've been enemies so long I can scarcely remember when we were not. But I didn't steal that formula from Dazzle. And I didn't know you were married to Mikki, or I never would have used your face or your name with our launch. Roger withdrew the product from the market immediately, and he refused to discuss his decision or to let me investigate the matter further.'' They regarded each other in silence.

"You know, Liz, you never ask about your father or Mimi when I come. Do you resent Mimi so much that you have decided to have nothing to do with your own father?''

Liz trembled. "I don't resent Mimi. In my short acquaintance with my 'real' father, I realized he is the kind of man who will always have a beautiful, smiling face before him. My mother once fulfilled that role—until she became pregnant with me. Now he has Mimi.''

Jock shrugged. There seemed nothing more he could say. The affection she'd felt for her real father after he'd found her and made her his heir seemed to be gone.

"So there's no chance for us?'' Jock asked at last, changing the subject.

She moved into the circle of his arms.

"If only it were you, and not Alexander.'' She kissed him gently then on the lips in parting.

A WEEK had passed since the night of terror, a week in which Juan had been arrested, a week of constant togetherness between husband and wife that had deepened the bond of love Liz felt toward Alexander.

Alex had come home from the hospital the day before, and though the child was pale and listless, he was improving.

Liz enjoyed tending to Alexander. She hoped that by showing him kindness, he would feel her love.

That particular evening Liz stepped into Alexander's bedroom to collect his supper tray and saw that he was sitting bare-chested at the writing table.

He looked up, and she saw a flicker of his old warmth and regard.

"Liz, I've got to go back to London, but I want you and the twins to come with me even though I can't—" He hesitated. He didn't want to hurt her.

She looked into his eyes and saw his doubt and desire and compassion. "Make promises that you can't keep," she finished.

"God help me, Liz, I can't go back without you," he muttered raggedly.

"It won't be easy for you, Alexander. Your family, everyone at Dazzle believes I betrayed you."

"No," he agreed, "it won't be easy—for either of us."

She thought of the long, empty years that had separated them, of the gulf of misunderstanding that still separated them. Quiet tears filled her eyes. She would do anything, promise anything in order to stay near him. "Alexander, I'll come back with you."

HIS OLDER half brother, Paul, called the next day from Paris. Paul skipped the amenities.

"A most unpleasant rumor has come to my attention, Mikki."

"What, precisely?" Alexander drawled.

"That the reason you have been gone so long is that you have found Liz and have reconciled with her."

"What if I have?"

"It's the end of your career at Dazzle. The board cannot forget she almost ruined the company."

"That was never proven in a court of law," Alexander stated coldly.

"Liz is Roger Chartres's daughter and his chosen heir to Radiance. She sees Jock on a regular basis. But, of course, you cannot be ignorant of that fact. Jock was in Mexico visiting her not six days ago. Don't tell me he managed that without your knowledge. There was a time when you would not have stood by—"

"Shut up, Paul, damn you."

Alexander swallowed the bitter bile clogging his throat. Jock here? Was his wife such a skilled liar that she could go from one man to another?

"If you bring Liz home with you, no one here will trust you."

"Not even you?"

There was a silence before the line went dead.

*

LIZ AND Alexander ate dinner in the dining room that night. When she entered the room, he glanced at her warily. Liz's smile was soft and warm and beautiful, and Alexander was caught for a moment in the spell of it before he reminded himself she probably smiled just as warmly for Jock.

Liz's joy at seeing him was instantly dashed when his dark, brooding face hardened with contempt.

They ate in awkward silence.

"What time should I have the children ready tomorrow?" she ventured.

"As early as possible," came his terse reply.

"I'm looking forward to going home," she said shyly, trying to make light conversation.

He shot her an odd look. "Really? Why?" He wondered if she was thinking of Jock, who would be more accessible to her when she was in London.

"Because of you—to try again."

"To try what, my love?" He flashed her a look of deep bitterness.

"Alexander, I don't understand why you're so angry," she began uncertainly. "What have I done?"

"I will tell you nothing," he growled. "And I will take you with me only on one condition."

"What condition?"

"You are not to see or even to speak to Jock again. Nor do I want you to communicate with your father."

A GRAY slanting rain was falling when the Vorzenski jet touched down in London's Gatwick Airport. Liz felt weary and wrinkled from the flight. Alexander helped Liz and the children disembark. They were instantly surrounded; microphones were thrust in front of their mouths. Flashbulbs popped in their faces as rapidly as the reporters' questions. The boldest journalist, an aging, obese man, jumped in front of Liz. He leered into her face. "Princess, why did you run away seven years ago? Is it true that you married the prince to steal Dazzle's formula? Isn't it a fact that you're still determined to ruin him?"

Alexander stepped between Liz and the man, grabbing the burly fellow by the lapels. A hundred flashbulbs burst at once.

The door of the silver Rolls swung open and Liz

stepped thankfully inside, the wide-eyed twins and Alexander right behind her.

"It seems that I make things worse for you without even trying," she said in a small voice.

"That scene was nothing compared to what will take place when I face the board tonight."

"Tonight?"

He nodded grimly. "My enemies are going to demand my head on a silver platter."

"Because of me?"

"You're one of the reasons." Glinting gold eyes swept her solemn face in cold amusement. "It's a pity you won't be there to witness my execution, love."

She gasped. Her face turned ashen.

His thoughts plunged him into an utterly black mood, and he forced his gaze away. Never had London seemed more dismal to him. Rain slashed against the hood as the Rolls sped toward the town house that Alexander leased on a quiet back street a short distance from Hyde Park.

Liz was a part of him, albeit an unwanted part, and when he hurt her, he hurt himself. Damn it to hell! He loved her.

*

THE SHADES were drawn and the elegant silver room was dark and silent except for the blare of the newscast. Liz Vorzenski's ravished white face filled the screen before the camera was jostled. Another camera caught the scenario of the prince dramatically protecting his wife from an overly zealous newsman.

The person on the brocade sofa in the dim room leaned

forward tensely, hands clasped on knees, brows furrowed
when the newscast ended. The set was switched off by
fingers that shook.

Liz had come back. She didn't look as radiant as she
had as a bride seven years ago.

The person in the room felt like God. Hadn't the Vor-
zenskis suffered enough? Should they now be allowed a
normal life? The mere thought bit like the pain of a dagger
in an unhealed wound and brought the stifling feelings of
the old madness and hatred. The possibility of any happiness between Mikki Vorzenski and Liz was as unendurable as it had always been.

"Never! Never will I allow it."

Gloved fingers reached for the telephone and dialed.

THE BUZZING phone seemed as agitated as Liz's thoughts,
but she did not answer it because in Alexander's house
the phone calls were always screened by the staff.

Alexander's lavish suite included two bedrooms, two
baths, two dressing rooms and a sitting room between the
bedrooms. If Liz had not been so upset she would have
thought the rooms beautiful.

She paced restlessly. She didn't know what to do with
herself in this grand, orderly house. Ana Lou had taken
over the children, and for the present Liz was relieved
about that.

Liz's thoughts turned to Alexander. An hour ago she
had stood forlornly at the windows and watched the rain
spatter his ebony hair and the expensive coat covering his
broad shoulders as he leaned down and stepped once more
into the Rolls. He'd never looked up or given a thought
for an affectionate caress or goodbye kiss from his wife.

Alexander had said he would be crucified by his family

and the Dazzle board tonight because of her. Was there nothing she could do to improve his situation? What if she went and pleaded with the board on his behalf? What could it hurt?

A knock sounded on the door and the housekeeper's muffled voice from the hall interrupted her thoughts.

"Mr. Jock Rocheaux is on the phone, madam."

Liz lifted the extension. Her hand was shaking. "Jock!"

"Hello, Liz. Your father wants to see you. He saw you on television, and he has asked me to bring you to Paris."

"Oh."

"Liz, the man's brokenhearted. He said you believe he is responsible for wrecking your marriage to Mikki. He wants to explain and to apologize."

"So he admits he's responsible?" Liz asked dully.

"Not in so many words. You know Roger is hardly the kind of man to lay his feelings out on the table for my perusal. But, yes, he feels responsible."

"Jock, I made up my mind a long time ago that I didn't want to have anything more to do with a man who destroyed the one thing in my life that mattered to me. Even if he is—" Her voice broke. "I can't see either of you because I promised Alexander I wouldn't."

"Liz—"

"Goodbye, Jock."

Liz was in the foyer waiting for a cab when the stony Mrs. Benchley came to her and told her that Jock was on the phone again.

"Please tell him I'm not at home. I've got to make that board meeting on time."

The housekeeper opened her mouth to say something, but Liz had already run out the door.

ALEXANDER SAT at his desk, which was piled with mail, contracts and reports. Michelle, his secretary, was trying to explain the chaos.

Finally he stopped her in midsentence and snapped in his deep, thundering baritone, "Save your breath, Michelle. You may need to explain this to the new president if I'm sacked tonight."

"Surely they won't do that, Mr. Vorzenski."

"I'm not so sure." He managed a smile. "Run along now, and type that one report I asked for, if you don't mind. I need to organize my thoughts before the board meeting."

Alexander lifted his gaze thoughtfully to the portrait of his grandfather. The painted eyes of Philippe Rocheaux, who had founded Dazzle, Ltd., ninety years ago, met his. Alexander smiled craftily to himself. The intercom sounded, and Michelle informed Alexander that everyone was in the boardroom.

LIZ'S TAXI slowly threaded its way between red double-decked buses and black taxis onto Piccadilly. Once England had meant Cornwall and her beloved Killigen Hall to Liz, that superb feeling of being part of a family that had endured for generations. Those illusions had been stripped from her by Ashley's death. She could almost smell the tang of cooking over furze fires on summer evenings when she and Ashley had camped out and lain beneath the stars, and he'd told her stories of knackers and tin miners. She'd assumed he was her father. Funny, how she'd taken it for granted. She'd lost Ashley first. Then her mother had sold Killigen Hall and run off to France with her young man, in the futile search for her lost youth and beauty. The distance that had always existed between Liz and her mother became estrangement.

Liz swallowed the dry lump in her throat. She wanted to remember that time of love and security. She had the feeling that if she fought hard enough today, and if she could win Alexander's love, she might be able to give that kind of life to her own children and to Alexander.

The taxi driver braked sharply and came to a standstill. When Liz realized that the traffic ahead was impossibly jammed, she tapped on the glass behind the driver. "Let me off here," she said. "I've decided to walk the rest of the way."

In front of the Dazzle building a Volvo had crashed into a bus on Regent Street, and the bus had plowed into a building. The smashed car was abandoned.

A grandmotherly woman behind Liz said crisply, "I seen it happen, you know, the accident. Almost looked as if the man in the car did it on purpose, the way he ran into that bus. He ran off the minute it happened, him that done it."

Bobbies ran about whistling and barking orders. When Liz walked into the Dazzle building, no one was at the desk to question her. She decided to take the stairs. Inside the stairwell Liz heard the sound of high heels skittering on the concrete stairs high above her, sharp, panicked beats like the pounding of her own heart. A door opened and closed, and then there was silence.

When she reached the top floor, she marched purposefully to her husband's office. The outer office was empty. Liz opened the door to Alexander's office and stepped inside. She heard a choked gasp from the darkened corner behind Alexander's desk.

"How did you get in here?" Michelle asked in a

shaken voice. The secretary stepped into the light. She clutched a sheaf of papers beneath her breasts.

"I came to see my husband," Liz said, moving to the door of the boardroom and lifting the handle.

"You can't do that!" Michelle cried.

"I just did," Liz said with a bold smile as she swept into the room.

Princess Vorzenski, the family matriarch, halted her speech in midsentence. Alexander stood up slowly, and said smoothly, "Ladies and gentlemen, may I introduce you to the lady we've all been so avidly discussing. My wife, Liz."

She felt their eyes boring into her, assessing her, distrusting her.

Princess Vorzenski regained her tongue and attacked. "So this is your impossible wife, Mikki? The wife you promised us you would hide in the country while you smooth everything over. I knew I was right. You should be removed from the presidency until you recover your sanity where this woman is concerned. Maybe now everyone will listen to me."

"Won't anybody here listen to me?" Liz cried. "I know you're against me. I know you want Alexander to divorce me, but I love him. I never did anything to hurt him or you. I came here today to tell you that I am innocent. And so is he."

The princess spoke. "If you're innocent, Liz Chartres, why didn't you come to the board seven years ago? Why did you run away?"

"Alexander wanted me out of his life. I was pregnant, and I thought he did not want...children from me, that he could not really love them." Her last sentence was a dying whisper. "But I was so very wrong...about everything."

"Liz—" Alexander's voice betrayed more warmth than he would have liked. Doubtless she was wielding the deathblow to his career, but it didn't seem to matter.

"Don't try to stop me, Alexander," Liz said softly, speaking at last to him. "I'm going to find out for sure who stole Paul's formula and deliberately framed me, because I know you won't believe me unless I do."

Liz swallowed. No one believed her.

The princess said, "Give Mikhail up before you destroy him. Go back to Mexico and make your puppets again."

"You've made your decision then, I see," Liz said in a strained, low tone. "It's useless to talk further."

She could bear no more. She spun on her heel and dashed into the hall. A hammer pounded inside her brain. She'd been wrong to come. She pushed the button for the elevator.

Alexander came out of the boardroom looking weary and drawn. "I'll take you home," he said grimly.

"So that I won't get into trouble? Alexander, I'm sorry I came. I shouldn't have provoked your mother. I'm worried that now she'll find it hard to forgive me."

He laughed shortly. "Maman does not have a forgiving nature. I had hoped to bring you two together under different circumstances. As it is, you collided. Now we must deal with the consequences."

"I thought only to—"

He was determined not to let her pretend she had had his interests at heart. "Liz. Don't. I'm taking you home."

She saw that he wouldn't believe in her. "Alexander, tonight I need to be alone, to try to think what to do. Please, let me leave by myself."

"If you won't come home with me, at least let me see you safely inside a cab," he said wearily.

The doors of the elevator opened. Alexander had every intention of following her, but when he glanced at the man who moved toward the doors, he recognized his cousin, Jock Rocheaux.

As Liz stumbled into Jock's waiting arms, the doors closed. Alexander rushed blindly toward the stairwell. Inside the elevator, Liz pressed her shaking body against Jock.

"Oh, Jock, I've made such a terrible muddle of my life. I've hurt everyone—even you."

"You can't be in love without hurting people. I should know. I'm an old hand at hurting. Here...." He handed her his handkerchief. "Liz, I snuck inside Dazzle tonight to find you. We have to talk—now." His golden face was more urgent than she'd ever seen it. "You've got to come to Paris with me." The doors of the elevator opened, and a powerful arm reached inside and wrenched Jock bodily from Liz.

"Paris! If you think for one minute I'm going to let you sail off into the sunset with my wife, Jock, you are deranged," Alexander snarled.

Four uniformed men surrounded Jock. "Mikki," Jock stalled. "I have to convince Liz to come to Paris. What I have to say can only be said privately—to her."

"I never doubted that for a minute."

The four guards hustled Jock down the hall to a small office. Liz wasn't up to any more quarrels tonight. She seized the opportunity to escape.

Jock was the first to notice that Liz had not followed them into the office.

"Where's Liz?" he demanded, his voice urgent. "Mikki, you've got to find her. It's a—"

Alexander had already run out of the office and down

the hall into the rain. He didn't hear the end of his cousin's harshly expelled sentence.

"It's a matter of life and death."

LIZ WAS trembling with fatigue and nervous strain. She trudged up to her bedroom feeling a stifling sensation of aloneness. As she went to bed, her mind was still a jumble of remorse over what she'd done.

Later, in the darkness, Alexander's voice came to her. "Liz, are you awake?" His hand gently smoothed her hair from her forehead. "I don't blame you for not wanting to talk."

She began to cry. "Tonight, when I went to Dazzle, I wanted only to help you, Alexander, and I ended up hurting you." More tears fell.

"I've been hurt before. I'll survive." His voice was infinitely gentle.

"I guess now it will be difficult for you to convince the board you can manage me."

"Quite difficult."

"I'm sorry. Can you believe me when I say that I didn't mean to make things harder for you?"

"Honestly?" His hand in her hair was still.

"Honestly," she said.

"I don't know."

"Alexander, how can we go on like this, when you have all these doubts?"

"Because not going on would be so much worse. I learned that much tonight when you ran out into the rain." His warm fingers moved on her, this time in a caress upon her shoulders beneath the heaviness of her hair. "I'm sorry," he said.

"Even about Jock?" she asked.

"Even about Jock." He had tensed, but his voice remained easy. "I was…I am…jealous. Because I knew he was with you in Mexico, and you didn't tell me."

Liz's hand slid low over Alexander's flat belly, deliberately stirring him. "You have nothing to be jealous about."

He held her in silence for a long moment. Then the phone began to ring.

"Oh, dear," Liz cried, jumping from the bed. She had forgotten not to answer it. "Hello," she whispered.

Princess Vorzenski's shrill voice exploded into the phone. "Let me speak to Mikhail."

Without a word, Liz handed Alexander the telephone.

As he listened to the princess, his expression darkened. When at last he hung up, he stared at his wife, and his eyes were as cold and hard as stones. "Paul's formula was stolen tonight." In his voice there was a deadness that she had never heard before. "I have lost the presidency of Dazzle. Maman has filled the office herself."

"And you think I took the formula, don't you, Alexander?" He stared at her in silence. "Don't you?"

In his eyes she saw the unspoken accusation. She turned her face to the wall so that he could not read her face. If anyone knew what had happened to the formula, her father surely must.

"You realize," Alexander said grimly, "that if you run away this time, to Paris or anywhere else, everyone will be convinced you had some part in this."

"I—I—" She couldn't utter a sound. She would not let Roger get away with this a second time. Even if it cost her her marriage.

"Liz—"

His eyes captured hers in a hard and relentless gaze

that stripped away her defenses, leaving her shatteringly vulnerable.

"I was a fool to make that promise to you," she admitted at last.

"I see," he said in a low, dead voice. "If you go to Paris, I hope you understand it will be the end of…us."

Oh, she understood. She met his deep, dark gaze. The vision of his too-dear features wavered. She knew Alexander was lost to her forever.

*

WHAT DID ONE say to a man as callous as Roger? Once Liz had not thought her father callous. How different she had felt that last time when she'd secretly flown to Paris to tell Roger of her marriage.

Shocked at first, Roger had pretended to understand. He'd gathered Liz into his arms, kissed her, acting as if he shared her joy. He had even gone as far as to say he hoped that this marriage could bring a reconciliation between himself and Alexander's family.

A week later Paul's formula had been stolen and Radiance had launched the pirated perfume under the name Liz, using publicity pictures that had been originally intended for another Radiance fragrance, pictures Roger had promised to destroy when he'd learned of her secret marriage.

After what Jock had said yesterday, Liz was convinced that what she'd always suspected was true, that her father had been behind the theft and launch because he wanted to break up her marriage.

The car she'd rented thrust its way down the confusion

of the Rue Royal and then onto the great expanse of the Concorde where the Crillon was veiled with leafed-out chestnut trees.

Soon after that, Liz reached her father's opulent Paris flat, and Armande let her inside and showed her to her father's study. Liz paced before the long windows overlooking the Rue du Faubourg Saint-Honoré.

Armande returned. "*Madame*, I've reached your father's office. Monsieur Chartres is on the telephone."

Liz lifted the silver receiver. It was as cold as ice in her shaking fingers.

"Liz!" The deep, sensually accented baritone was warm with welcome. "Did Jock tell you I wanted to see you?"

"Yes."

"And is he with you now?"

"I'm alone."

"Odd." There was the faintest trace of alarm in his low voice.

"I did not come because of Jock or you. I came to stop you from hurting Alexander again."

After a long pause, he said, "I see."

"Jock said you admitted having stolen Paul's formula seven years ago."

"In a way I do feel I am responsible. I—"

"When Paul's formula was removed from Alexander's safe last night—"

"Paul's formula? Last night?"

The line went dead.

"Father?"

There was no dial tone. Liz called for Armande.

Upstairs a door opened. A velvet reply rippled down the stairs.

"Liz, I was asleep when you arrived." Mimi swept into the room.

"Mimi, I was talking to Roger. The phone went dead before we had finished speaking."

"It happens. There is some construction in the area. Let me check the other line for you and see if I can reach Roger."

Mimi left the room. She returned with an opened bottle of Burgundy in one hand.

Mimi smiled. "Roger wants to meet us at Charmont in an hour." Charmont was Roger's château not far from Paris. Mimi poured a glass of wine and handed it to Liz. "This will give us time to visit. You need to relax before you see Roger." She poured the wine. So, Mimi did realize how she dreaded seeing Roger. The wine was her way of being thoughtful. Liz did not have the heart to refuse her. Some time later a horn sounded outside. It was Armande with the car.

With Armande at the wheel of Roger's Lincoln, the suburbs of Paris swept past in a blur. Liz felt woozy. The road seemed to be a perpetual zigzag, and Liz felt less and less well. Then Charmont burst into view. The car shot through the tall, powerfully fortified gate. Armande parked the Lincoln in front of the enormous south door.

Liz felt so weak and shaky she almost fell when she tried to get out.

"Liz, you're as white as a sheet," Mimi said, taking her by the hand. The house was still, so unlike the Charmont she remembered. The air was damp and musty, as if the house had been shut up for a long time. Something felt terribly wrong.

Vaguely Liz was aware of Mimi leading her up the stairs to the bedroom she had always used when she had come to Charmont with Roger. It seemed to her that the two of them floated weightlessly as they mounted an endless white staircase. Once inside the bedroom, Liz sank down upon the elaborate bed. The room began to spin.

Mimi said, "I think I will call the village doctor. Just in case."

Liz heard the retreat of Mimi's footsteps on the carpet and then the rapid, gunfire taps on the marble stairs. The sound reminded her of something. Liz focused upon the golden phone on the gilt table by the window.

There was a phone in the room!

Muddled as her mind was, somehow she knew something was wrong if Mimi had gone downstairs to use a phone when there was one right there.

Liz rose and stumbled across the thick flowered carpet to reach the phone. She pulled the cord and the telephone crashed onto the floor. She lifted the receiver and held it against her ear. The phone was dead.

Liz heard the Lincoln's engine roar in the drive downstairs. Armande was leaving! Mimi had gone downstairs to send him away.

Liz collapsed onto the floor. She heard the staccato tapping of the heels downstairs, and she knew where she had heard it before. In the stairwell at Dazzle's office building. Mimi had been there that night, the night the formula had been stolen.

That car accident had not been an accident. Mimi had deliberately planned it as a distraction so that she could enter the Dazzle offices undetected. It was Mimi. Not Roger. Mimi had wanted to destroy her marriage. Liz felt herself sinking.

Liz didn't know how much time had passed, but she

managed to focus on Mimi when she returned. Her golden face was naked with hatred.

"Why, Mimi? What have I ever done to you?"

The purr of her voice was filled with bitter sadness. "My sister died of an overdose—"

"W-what do I have to do with your sister?"

"Rochelle was my little sister. For her I climbed from the gutter to stardom. Then Jock Rocheaux and Mikki Vorzenski amused themselves and made a game of my sister's love, and she died. She was so idealistic. After my wedding, she took pills because she was too excited to sleep. Or so the authorities said. My last words to her were said in anger. You see, she did not approve of my marrying a count, simply because he was a count."

"Rochelle's death must have been no more than an unfortunate accident," Liz murmured.

"I slept with Sasha Vorzenski, and I told him that I was sleeping with his cousin Jock as well. Sasha was so jealous that he tried to kill Jock on the racetrack the next day, but he died himself."

"Mimi, how could you...so coldly..."

"Mikki Vorzenski then suffered as I suffered." Mimi's eyes were glazed. "I became Roger's mistress to get close to Jock. Then you came to Paris. When Jock fell in love with you, I took you down to Deauville so you could meet Mikki Vorzenski. Then when there was to be a Dazzle launch, I had my cousin, Michelle, steal the formula, and I substituted it at the last minute. Jock was nearly ruined because he used your publicity pictures. I had torn up Roger's orders not to use them. Mikki Vorzenski nearly lost his presidency. The only problem was that Roger found out what I had done. He took the perfume off the market. But he still wanted me enough to forgive me.

"Michelle and I took the formula last night, and then I helped her run away. Soon it will be discovered that Mikki Vorzenski's car ran Jock down. Mikki will lose you. He will be accused of murder. His career will be ruined."

The words were a jumble in Liz's weary brain. She had to stay awake. Sleep was death. She knew she'd been drugged.

Mimi fled the room, turning a key in the lock, imprisoning Liz. High heels clattered on the stairs.

Groggily Liz dragged herself to the window. The cool air revived her as she leaned out. In the distance she saw white, darting lights on the Charmont road.

Beneath the window was a ledge. The windows of the bedroom next to her had been thrown open. If Liz could walk along that ledge the ten feet to the next window and crawl inside, perhaps she could get downstairs.

The car lights twinkled on the road. The car was coming to the château. Liz pulled herself up onto the windowsill and swung her feet outside, sliding her body out the window until her toes touched the ledge. She could scarcely stand, but somehow she managed to inch her way to the other window.

The car was in the drive. A terrible blackness swamped Liz, but she forced herself to keep moving. At last her hand curled over the windowsill. It took all her strength to pull herself inside. She collapsed headlong onto the floor. The room was a blur. The blood in her head seemed to be a pounding force. Gathering her remaining strength, she staggered to the door. When she twisted the doorknob, it opened.

Deep baritone voices thundered from below. Liz crawled to the landing and pulled herself up.

Liz lurched toward that welcome sound of voices. When she reached the top of the stairs, she clutched the newel post. ''Alexan—'' Again no sound came.

In her panic, Liz let go of the newel post and lost her balance. She screamed. The frail sound cut the air like the thinnest blade.

Alexander glanced up, his eyes filling with terror. He raced swiftly up the stairs, taking them two at a time, as Liz fell.

A violent stab of pain jolted. She rolled over and over until her soft body reached Alexander, who had climbed halfway up the stairs.

He wrapped her unconscious body in his arms and bent his black head very close to her face. He searched for her pulse, and when at last he felt the weak throb, he began to weep, his tears falling upon her face, which was as cold and still as death.

*

THE SOUND of music filled the sun-splashed villa that perched on the sculptured edge of a cliff high above Sardinia's Porto Rotondo.

A thousand bejeweled guests were crammed inside the villa or clustered upon the wide decks around the aqua expanse of the glistening pool. Samantha and Alex were splashing in the pool. From her balcony, Liz watched the milling crowd—executives from the highest echelons of both Dazzle and Radiance.

Liz smiled as she watched Jock limp across the deck and join her father. Somewhere in the press of people was Jock's new wife, Sarah, the lovely English nurse he'd fallen in love with when he was recuperating. So much had happened in the month since Alexander had driven to Charmont with Roger and saved Liz from certain death. Mimi had been institutionalized in Switzerland. Michelle was behind bars. Roger had confided that Mimi had been repeatedly hospitalized for psychiatric reasons over the past few years, but that he had not realized how dangerous she was.

He said that in reality Mimi had blamed herself for Rochelle's death, but she'd tried to convince herself Jock and Alexander were to blame. The night Mimi drugged Liz, Roger and Alexander had forced Armande to tell them that Mimi had taken Liz to Charmont, which had been closed for over a year because Roger was planning to renovate it.

The formula that had been stolen the night before Mimi tried to kill Liz had been a fake substituted by Alexander as a precautionary measure. Liz had recovered after two nights in a Paris hospital. Roger told her that Alexander had hovered at her bedside until she was out of danger, but that when she had regained consciousness, he'd left Paris and returned to London. His leaving her had ripped her heart to pieces.

A letter from Alexander came to her in Paris. He offered her his villa in Sardinia to recover. When she accepted, in the hope of seeing him, he sent Ana Lou and the children to join her. But he had not come himself.

The only letter that came from him was one he forwarded from Manuel, who wanted to buy the doll factory.

Within a week, Liz had decided what she would do. She called Roger in Paris and invited him to Sardinia.

The night Roger arrived, Liz asked for his help. "Because of me, Alexander has lost the presidency of Dazzle.

I know that everything regarding the explosion has been resolved, that all charges against him have been dropped. But the news stories in the papers were so lurid, his career may never recover.''

"Men like Mikki Vorzenski have a way of landing on their feet. Give him time, my child.''

"But, don't you see, he's not fighting, and his mother will never give him a chance.''

"What do you want me to do?''

"Could you... Could we buy Dazzle?''

"And they call Mikki Vorzenski a pirate.'' Roger began to laugh, but his eyes were filled with love.

"Alexander owns a great deal of stock in Dazzle, Father. So does Paul. Perhaps you could approach them?''

"Perhaps....'' Roger folded her hand in his. "You do realize you might be making a very grave mistake. Some men do not like to be bought by a woman.''

The memory faded and the present came back with violent force, but Roger's words lingered.

Some men do not like to be bought by a woman.

This party was in celebration of the upcoming merger of two of the greatest names in the perfume world—Dazzle and Radiance. The financial papers had made much of it.

Suddenly a hush swept the party, and Liz saw a very tall black-headed man leading a silver-haired woman on his arm. Alexander and the princess. Roger extended his hand and Paulette took it. After a long while she knelt and leaned over the pool. She didn't seem to mind that the children splashed her when they swam near. The princess's smile was radiant.

Liz remembered something Alexander had told her

once about his mother, that she was always on the side of the winner.

Liz was the winner.

As if drawn to a magnet, Liz's gaze melded with Alexander's. For a long moment he stared up at her. He was as still as a statue, and then he was running.

And so was she.

High-heeled sandals scampered down red tile stairs. Liz flew into his arms. He was kissing her, whirling her in his arms.

"I love you," he said. "I don't know if you can ever forgive me for being so stupidly blind to the truth."

"I thought you were mad because I bought Dazzle."

"Mad?" He threw back his black head and laughed. "Mad? I thought it was one hell of a way to tell a guy you love him. It was insanely reckless, of course. I don't deserve you," he said, "but, Liz, I can't live without you."

"Nor can I."

"So I'm to be president of your company?" he murmured.

"Our company."

"I bought you a gift, too," he said.

Her eyes flashed with excitement. "What?"

"I went down to Cornwall and bought that crumbling antiquity you're so insane about."

"Killigen Hall?" She shrieked with joy.

"Ghosts and all."

"How did you manage it?"

"By paying three times what it was worth."

"Whatever you paid, I'll make it worth it." She began to laugh as he lifted her into his arms again. "Where are you taking me?"

"Somewhere private where you can start earning your keep."

He began to walk up the stairs to the sun-drenched terrace outside the master bedroom.

They kissed, surrendering at last to the brilliant and fulfilling dazzle of their everlasting love.

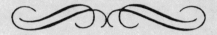

MARRIED TO THE ENEMY

Ann Major

"Faster, Daddy! Faster!" Stormy cried, wild with childish delight from the exhilarating speed. Traveler's galloping hooves were crashing into the hard, dry earth. She was flying on that magic, darkening wind, as she had so many times before.

When he drew in on the reins instead of obeying her, she whirled around in the saddle indignantly. It was of no importance that Hugh Jones was master of a hundred thousand acres of Texas ranch and oil land. To his five-year-old daughter he was her adoring father, and therefore hers to command. She dug her heels into Traveler defiantly. "Daddy, I told you faster! I want to fly to the other side of the moon."

"Tonight was our last time to fly, Stormy," he said gently, taking her hands in his. His handsome face was drawn and still. Then, for the first time in his life, his broad shoulders sagged.

Hugh Jones turned Traveler back toward the ranch house, bending his head over hers, talking softly and slowly, trying to make her understand the way her life was going to change. All she heard was the sadness in his voice.

All she knew was that this had something to do with her mother. Thus, when her mother ran out of the ranch house, lifting her arms toward her child, Stormy clung to her father weeping. As he handed his daughter into those outstretched arms, Stormy's eyes blurred with tears.

Then she heard the squeak of leather as Hugh leaned down from his saddle again. "Don't cry for me," he said gruffly.

When Stormy began to weep more loudly, he dug his

heels into Traveler and flew away into the magic darkness on the other side of the moon without her.

"Dry your tears, dear one," her mother said softly in that awful, unearthly whisper Stormy had come to dread.

Her mother took her to a strange land near a cold sea. As the nights passed, Stormy wept into her pillow. Her mother would come to her and tell her that she must forget him.

But Stormy couldn't forget; she wouldn't forget. Until one day her mother told her her father was dead.

*

LOOKING desperately beautiful in a sparkly silver dress that fit her like a glove, Stormy Jones stood on the landing alone, gazing down at the crowd clustered beneath her paintings. Stormy was the artist. This was her show. She should have been the one to shine tonight. As usual, all attention was focused on her famous mother.

The airy splendor of the fashionable Beverly Hills gallery was crowded with too many women in beige gowns, her mother's fanatical followers. The guests seemed more absorbed in debating each other than in Stormy's paintings. And no wonder.

All Stormy's subjects were passionless women who seemed to float away in a beige void. They were lost, disconnected—as she was.

Maya moved majestically through the throng in her flowing beige robes and climbed to the dais.

"Dear ones..." floated the soft, famous voice that her followers loved. The press moved closer with their cameras and microphones, notepads and lights. "Dear ones, motherhood is the single most important event in a woman's life. Children are our product. But like the poor lost creatures in my daughter's paintings, we have no true status in American society...."

Tomorrow Maya would be in all the papers and on all the television channels. Her daughter's art show would scarcely be mentioned. Stormy felt curiously deflated.

The all-too-familiar scene beneath Stormy began to blur before she turned and went down the hall to the upstairs room. She opened the door and slipped inside.

One minute she was safely alone in the hushed darkness, then *he* stood silhouetted in the doorway, a dark cowboy-pirate filling that suddenly too-small space. He removed a battered, sweat-stained Stetson and bowed slightly in her direction. A memory clicked in her mind, elusive and yet powerful, and into her heart came a sudden strange hurting warmth.

Diamond-hard black eyes made their piercing study of her. She had the uneasy sensation that her silver dress had been stripped away; that he knew secrets about her even she was unaware of....

"Do I know you?" she murmured.

"I don't believe you've had the pleasure," he drawled.

He was dangerously dazzling in a rough-hewn way and as out of place in this tony gallery filled with Mothers-of-the-Earth members as they would have been in his rough masculine world. He was exactly the kind of man her mother had warned her to stay away from.

Her mother had been right to rear her so protectively in that all-female commune and send her to that all-girls school if there were many men like him inhabiting the planet.

"Who are you?" The whisper floated across the room.

He took a single step closer. There was a burst of laughter from the lower floor. He hesitated and seemed to catch himself.

"Sorry, ma'am, to have bothered you. Wrong room." He tipped his hat back. Then he was gone.

Stormy felt a bitter pang of disappointment.

Moments later, Lisa, with her platinum white hair and her black dress, came rushing up the stairs and cooed, "There you are, darling." Lisa was the gallery owner who had arranged the show. "You're to pose for the photographer."

Lisa tucked her arm through Stormy's and they glided down the stairs together toward Maya.

Maya embraced her showily. "You were wonderful, dear one."

"You were you, Mama." But as Stormy welcomed her mother's embrace, her daughterly love took the sting out of the barb.

Maya finished her champagne, and they began to pose together for the cameras.

Dozens of lights went off, blinding Stormy.

She blinked, and *he* was there again—tall and dark at the center of the white dazzle. For the first time in her life, she outshone her mother. She threw back her head, and her thick sleek hair flowed down her naked back in a river of shining silken ink.

Perhaps it was the artist in her that was so attracted to his scorching black eyes, his angular face, his wide, sensual mouth and the not-so-subtle strength of his powerful body. But the quiver in the pit of her stomach told her it wasn't the artist. It was the woman.

Suddenly Maya spotted him. "Who is that man?"

Stormy yawned and looked in the wrong direction.

"No! Over there, dear one. The cowboy. I'm sure he wasn't on my invitation list."

"But isn't he gorgeous, Mother?"

"I don't like the way he was looking at you. Stay away from him, dear one."

"One of your orders from on high, Mother dear?"

"Stormy—dear one, you should listen to the voice of experience."

"Perhaps I want experiences of my own," said Stormy rebelliously.

"I want to save you from all that."

Stormy cast a lazy glance toward the handsome stranger. Her pulse accelerated. Stormy knew she was out of her depth, that she was playing a dangerous game, but she didn't care.

"Mother dear, I'm not at all sure I want to be saved... from all that."

STORMY'S FINGERS tightened on the steering wheel. It was late—nearly 3:00 a.m. There had been a party in Malibu after the show. When her mother had offered her the limo in that high-handed way of hers, saying, "Dear one, I don't know a single decent person who drives her own car in this dangerous city after midnight," Stormy hadn't been able to resist one of her rebellious "I'm on my own now, Mother" performances.

Delicious as that infantile scene had been, Stormy regretted it now, because ever since she'd left the party, she'd had the terrifying sensation she was being followed.

She wrenched the Volvo, tires squealing, around two more cars and took a side street to her apartment complex. When she glanced back, the other headlights were gone.

When Stormy reached the complex, the parking lot was dark and deserted. She felt the urge to drive to some well-lit hotel. Instead she parked the Volvo in her assigned space.

She didn't notice the low-slung car with the tinted windows ooze stealthily into the darkest shadows at the far end of the parking lot. Nor did she hear the car door open or see the menacing figure that crept out and kept to the shadows.

Her hurried footsteps rang loudly in the darkness. When a gust of wind sent a paper cup skittering noisily across her path, Stormy jumped. She fumbled for her house key.

A sweaty palm snaked out of the dark shrubbery, covering her mouth, muffling her strangled scream. The hands around her neck tightened into a vise. Her lungs felt as if they were bursting.

"Let her go!" thundered a voice, the roar so loud it penetrated even Stormy's fading consciousness.

In the next instant the crushing hands at her throat were ripped away. A battered Stetson spun to the ground beside Stormy. Gulping in air, she looked at it dazedly.

The owner of the Stetson swore viciously in a deep, low-pitched drawl. She could see nothing more of him than his flying boot heels and the cuffs of his jeans. He used his advantage of size and strength with ruthless expertise, slamming fist after fist into the other man's jaw.

"So, you like terrorizing women—" The stranger roared as he drove a boot hard into Stormy's attacker. "Go on. Get the hell out of here."

Stormy heard tires squeal and gravel spin, and she sank dizzily against the wall.

"Ma'am, are you okay?"

Tight denim stretched across his bulging thigh muscles as he stooped and retrieved his flattened hat and her keys from the dirt. He turned, and she recognized her cowboy from the gallery.

She managed to nod mutely as he helped her up and unlocked the door. Just his nearness made her slightly breathless.

Stormy's apartment door swung open. The single lamp on a low table backlighted his rugged profile. The cowboy tipped his hat back and looked down at her from beneath the brim, as if waiting for her to invite him in.

All she had to do was step in front of him, block the doorway, thank him, and he would go.

He smiled as if her indecision amused him. "You look like you're wondering if I'm the big bad wolf in sheep's clothing." When she said and did nothing, he said, "I'm not the wolf."

In a dazed state she turned on more lights. Her head felt groggy and her legs were unsteady.

He crossed the room and sank onto the sofa, his lean body sprawling. He picked up one of her mother's news-letters from the commune and leafed through it, his gorgeous mouth tightening. With sudden violent disgust he tossed the newsletter back on top of a dozen other pamphlets about Mothers-of-the-Earth philosophy that littered the coffee table.

"When Mother visits me, she leaves those pamphlets."

"You leave them out."

"If I don't, she brings more."

He sprang up with an easy, pantherlike grace. The closer he came, the more primitively male he seemed. She backed away from him until her heel hit the wall. When his brown hand reached toward her bruised cheek, she twisted wildly away.

"Hey, hey, it's okay," he murmured softly, as if to a frightened child.

Then his callused fingertips brushed her cheek. "He cut you. I should have killed him when I had the chance." There was savage hatred in his soft, barely controlled tone.

"I'm okay."

"You're sure?"

She nodded weakly.

"He followed you from the show."

A chill swept her. "You followed me, too. Why were you there? At my show?"

His mouth curved. "Would you believe I have an interest in your art?"

"You don't look the type."

He ran splayed fingers through his unruly hair. "What type am I, then?"

"The type of man my mother taught me to run from."

Suddenly he laughed, and the faintly self-derisive sound was warm and pleasure-filled. "Honey, those are usually the most interesting men."

"I wouldn't know. I'm afraid I don't know much about men. My mother raised me at the commune with women."

"Right," he muttered, a note of cynical derision in his voice. "If only it were so easy to avoid women."

"You've had bad experiences with women?"

"Only with one. But once was enough. I made the mistake of marrying her. Of having a child."

"Then you're a father?"

"Of sorts." There was something sad about his brutally clipped answer.

"You're divorced?"

"If only it were that simple." His voice was curt and flat, dark with hidden meaning. "I'm a widower."

"Perhaps you shouldn't judge all women on the basis of one," Stormy said.

"Honey, perhaps you shouldn't judge all men on the basis of none." His insolent eyes devoured every curve encased by her tight silver dress. Then he shrugged. "I could do with a drink before I go."

Her face flaming, she went into the kitchen. "I've got cola, iced tea, coffee—"

His deep husky laughter made her shiver. "That's not exactly what I had in mind."

"Oh, you mean...alcohol. I don't think I have—" Then her face brightened. She opened a cabinet door and grabbed a bottle. "Oh yes, I do. A bunch of musicians left this when they were down here the other night."

"Tequila," he murmured, reading the label. "Hey. This is dangerous stuff." He was looking at her, not the bottle. There was a smile in his voice.

Quickly she handed him a glass. He splashed two shots of tequila into it and drank deeply.

She was pouring herself a soda. He had finished his drink and started toward the door.

He stopped abruptly. "Tonight was a setup. I really think you should call the cops."

She set her soda down. "No."

"Why not?"

"Because then my mother would find out and she would make me move back to the commune."

"Maybe that's where you belong."

"No!" She glowered at him.

"Honey, that man followed you here."

"No."

"Okay. It's your funeral." He shrugged lazily and undid the door latch.

Suddenly it hit her—everything that had happened. The show. Her close brush with death. And the fact that this gorgeous man who had saved her was about to walk out of her life forever.

She stepped toward him. "I—I don't want you to go." Soft tears began to trickle messily down her cheeks.

For a long moment he stared into her sad, glistening eyes.

"Hell." He closed the door and stood there.

Without thinking, she flung herself blindly into his arms. His body was as hard as stone and blazing hot, and infinitely, wonderfully comforting.

He cradled her against his wide chest, rocking her, smoothing her hair. The more she wept, the more overwrought she became. He drew her with him into the kitchen and poured himself more tequila, downed a glass, then poured another, ordering her to take a sip.

"No..." she whispered.

"It will make you feel better." He brought the glass to her lips, and she gulped, strangling on the fiery stuff as it slid down her throat. He wouldn't let her stop until the glass was empty. Then he lifted her into his arms. "Now you're going to bed."

Her sobs turned into giggles. A dangerous sign. He carried her into her darkened bedroom, where he laid her down upon her bed.

"What do you think you're doing?" she murmured carelessly when she heard him undo the zipper of her dress. He peeled the glittery garment from her body, his knuckles rasping against her bare skin.

She heard the scrape of wood against wood. He ripped open a drawer and slammed it shut. Then something soft and silvery—her flimsy cotton nightgown—sailed across the darkened room and landed beside her.

"I think you'd better take it from here," he muttered through gritted teeth as he turned toward the door. "I'm sleeping on the couch."

The tequila made her feel hot—warmly aglow. All her fears seemed to have vanished, and she was filled with that wanton, unnamed, never-felt-before yearning.

"Stay," she whispered, gazing pleadingly at his starkly etched face.

"If you had a grain of sense where men were concerned, you'd tell me to go," he replied hoarsely.

She licked her dry lips, and he watched the darting flick of that velvet tongue. Then, with a husky groan, he backed out of the door and slammed it quickly.

JONATHAN McBride sank wearily onto the recliner and propped up his scuffed, sharkskin boots. Just the memory of her satiny body nestled on those lace sheets was enough to make his muscles knot again with hard desire.

Damn. The last thing he needed was this hot, all-devouring yen for some oddball, commune-taught female who, damn it, just happened to be his boss's daughter—the one woman his honor forbade him to take.

Well, he would keep his distance. He would tell her what he'd promised Hugh he'd tell her and then he'd get the hell back to Texas. What she and Hugh did then would be their own business. Jonathan took a comforting pull from the bottle of tequila.

Except for her dark hair and eyes, she looked like Lylia, the woman he'd hated, the woman he'd married. The woman who had ensnared him body and soul and made him swear off women for good. The woman who'd borne him a son, Daniel, who was so unlike himself and so like his mother that Jonathan could hardly bear the sight of him.

He'd loved Lylia once. She'd lied to him, cheated on him. She'd died in a terrible way. He remembered the hellish months afterward, when he'd been blamed. In life and in death, she'd come as close as anything ever had to destroying him.

Never again would he allow a woman to get close to him.

And then Stormy screamed.

Jonathan bolted out of the recliner. The next instant, he was pushing her door open. The windows were tightly sealed, the room secure. She was only having a nightmare. He had to go.

But he stood frozen where he was, his devouring gaze ranging the length of this splendid, voluptuous beauty.

Then she cried out again, and the tortured tone tore

through him. He went to Stormy and sank softly down beside her. She was trembling.

"It's me—Jonathan," he whispered in his low, comforting drawl.

Gradually she stilled. "Jonathan." She slurred his name drowsily, saying it in wonder, never having heard it before. She reached for him, groping wildly until she could bury her face against his warm throat.

"You had a bad dream, honey. That's all."

"But you're here."

"Yes."

"Promise me—" she began.

"What?"

"That you'll stay."

"Honey—"

"I'll be so scared if you go."

"Dear God…" He buried his lips in the sweet-smelling mass of her hair, murmuring reassurances. Every time he tried to move away from her, she clung to him more deliriously. For the first time in years he yearned for tender closeness with a woman. She seemed to drag all the loneliness and all the bitterness from his soul.

"Don't leave me. Please don't ever leave me again. I've been alone so long."

Hell. So had he. Instead of going, he wrapped his arms even more tightly around her. Then his mouth was on hers. Jonathan McBride was lost. All logical thought, all honor was thrust aside.

His desire built like a tumultuous wave that hovered high on the brink of final explosion. He was ripping off his shirt, fumbling with his silver belt buckle, when her fingers closed over his. She dragged his jeans off. Her fingers, blind in the silvery darkness, slid unknowingly over his thighs and against his manhood, causing his desire to pulse with unendurable urgency.

He grabbed her when they were both naked and ran his mouth greedily over her silken throat, her breasts, over every part of her.

He would have taken her then, but she stopped his exploring mouth.

"No. It's my turn to kiss you," she said, her voice thick with passion.

She was an innocent. But her tongue and mouth were not. Dear God. How did she know what to do?

He was gasping when she stopped and fell back into that lacy tumble of pillows and sheets, her dark eyes shining with wonder as she waited for him to slowly lower his body over hers. Only in that last minute did he remember that he had to take care of her. He leaned across her and fumbled on the floor for his wallet, easing it from his jeans.

"What are you doing?" she whispered.

He ripped open a wrapper. He touched her cheek very tenderly. "Honey, I have to protect you."

When he took her, she cried out once, and he stopped, waiting until that first flash of pain dulled, kissing her feverish brow until at last she sighed, having grown accustomed to him. Then slowly he began to move, faster and faster, until she moaned in sudden bewildered joy and clutched him closer, her whole body trembling. Never had it felt remotely this good. He gathered her in his arms, and let her cling to him afterward. Which was not his custom. In the darkness her lips grazed his neck, his shoulders.

He stared down at her. "You are beautiful," he whispered. "The most beautiful woman I've ever known."

She buried her face trustingly against he neck. "Next time I'll be better...."

"Honey, you were perfect."

"So were you," she whispered drowsily.

He wound protective arms around her and drew her closer, holding her until she fell asleep. Tomorrow when she found him gone would be soon enough for her to find out what a coldhearted, selfish bastard he really was.

There was no way he could tell her Hugh's news now. Hugh would have to find the strength to do it himself. And if he ever found out that McBride had slept with his daughter and then run out on her afterward, there would be the devil to pay.

Well, Hugh must never know.

Shakily, Jonathan eased himself free of Stormy's perfumed limbs. When he looked down at his own body, he saw with horror that the protection he'd used had broken. Dear God. How long had the thing been in his wallet? Years, probably.

Slowly Jonathan rose and picked up his wallet, jeans, shirt and boots. His only thoughts were on the horror of what he'd done.

THIS WAS the protected house of her childhood. Her mother's house was a place of tall, airy ceilings, of natural woods and fibers, a house through which the beige ghosts drifted silently, speaking only when necessary in soft, nonviolent whispers.

Every day of the past month had been hell. Stormy had sat on the cliffs, the cool wind in her hair, and had watched the waves and the sea gulls, envying them. At night she watched the moon.

Not that anyone had understood her depressed moods, her unwillingness to paint more women floating away in their filmy gowns.

"You can paint here as well as anywhere, dear one."

Stormy had finally relented. "Perhaps you are right."

But she had rebelled and painted *him*.

Even to look at his picture gave her a physical ache

and made her long for him. Just to glance at his dark eyes made her remember that wanton night and the way he'd taken her with such unbridled abandon, made her wonder again why he had walked out.

She felt her stomach. A heady sense of power and wonder at the marvelous possibility of some unforeseen destiny possessed her.

Why hadn't she ever imagined such a consequence?

Because he'd said he'd used protection.

With a blush she remembered the wildness of their blazing passion. Something must have gone wrong.

She stared out the window and watched the beige ghosts below, floating on the lawn. She didn't want to be one of them. Nor did she want her child to be.

The cool wind blew through the open window, and she shivered with cold. The thought of raising her child without him brought a terrible, empty ache in her heart.

She heard the rumble of thunder. Only, the thunder wasn't thunder. The roar came from the lower floor. Instead of whispering, the ghosts were shouting.

Then she heard *his* drawl resounding against the wooden walls. "Where the hell is she?"

She stared across the room at her French easel, at the craggy male features she had captured on canvas, and the sight of his painted likeness and the sound of his voice made her heart flutter chaotically.

He had come.

Her mother's voice crackled. "Men aren't allowed here. Especially not you, McBride."

"McBride. His name is McBride," Stormy murmured softly. It was an honest name. A beautiful name.

"I don't give a damn about your rules," came more of his thunder. "If I have to tear this place apart board by board, I'm not leaving until I see her."

"She's not here. And even if she were, you are the last person she would want to see."

"Oh, yes, I am here! Yes, I am!"

Then she was flying down the stairs, only to find him halfway to the landing himself, having hurled his great body up the stairs two at a time the instant he'd heard her voice.

"I didn't know if I'd ever see you again."

His fathomless black eyes seared her. "You'd be better off if you'd never had to."

Her heart pounded with fright. "No..." she gasped.

"It's the truth. What happened between us...it was because of the tequila—I didn't mean for it to happen. I swear it. I've never been sorrier about anything in my life." His dark face was a cold, brutal mask.

Her soul seemed lost in some dismal aching void as she stared at his broad shoulders, at his lean waist, at the way sunlight made glossy ribbons shimmer in his blue-black hair.

"So why *did* you come?" Stormy managed at last, after an interminable agony of silence.

"For the same reason I came the first night. Stormy, I'm not just some stranger who walked in by accident and saved your life."

She was stunned. "Then who are you?"

"I work for your father."

Some vague, sad memory stirred to life. Then a convulsive shudder of denial raced through her. "You're... lying! My mother told me he died. Years ago."

"For all practical purposes he was dead—to her," came Jonathan's gentler voice. "But he's never forgotten that he had a daughter. He wants to see you, Stormy. And I've come to take you to him." There was a dreadful, telling pause. "Hell...he's dying, Stormy."

At Jonathan's dark, lost face, she felt a sickening coldness in the pit of her stomach. She believed him.

Although she was nothing to Jonathan McBride, she would go with him anyway. Not just because she had to know her father. But because she had to know Jonathan. She had to understand what lay beneath the hatred in his eyes before she could say goodbye to him forever.

*

BEAUTIFUL TWINS—Maria, who was sulkily dark and seductive, and Risa, who was more childlike and high-spirited—had helped Stormy unpack. They were the daughters of Jose, her father's foreman. Risa had admired all the garments she took out of Stormy's suitcases before she'd carefully hung them up or placed them in drawers. Maria had seemed to dislike the pretty clothes and to dislike Stormy even more.

After the girls left, Stormy crept into her father's room and stood at the threshold, a slim awkward figure struggling to compose herself. There was an odd smell about the quiet room, the mustiness of age and decay.

"I used to read to you in this room," came a gravelly voice from the bed.

She started. "Yes," she said softly.

Like one in a dream she moved mechanically toward the shelves and was surprised that she knew instinctively where to find a dusty copy of *Treasure Island* and another of *The Black Stallion*.

"Step into the light," commanded her father's disembodied croak. The shadow of a skeletal finger on the wall directed her to a pool of light at the foot of his bed.

"You look like your mother," he concluded with a weary sigh, sinking more deeply into his shadowy pillow.

"Before she got all hot and bothered by all those crazy notions."

Stormy laughed nervously. "Is that good or bad?"

"Your mother was a fine-looking woman. She still is," he admitted.

"You've kept up with her?"

When Stormy knelt beside him, he tried to sit up, but his gaunt body collapsed weakly back against his pillow. The only parts of him that seemed alive were his fever-brilliant dark eyes.

"I've kept up with you, too. Through the years she sent me pictures, even a letter now and then."

"She told me you were dead."

"Because I told her to," Hugh replied with gruff honesty. The gnarled, icy fingers tightened around hers. "I loved you more than anything in the world. But things went wrong between Maya and me. All the things that set me free—the open spaces, the isolation—made her feel trapped. She grew so unhappy, she was of no use to herself, let alone to me. So when you were five, I let her take you, because we'd have torn you apart fighting over you. Better you thought I was dead."

"No, it wasn't.... I always felt there was something missing from me. And I didn't know what it was."

"There was damn sure something missing for me," he growled. "I used to take you everywhere. You loved roundup and everything else about ranching. Sometimes we'd pretend we were flying to the moon."

"Flying... I—I don't remember anything. How could I have forgotten you, or my home—my life?"

"Probably 'cause it would have made you too unhappy to remember. Forgetting is the one thing that eases life's most terrible tragedies. You can't change them. You just outlast them. I keep trying to teach Henrietta that. She was always jealous of me for being the male."

"Henrietta?"

He didn't hear her. "There was only one tragedy I never bested or outlasted. I wanted sons—to pass the ranch to. I wanted to continue the dynasty. My father had left me the ranch, as his father had left it to him."

A desperate idea flitted through Stormy's mind. She leaned closer, anxious now to regain his attention.

"There's something you don't know...something that would matter to you. Hugh!"

"What could possibly matter to me now, child?" he asked in a faint voice.

"I'm pregnant."

Fever-bright eyes snapped open and stared at her fixedly.

"It's Jonathan's baby," she whispered.

Hugh's fingers gripped hers. "Jonathan...and you?"

She nodded.

"When Jonathan came to California the first time, I was mugged outside my apartment. He saved my life. We made love. It was more my fault than his, and he doesn't know about the baby. I've been afraid to tell him."

"I never was one to believe in miracles, but this is nothing short of a miracle." Hugh pondered the wonder of it. "Jonathan and you. A baby. My grandson."

"We can't be sure it will be a boy."

"Then the next one damn sure will be."

"Oh, there won't be a next one."

Hugh's weak voice cracked. "Don't tell me you've got those same crazy notions as your mother."

"No. It's just that Jonathan doesn't like me."

"After I'm done with him, he will make up his mind to like you."

"Oh, please, please, don't tell him about the baby. I want to find the right moment. You see, I want him to be happy about it. I don't want him threatened."

"As you wish. I never intended to threaten him, and you can tell him about the baby on your own." Hugh closed his eyes again. "Leave me, girl. I'm tired. Very tired." His voice seemed to fade away.

"Sleep well," she whispered, kissing him gently on his cold forehead before she tiptoed out of the room.

His black eyes flew open the instant he was sure she had gone. Tomorrow, maybe, he could sleep forever. But not tonight.

HELICOPTERS filled with the ranch's lawyers, their brief-cases bulging with complex legal documents, roared back and forth between the sprawling Spanish colonial ranch house and San Antonio that night. Stormy slept as soundly as a child through these frantic comings and goings.

In the gallery she had found a magnificent oil painting of her father cradling her against his chest as his stallion reared above a coiled rattlesnake. The artist had captured the horse's wild fear, her father's rugged, protective bravery in the face of danger and the child's fearless love and faith in this awesome man.

That night she dreamed of her lost childhood. She remembered Hugh holding her patiently on his knee. She remembered her Shetland pony, her saddle with the silver trim. Most of all she remembered the way they had flown together to the other side of the moon.

Dreaming deeply, she slept for hours, until some slight, nearby sound awakened her. She sprang from bed, the memories of her childhood still fresh on her mind. She was anxious to rush to Hugh and tell him that she had remembered everything.

But when her bare feet touched the cold wooden floor, a tall dark figure stepped out of the shadows and blocked her headlong flight toward the door.

Jonathan had been standing in Stormy's bedroom for

more than an hour, his heart filled with a morose, choking grief. Hugh, his one real friend on earth, Hugh, the champion who had pulled him up from the gutter and saved him, was dead.

The only thing in this bleak night that offered him the tiniest comfort was being near Hugh's daughter—the one woman Jonathan should have wanted to avoid. The one woman he should hate because she'd told her father that Jonathan had betrayed him and slept with her. The one woman he could never again avoid.

Hugh and his lawyers had seen to that.

The memory of Jonathan's last moments with Hugh at his deathbed had been ruined because of Stormy's rash and selfish confession. Jonathan imagined she had done it to bring him to heel. To control him. To make him pay.

These thoughts were whirling angrily in his mind when she sprang up.

She gasped when he continued to block her escape, her huge dark eyes pleading with his. Sensing instinctively his terrible reason for coming to her, she hesitated only the briefest moment before flinging herself into his waiting arms.

No words were needed, but Jonathan struggled to say them anyway.

"Hugh's dead."

The profound sorrow in her low cry mirrored his own.

HER FATHER was dead. His gravesite was surrounded by banks of white lilies. Hugh's only sister, Henrietta, who owned the ranch next door, sat beside Stormy, along with Jonathan. On the other side of Jonathan sat his six-year-old son, Daniel, whom Jonathan had reluctantly introduced her to after the funeral.

The preacher began to read the Twenty-Third Psalm.

The familiar words that should have offered comfort
served only to emphasize Stormy's profound aloneness.

The casket was being lowered. Dirt was being thrown
upon the satiny pink flowers. She brought a handkerchief
to her eyes, her hands visibly trembling.

When she began to weep soundlessly, Jonathan pressed
her black head against his muscled chest. Her wonder at
the unexpected tenderness lessened her grief as nothing
else could have. When the service was over, Henrietta
slapped Jonathan jarringly on the back.

"Hugh wouldn't like us to waste ranch time on tears.
Least of all you, Jon," Henrietta said in a brisk voice,
gravelly from years of whiskey and cigarettes. Her body
was big and tough, her silver hair as short as a man's, her
skin leather-dark from the sun. "Give Stormy to me and
get on with more important things."

Jonathan grimaced as if he didn't like being ordered
about by Henrietta, but his comforting hands fell like
stones to his sides as he released Stormy.

As Henrietta began to fuss in her rather tactless, overly
possessive way, Jonathan ripped off his suit jacket and tie
and rolled up the sleeves of his white dress shirt.

Then Jonathan was in the saddle, digging his heels in.
Without even a backward glance in Stormy's direction,
he galloped away across the wide, empty range, leaving
her behind by her father's grave.

Stormy watched numbly until he disappeared. When
she turned away, desolate, she noticed Daniel cowering
beside a nearby tombstone and staring after his father with
big, dry eyes.

"Poor little thing," Henrietta said of the boy. "That's
his mother's grave. Hugh adored Daniel. The boy has only
Jonathan now. He would worship his father, if only Jonathan would let him."

"Jonathan makes himself hard to love."

Henrietta threw her cigarette down and squashed it with her boot. "I'll tell you what I told Hugh more than once. Jonathan McBride's a lost soul, past redemption."

"I don't believe it," Stormy whispered.

"Hugh wouldn't believe it, either, but he was wrong."

Stormy knew her aunt was trying to warn her out of kindness. Henrietta might have argued further, but they were interrupted by a sullen Maria, who informed them that food was ready to be served at the ranch house.

"I'll see to Daniel, Henrietta," Stormy said, glad their discussion was over, "if you'll see to everyone else."

Stormy knelt beside the child. The boy's blue eyes were solemn.

"You can cry," she said softly. "It's okay to cry when you're sad."

His huge eyes rose to hers. "They say he killed my mother. They say he hates me 'cause I remind him of her."

"Oh, no. You mustn't believe that."

"Why not, if it's the truth?" he lashed out.

"I'm sure Jonathan doesn't hate you."

"Oh yes, he does." Daniel's voice trailed off. "Ask Henrietta!" A shadow passed over his face. "He hates me. And he hates you, too. Just like he hated my mother."

*

STORMY got out of the plush leather chair and threw Hugh's will back onto the lawyer's desk in disgust. It was her own fault. She knew why Hugh had done it—because she had foolishly told him about the baby.

The lawyer picked up the document. "By the terms of your father's will, if you choose to marry McBride, and you and he live together as man and wife for one year on the ranch, you will each inherit fifty percent of it. Livestock, mineral rights. There's a fortune in the minerals alone. But if either of you fails to agree, the other gets everything.''

''This is a monstrous document.''

His fingers flipped quickly through a second document until he came to the last page, which he handed to her. ''This may interest you.''

She lowered her gaze and beheld a bold black signature at the bottom of the milk-white page.

''As you can see, Miss Jones, McBride has already signed.''

STORMY FOUND Jonathan in Marengo's stall.

One look at her flushed face and fiery eyes, and Jonathan eased his saddle slowly back down onto the sawhorse.

''I've been expecting you.''

''That's probably why you were riding away!''

''No.'' He patted the beeper fastened to his belt. ''Jose just paged me. There's a calf lost in the south pasture—''

''You planned this,'' she hissed, attacking him in midsentence, throwing the will at him. Marengo snorted wildly at her raised voice.

Jonathan leaned his muscled frame against the door of an empty stall. ''I guess you're furious because Hugh didn't leave it all to you.''

''I'm mad because I think you planned this. I bet you wanted this ranch for years and years.''

''You're right there.''

''It's a wonder my father never saw through you.''

''He did. He knew I could handle the ranch, even if he couldn't be certain how I'd handle his daughter.'' His black gaze swept her in slow, sensual appraisal.

"Your father loved this place. He would have done anything to keep it together. And so would I."

She swung away. "You want the ranch so much, you'd even marry a woman you hate to get it."

"I don't hate you," he said quietly.

"You sure don't love me."

"No," he said levelly, without a trace of remorse. "I loved my mother, and she kicked me out when I was ten so she could chase after some sailor. I loved my wife, and our marriage was hell. Honey, I learned the hard way not to set much store in the love of women. But if I have to marry again, you'll suit me better than most. You're the pretty wrapping on the one gift I've always wanted."

"Pretty..." The way he said the word hurt. "Pretty paper you'll rip apart and discard as soon as you get your hands on what you really want?"

His voice grew gentle. "Honey, I have no intention of discarding you."

"Well, I don't believe you," she said stiffly. "You disgust me."

"Really?" There was a dangerous glint in his eyes before his hand snaked across the short distance that separated them. He dragged her against his hard, muscled frame.

He captured her mouth in a long, searching kiss, as he used his expert hands to mold her so closely she was left with no doubt about the extent of his arousal. Her senses swirled. His lovemaking brought a pleasure so intense that she could only tremble with wanting as his warm hands moved inside her silk blouse to cup her breasts. His callused fingertips brushed her nipples into hardened buds of desire. A soft sigh escaped her lips as she arched her body against his.

His rough hands moved over her quivering body as if she were his possession and he could touch her anywhere.

"I could take you in this stable and you'd love it. Disgust? Honey, you shouldn't insult the man you're going to marry when you're guilty of the same crime."

She slowly, dazedly came back to her senses. Anger and shame burned through her.

"I won't marry you."

"Good." He sounded so delighted, she looked up again, straight into his taunting black eyes. "Then I'll get the ranch the easy way."

Furious, Stormy charged from the barn. As she stepped out into the sunshine she was momentarily blinded, but not so blinded she didn't see a small blond figure scurrying away.

Daniel… Stormy reddened with shame when she recognized the boy's golden head. How much had he heard? How much had he seen?

In no mood to face anyone, least of all Daniel, Stormy went to her room. Her hands wouldn't quit shaking.

Stormy thought of her baby, of her father and the ranch. Last of all, Stormy thought about Jonathan and the fierce passions that erupted every time they were together.

Defiantly she grabbed her French easel, her sketch pad, pencils and pastels, and stormed out of the house.

She tiptoed into the darkened garage from a side passage. Shakily, she got into Jonathan's pickup. She felt a curious comfort when she saw his pistol on the floorboard and his rifle and scabbard securely fastened in the gun rack.

She was in such a rush to drive away that she never looked back. But she had the oddest feeling that unseen eyes watched as she vanished in the thick brush.

WHIRLS of hot dust enveloped her as she jounced to a stop when the mile-long road dead-ended in front of a quaint adobe cabin beneath a windmill. Most of the windowpanes were either missing or broken. Stormy found its isolation soothing.

She sat on the porch and began to sketch. An hour passed. Then another. She drew cactus and mesquite, forgetting Jonathan and the haunting indecision in her heart. The sun began to go down, and she grew enchanted with the magic play of vivid color and light. Stormy used her pastels and sketched wildly.

All too soon the magical colors faded. Long shadows fell across the porch.

From behind her there came a stealthy crackle of undergrowth in the shadowy mesquite thicket. Stormy's interest in her art fled. The isolated setting took on a threatening aspect. From the bush burst the song of a startled whippoorwill. Then all was still.

Stormy threw her art things down and raced back to the pickup, telling herself that she was crazy to feel such fear.

The door stood ajar. Jonathan's rifle was gone from the rack. Gone, too, were the pistol and truck keys.

Suddenly there was a wild thrashing in the mesquite nearby. She jumped away from the truck and charged into the most tangled part of the thicket, heedlessly stumbling over rough ground, fallen branches. Whatever stalked her soon began to gain on her.

Stormy plunged deeper into the dense brush. In her terror, she stumbled over a gnarled root. Her attacker loomed out of the blackness.

She half dragged herself, half crawled across the rough ground away from those black-booted feet.

The sound of leather sliding the length of a rifle barrel rang like a death knell. Behind her she heard a loud crack. Then she pitched face forward into the earth, and her world grew dark.

STORMY WAS spiraling down into a hot, black tunnel when a hard hand clamped around her waist. She shrieked in terror and tried to claw free as strong arms pulled her to safety.

"Stormy…" The silken male drawl was low and familiar, and stilled all her fears. "Honey…"

She opened her eyes and saw Jonathan there, tucking a pistol into his belt, kneeling over her and gently shaking her.

She reached out her hand like a blind person. "Jonathan…it's really you." Her mind spun. "I thought I heard a gunshot."

"I heard you scream, and I fired a warning shot. I saw the truck at the cabin. Your easel and paints were scattered all over the ground."

Blindly she reached for him. "You're always saving me," she whispered against his throat. "Someone followed me here and he would have killed me, if you hadn't come. He took your rifle and your pistol. Your keys, too…" The chilling words were muttered shudderingly into the massive warmth of his broad chest. "All I saw were black boots."

His fingers ruffled her snarled hair. "Well, I'm here. And I'm not going to let anything happen to you." His hands slid to her waist. "Do you think you can stand?"

When she tried, her ankle crumpled. He lifted her as if she weighed nothing.

When they reached the truck, he set her down. "It'll just take me a minute or two to hotwire—" As he spoke, he reached inside the truck. He drew his hand back with the keys.

"No…" A chill of horror went through her. "They were gone," she insisted.

He grabbed the saddle scabbard with his rifle, his other pistol in its holster, and held them out for her to see.

She shrank from him, more frightened than ever. "I tell you they were gone. Someone took them."

"Who? I didn't see anyone else when I got here."

Suddenly she was staring into his face, her wide eyes fearful. "How did you get here?"

"I rode Marengo."

"Then where is he now?"

"Most likely galloping hell-bent for his stable."

"Why did you ride this way?"

"Daniel paged me and said you'd driven off. He said you hadn't come back. I was worried about you." His penetrating gaze rested on her pale face. His eyes blazed darkly with sudden anger.

With a single ruthless movement he yanked the door open and lifted her into the truck. She scrambled across the seat as he hurled himself after her, slamming the door so hard the whole truck rocked. "You're wondering if I want the ranch so badly I would kill to cut you out of the half that is yours. Dear God," he muttered fiercely, pulling her against him in the hot darkness. "Will I never be free of the past? Will it taint everything I love?" His desperate gaze sought hers.

Even through her own fear and bewilderment, she felt his pain. "Someone was here."

"It wasn't me."

They looked at one another for a long time. Then, with uncertain, faltering fingers, she touched his face. "Jonathan, I want to believe in you. I want to understand you, but you keep pushing me away."

"I've been a fool." Then he was kissing her as if she were life itself.

"Dear God, if anything had happened to you—" His mouth traveled from her lips to her throat. "I didn't kill Lylia, and I would never hurt you," he whispered. "I would kill anyone—with my bare hands—who hurt you.

Marry me,'' he pleaded. ''Marry me...because I'll die if you don't.''

The answer she gave him was carried away on the wind.

WHEN JONATHAN strode toward the veranda with Stormy cradled possessively in his arms, the outside lights flashed on. Henrietta and Daniel came running out. The dark shape of a woman's shadow hovered against a long window. There was something about the sullen figure that made Stormy know it was Maria.

The fluorescent glare washed all color from Henrietta's face. She looked tired and old.

''For the love of the Almighty, what happened to her?''

Jonathan stared at the woman with a dull, blank face. ''I'm not sure. Open the door, Henrietta.''

Henrietta stood like a stone in his path, not budging, but Daniel went flying behind her and flung the door back wide. Jonathan gave Henrietta a long look and then stepped around her.

''Is Stormy okay, Dad?'' Daniel queried.

Jonathan's manner gentled. ''Yes. Because of you, Daniel.'' He paused. ''Only because of you—son.''

Daniel beamed up at his father, then came up to Stormy shyly, as pleased as a puppy when she stroked his golden head.

Without another word Jonathan swept past him and proceeded up the stairs to Stormy's bedroom, with Daniel and Henrietta racing behind them.

''She's obviously had a terrible shock.'' Henrietta's voice floated from the shadowy threshold like a disembodied sound carried on dark wings.

Jonathan was smoothing Stormy's hair against her pillow. ''Yes,'' he said, his voice harsh. ''This isn't the first time. Stormy was attacked in L.A., too.''

"Jonathan saved me that night, too."

"That night, too?" After Henrietta's tactless question, disquieting silence fell. For a long moment there was only the sound of the hot wind rattling the windowpanes. "What an odd...coincidence."

"I thought so, too." Jonathan's voice seemed very tired.

"Jonathan has asked me to marry him," Stormy said.

Henrietta turned a ghastly gray. There was another silence. "If there's anything I can do," her aunt finally said. Her hands shook with the palsied rhythm of an old woman's.

"If you really want to make yourself useful, you could call Dr. Morris," Jonathan muttered sharply.

Henrietta pursed her thin lips. "I know as much as that old quack Morris."

"Aunt Henrietta learned everything she knows by watching the vet," Daniel said authoritatively.

"And that's why she's not laying a hand on Stormy," Jonathan said, a taut smile thinning his lips.

"Well," said Henrietta with sudden passion, "there are those who might be smart to prefer me laying a hand on them than you, Jonathan McBride."

Jonathan went very white. "You're tired. Why don't you go to bed, Henrietta?" His voice was softly threatening.

Henrietta looked terribly old, thin and shaken.

After she and Daniel left, Jonathan shut the door. He leaned heavily against the frame for a long moment. "Stormy, if you want me to go, I will. You can have the ranch, everything, my darling."

Confused emotions coursed through her—terror, love, hope—and then came the blinding knowledge that she would risk everything for a chance at happiness with him. "Jonathan, come to me." Her tone was rushed and breathless. "Hold me." In a single stride he was beside her. She brought her hand to his brow and smoothed back an unruly, blue-black lock. "What would the real killer do if you left me?"

He drew her into his arms then and held her close. She felt the bitter pounding of his heart.

*

STORMY'S wedding day was leaden gray like the day of Hugh's funeral. Maria sullenly packed Stormy's suitcase for her honeymoon while Risa fingered the delicate lace of Stormy's veil.

Stormy turned to her mother, who wore a long, flowing black robe.

"Mother, couldn't you have at least worn beige? You look as if you're going to a funeral."

"Exactly, dear one."

"Mother, please. I know what I'm doing."

"That's what you always say before you make the worst mistakes. But this... Dear one, Henrietta says there have been two attempts on your life, and he was there both times."

"If Jonathan wanted to kill me, why did he save my life twice?"

"Henrietta says—"

"Henrietta?" Stormy exploded. "Who says she's the gospel? What makes you so sure you can trust her?"

"Henrietta?" Maya laughed with contempt. "I trust Henrietta because for all her tough blustering, she's weak and spineless. When Henrietta chose not to marry and have children, her father passed over her and left the bulk of the ranch to Hugh. She didn't like it, but do you think she did anything? No."

"Maybe she really didn't mind."

"Oh, she minded. Not that she ever said a word to the men. But she complained to me." Maya paused. "Your precious Jonathan came here with nothing. The only thing that stands in the way of him having everything is your life. I'm afraid, Stormy. I want you to come back to the commune, where you'll be safe."

"Mother, why can't you see that I can't? No one's ever believed in Jonathan."

"Maybe there's a reason."

Stormy closed her eyes. "I love him, Mother."

"So much that you're willing to die for him?"

Stormy's voice was faint. "Mother, please—"

There was a sound. Stormy opened her eyes and saw that Jonathan had opened the door behind them. She met his icy stare. For an instant it seemed that time had frozen.

Jonathan's forced smile only made him look grimmer. "Your mother has a point, darling. You can still change your mind."

Her body trembling, Stormy ran to the window, away from him, and looked out. Jose was directing traffic into a pasture.

"There are so many cars," she murmured. "I never thought so many people would come to our wedding."

"The terms of Hugh's will aroused a rather lurid curiosity in the minds of many of his friends and business associates. People haven't forgotten what happened to my *dearly beloved* Lylia."

Stormy felt blind panic. "Don't, Jonathan. Please…"

"People have a morbid curiosity about us—about me. From the looks of those cars, people will be packed into that chapel like kids lining up for a dangerous ride at a carnival."

JONATHAN'S cynical assessment proved all too true. Fewer than a third of their wedding guests could fit into the crowded chapel.

Perhaps it was only Stormy's imagination working overtime, but it seemed to her that Lylia's uninvited ghost hovered beside Jonathan and herself as they stood at the altar. The minister droned on, and Stormy felt hundreds of eyes boring into her back.

As the ceremony drew to a close there was a low rumbling of thunder. The sky blackened.

The shadowy chapel, Jonathan's chilling black eyes—everything seemed to spin in a sickening whirl. She willed away the morning sickness and her nightmarish fears, and clutched Jonathan for support.

"You may kiss the bride," said the minister, his voice tight with disapproval.

Jonathan crushed her to him in a fiercely possessive kiss. He seemed not to mind his gaping audience.

"Now you are mine," he whispered. "Forever."

A ripple of tension stirred through the crowd. People were remembering the sullen boy Hugh had brought home, one who'd had nothing but the ragged shirt on his back and chips the size of blocks on both his shoulders. No one but Hugh had liked him. Now every acre, every brick, every cow, every drop of oil and every atom of natural gas belonged to him.

The tension between the bride and the groom lasted as they fled down the aisle together, lasted as they stood beside one another stiffly at their reception, greeting an endless line of curious guests.

When they had greeted their last guest, Jonathan seized the first opportunity to leave her, and although his grim presence had been unbearable, his absence was even worse. The minute he was gone, Stormy's heart swelled with loneliness, even though she was surrounded by teasing well-wishers who kissed her, joked with her and hugged her.

At last it was time for Stormy to go upstairs and dress for her brief New Orleans honeymoon. Risa went up to help her change.

Inside her bedroom, Stormy tore off her white dress and ripped the veil from her head. Risa caught the filmy thing in midair and held it to her face. "Someday I will be happy like you and marry the man I love."

"I hope so," Stormy said quietly. Then she flung herself into her bathroom and began to cry. What kind of wedding day had she expected? Surely not one where her husband left her to face everyone alone.

Now that he had married her, perhaps he saw no reason to pretend. The ranch was his. What a naive, ignorant fool she had been. Stormy leaned back against the wall and began to weep in earnest.

Her wild tears were shattered abruptly by an explosion, then a muted cry.

Stormy flung open the door. Risa was lying facedown in a crumpled heap. A pool of red seeped from her ashen forehead, coating her long black hair, the growing stain reddening Stormy's white wedding veil.

Risa had been wearing Stormy's veil. Stormy went cold.

Then she began to scream for Jonathan.

He burst through the door. All color drained from his tanned face.

He was examining her injuries when Henrietta and Maria rushed in. Beneath his light probings, Risa stirred. Her lashes flickered.

Maria's expression darkened. She turned on Stormy, her anger hissing out of her lips like the quick rush of an explosive gas. "This is your fault. Whoever shot her was trying to shoot you. If you'd never come back, Jonathan

would have married me. He would love me. Me. Not you.
Before long he'll hate you the same way he hated Lylia.
You don't belong here. You never will."

Jonathan rose wearily to his feet. He spoke in a low
and gentle tone. "Maria, you must not say these things.
You must not even think them. Stormy is my wife."

Henrietta was staring at Jonathan with burning, hate-
filled eyes as if he were a monster.

Maria, looking bitterly crushed, sank hopelessly down
beside her sister.

Stormy dared not lift her eyes to meet Jonathan's for
fear she would see regret or something even more terrifying.

JONATHAN shuddered. The nightmare was happening
again. He was caught up in it, fighting for his life.

Risa had been taken to the hospital, and everyone was
assembled in the library. His rifle and his saddle scabbard
had been brought in and now lay on a low reading table.
These people were his enemies—ready to condemn him.

He had felt it all before—after Lylia's death—but he
was afraid, more afraid than he'd been then. Because he
had so much more to lose.

The sheriff and his officers, Henrietta, Maya—a dozen
others sat in a huddled, silent group, their cold stares judg-
mental. Looking lost and forgotten, Stormy sat apart from
the others on a low couch. Never had she looked so utterly
out of his reach.

The sheriff cleared his throat. "You've got some tall
explaining to do. A single round's been fired, McBride.
The bullet's the same caliber we dug out of the wall of
your wife's bedroom."

Jonathan swallowed hard. He felt like a cornered beast.

"Anyone could have taken his gun," Stormy cried,
running toward him.

Jonathan was so numb he barely felt her touch when she encircled him with her arms to shield him from the others.

"Do you really think that if he wanted to kill me, he would use his own gun and then hide it where we would find it? In Marengo's stall?" she pleaded desperately.

The sheriff moved threateningly closer. "Well, McBride? Where the hell *were* you?"

Jonathan felt the sick, familiar coldness in the pit of his stomach. "I don't have an alibi. I was in the stable with Marengo."

"On your wedding day? You're telling me you prefer your horse to your bride?"

The sheriff kept badgering him with questions. Jonathan barely heard him. He barely heard his own mumbled answers. All he saw was the icy pallor of his wife's face, the frozen darkness in her frightened eyes.

Without a word, Jonathan strode silently out of the room. The sheriff shouted at him to come back. But Jonathan kept walking. Out of the house, stumbling blindly through the slanting rain and thick mud to the stable again, where he saddled Marengo.

He knew he should go to his bride and try to gently persuade her to believe in him. But cold fear condemned him to ride out into the fierce wet night.

STORMY TOSSED and writhed, her dreams tormented nightmares. She didn't know that she cried out. Nor did she hear the hurried footsteps that rushed along the hall and then came into her bedroom. All she saw was the huge black shadow falling across her when she awakened.

A scream bubbled up in her throat, but a dark hand closed over her mouth.

"Hush, darling," came a man's husky, familiar drawl.

It was Jonathan.

She shrank more deeply into her pillows. "I waited and waited for you," she mumbled.

"I'm here now."

In the moonlight she saw that his handsome face was ravaged by loneliness and fear. What she felt for him went beyond doubt and common sense. If she denied him now, she would lose him forever.

"Darling," she whispered in a light, breathless tone. "In all the excitement we seem to have forgotten something."

The erotic promise in her whisper held him spellbound. "What?"

"It's our wedding night," she murmured, holding out her hand in the silvery darkness to draw him nearer.

"Dear God." With shaking arms he crushed her close. "I didn't think you'd want me near you."

She felt his warm breath against her throat. "I want you near," she whispered. "Tell me one thing."

"Anything, my love."

"What did Maria mean? Do you love her?"

Jonathan's hands grew still upon Stormy's hair. "She's had a crush on me for years. She thought she had a chance after Lylia died. Stormy, Maria was one of the only people who believed I hadn't killed Lylia. I was so grateful that someone believed in me that I didn't realize until it was too late that Maria was in love with me. She's been very upset ever since I told her I was going to marry you."

"Are you in love with her?"

A muscle worked tensely in his jaw. "You are the only woman in my life. Darling, I didn't kill Lylia, and I would never hurt you. I would defend you with my own life. You must believe that."

"I would defend you with my life, too."

"I must see that it never comes to that." His hands cupped her face as if she were very precious to him.

She stared up at him with blazing eyes. A look passed between them. Suddenly the time for words had passed.

*

STORMY AWOKE to find herself alone. The passion of the night seemed a dream. Jonathan was shutting her out again.

Where was Jonathan?

"Señor McBride left before first light to supervise the repair of some windmills on the northern division," Jose answered when she and Daniel found him in the barn. "Señor McBride think someone is playing bad tricks. He say sabotage."

"Sabotage?"

"He'll be gone all day, or they will no have water in the north pasture. I gotta take all my men...."

Jonathan would be gone all day. He'd left without saying a word to his bride.

Slowly she and Daniel walked back to the house.

There were hours of that long day that she would never be able to account for. Hours she passed sketching with Daniel. Hours she really spent waiting for word from Jonathan.

That afternoon Stormy drove into town to the hospital to visit Risa, who was doing fine. When she returned much later, Henrietta and Maria met her on the stair. Maria was like a silent angry shadow; Henrietta did the talking.

"Jon came home. The sheriff was here, too. They spoke in the library."

"What—"

"It was a private talk. Jon said he had something important to tell you. He seemed...upset."

Stormy's heart had begun to pound fiercely. "Where is he?"

"He had to go out again. You just missed him."

Made frantic by a bitter mixture of acute disappointment and dread, Stormy rushed past them up the stairs.

She saw the note on her pillow the minute she opened the door. She flew across the room. Dazedly she skimmed the brief contents.

Sorry we missed each other, darling. I have something to tell you. It will have to wait now. I have to make a repair on the windmill behind the adobe cabin.

Without a word to anyone, without changing her dress, she picked up her sketchbook and dashed out the back way.

She didn't know that Daniel's attention was caught by a glint of light from the truck backing out of the garage.

She didn't know that moments later he made a phone call, then ran as hard as he could away from the house, as if a dozen devils were after him.

WHEN STORMY reached the cabin, the sun was sinking in a blaze of red. The whining blades of the windmill made an eerie lonely sound. A faint sense of unease brushed her. Jonathan was nowhere to be seen. She climbed down from the truck to find him.

The light was fading. Long, clawlike shadows leaped from the trees. Stormy stood still. The birds had stopped singing. So had the cicadas. There was only the sound of the windmill. Terrible uneasiness lodged in the pit of her stomach.

Stormy forced herself to walk back to the truck as if she were unafraid. She opened the door. Then she screamed. A tangle of loose wires dangled like masses of spaghetti from under the dash.

Jonathan's note had been a trick. Whoever had tried to kill her before was out there now, watching her, waiting for complete darkness. Was it Jonathan after all?

Moving like an automaton, she stumbled into the dark thicket. Soon her ankles were bleeding from sharp branches in her path.

Behind her there was a stealthy sound.

"Jonathan…"

Stormy didn't feel the blow against her temple that struck her to the ground.

STORMY AWOKE to suffocating, acrid black smoke. Her body was bruised, as if she'd been dragged across rough ground. She was lying on the shattered fragments of a windowpane. Through the smoke she made out the sloping adobe walls and wooden floor of the cabin loft.

She struggled to sit up, only she couldn't because taut ropes bound her wrists and ankles. Smoke was everywhere. Someone had set the mesquite thicket on fire, and the wind was whipping it toward the cabin. She and her baby would be burned alive. Stormy managed to grab a piece of glass and work it against the rope that bound her hands. She cut her wrist and cried out.

"Jonathan…"

Suddenly he burst through the door, his shirt torn, his face dirty from the smoke. The fierce light in his eyes seemed to go out when she looked up at him.

Then something prodded him, and he stumbled inside.

Stormy made out the shadowy figure climbing the cabin stairs behind him—a figure who was pointing an automatic dead center at his heart.

Henrietta, crazed, grim-faced, pulled steadily, remorselessly on the trigger.

"Jonathan!"

Jonathan turned. The bullet blasted into his body. He pitched forward and lay still. Outside, the flames roared in the trees that backed up against the house. The roof had caught fire and so had a beam.

Henrietta was smiling down at her.

"I'm sorry you have to die with McBride, Stormy. You're my blood," she said almost kindly. "I tried to warn you. In L.A. Here." Henrietta spoke in that strange, terrifyingly controlled masculine voice. "But you wouldn't listen."

"Henrietta, I'm going to have a child. Hugh's grandchild. Your— You wouldn't just leave us to die?"

"I've done it before. I listened to Lylia scream when her lover strangled her because she'd taken another lover. She deserved to die."

"You let everyone believe Jonathan killed her?"

"I started the rumors—to drive him away. When you're both dead, everything will be mine."

"You have your own ranch."

"It was never enough," came her hate-filled tone.

The wind was sweeping the boiling-red flames up the back wall of the cabin.

"You wrote that note and left it for me to find?"

"Yes. Jonathan has a distinctive hand—easily forged. Then Daniel saw you leave. I listened at the door when he called Jonathan, who naturally came as fast as he could—exactly as I planned." Henrietta's face was loathsome, triumphant.

There was a sound behind Henrietta.

Daniel's golden hair was illuminated by the flames. "If you don't let them go, I'll tell on you, Aunt Henrietta," he said in a thin, frightened voice.

Daniel was standing at the top of the stairs, his chest heaving from his mile-long run. Smoke was billowing up around him. His face was as darkly grim as his father's.

"Damned brat!" Henrietta screamed. "I'll kill you, too."

Then three things happened at once.

Stormy sliced through the rope that bound her hands and scrambled toward Henrietta. Jonathan sprang up like a tiger. Henrietta lunged away from them both to grab Daniel.

As agile as a monkey, Daniel scampered out of her way. Stormy's hand closed around Henrietta's black boot. For one wild moment Henrietta clawed wildly for the door frame, for the railing, and missed. Then she toppled down the stairs backward, tumbling over and over, ending in a broken heap on the floor. It was obvious she was dead.

Flames were racing up the walls of the lower story and covering the ceiling as Jonathan, weakened by the bullet in his shoulder, half carried Stormy, half stumbled with her down the stairs.

When the three of them were safely outside, Stormy felt the most terrible heat crawling up her skin. She looked down and saw that her skirt was on fire. Jonathan and Daniel began smothering it with their hands. She was more afraid than ever before.

"The baby..." she whispered.

Jonathan knelt close, the blood from his shoulder wound soaking her dress. "What? I heard what you said to Henrietta, but—"

"Our baby… I hoped that if you couldn't love me, you could at least love our baby as much as I do."

The cabin and Henrietta and all the evil that had threatened them for so long was consumed in a final explosion of golden fire.

"I love you," Jonathan said. "I love you."

"I love you, too," Daniel whispered.

But the unconscious woman in Jonathan's arms did not hear them.

THERE WAS a blinding white light in Stormy's eyes. And at first she thought she was dead—in heaven. Then she saw Jonathan. He was shirtless, and a huge bandage covered his left shoulder.

"My darling…my beloved darling. You are safe. And so is our baby," he said.

She felt the warmth of Jonathan's arms around her, and for a long time he held her.

"And Daniel?" she asked.

"He's sleeping in the next room." Jonathan said. "He was incredibly brave."

"Did you tell him you thought so?"

"Yes." Jonathan smiled. "He is thrilled that you are safe, and that he is going to have a real brother or sister."

"Jonathan, in our excitement about the baby, we must not let him feel neglected."

"Never again."

"Then I have everything I ever wanted," she said. She closed her eyes. "Except one thing."

"What's that, darling?"

"You've never told me you love me."

"Oh, yes I have. You were too ill to hear me."

"Then you must tell me again."

"Anyone can say the words," he said as he brought his lips close to her ear.

She smiled up at him. "If it's so easy, why don't you say them?"

"Because it's not so easy. Not for me."

"That's why it will mean so much—for you to tell me."

He leaned closer and whispered the three most precious words in all the world into her ear.

"Someday, I want you to shout them," she said.

"Someday, we'll take our two children and ride together to the other side of the moon, and I will."

*

THE SAN ANTONIO art gallery was crammed with guests. Silver trays brimmed with caviar, crabmeat and other delicacies. Champagne fountains flowed. Maya had arranged everything—but this time without thought of stealing the show from her daughter.

The golden shimmer of Stormy McBride's gown spread about her as she stood on the landing gazing up at the magnificent painting of Jonathan backlighted by a fiery sunset. A dozen more of her paintings, all rich with vibrant color and detail of Western ranch scenes, hung on the walls.

A side door opened and a new, gentler Jonathan entered carrying their dark-haired baby, Jason. Daniel trailed behind him with a blanket and bottle.

Stormy forgot everything and hurried down to them. Stormy tenderly stroked her baby's hair, and he gurgled with pleasure as he beamed at his proud parents.

"Say Mama," Maya said, leaning jealously over her grandson.

"Jason doesn't like orders from on high, Mother dear."

"Say Mama."

"Dada," Jason replied with a laugh.

Everyone burst out laughing—even Maya. She lifted him from Jonathan's arms into her own, which freed Jonathan to embrace Stormy. Daniel snuggled against his parents. With wise eyes that seemed to see them in a new light, Maya looked from her grandson to Jonathan and Stormy.

"I'm very proud of you, Stormy dear," Maya whispered at last, "for possessing the brave soul of a true artist and finding your own path—even though it led to marriage."

Jonathan smiled grimly at his formidable mother-in-law. "A fate worse than death."

"Not for Stormy," Maya admitted. "Your love has enriched her. I never thought I'd say this, but I'm grateful to you, McBride."

Jonathan's arms tightened possessively around his wife. He leaned closer and kissed her.

"I love you, Stormy. I will love you till I die."

Passionate, Powerful, Provocative

Save $1.00 off the purchase of any 2 Silhouette Desire® titles.

$1.00 OFF!
any 2 Silhouette Desire® titles.

RETAILER: Harlequin Enterprises Ltd. will pay the face value of this coupon plus 8¢ if submitted by customer for this product only. Any other use constitutes fraud. Coupon is nonassignable. Void if taxed, prohibited or restricted by law. Consumer must pay any government taxes. For reimbursement submit coupons and proof of sales to: Harlequin Enterprises Ltd., P.O. Box 880478, El Paso, TX 88588-0478, U.S.A. Cash value 1/100¢. Valid in the U.S. only.

**Coupon valid until June 30, 2002.
Redeemable at participating retail outlets in the U.S. only.
Limit one coupon per purchase.**

108102

5 65373 00076 2   (8100)0 10810

Silhouette®
Where love comes alive™

Passionate, Powerful, Provocative

Save $1.00 off the purchase of any 2 Silhouette Desire® titles.

$1.00 OFF!
any 2 Silhouette Desire® titles.

RETAILER: Harlequin Enterprises Ltd. will pay the face value of this coupon plus 10.25¢ if submitted by customer for this product only. Any other use constitutes fraud. Coupon is nonassignable. Void if taxed, prohibited or restricted by law. Consumer must pay any government taxes. Nielson Clearing House customers submit coupons and proof of sales to: Harlequin Enterprises Ltd., 661 Millidge Avenue, P.O. Box 639, Saint John, N.B. E2L 4A5. Non NCH retailer—for reimbursement submit coupons and proof of sales directly to: Harlequin Enterprises Ltd., Retail Marketing Department, 225 Duncan Mill Rd., Don Mills, Ontario M3B 3K9, Canada. Valid in Canada only.

Coupon valid until June 30, 2002.
Redeemable at participating retail outlets in Canada only.
Limit one coupon per purchase.

5 2 6 0 4 1 5 3

Silhouette®
Where love comes alive™

Sassy, Sexy, Seductive!

HARLEQUIN® *Temptation.*

Save $1.00 off the purchase of any 2 Harlequin Temptation® titles.

Visit Harlequin at www.eHarlequin.com
T5V6CHTUS
© 2001 Harlequin Enterprises Ltd.

HARLEQUIN® *Makes any time special ®*

Sassy, Sexy, Seductive!

HARLEQUIN®
Temptation.

Save $1.00 off the purchase of any 2 Harlequin Temptation® titles.

Visit Harlequin at www.eHarlequin.com
T5V6CHTCAN
© 2001 Harlequin Enterprises Ltd.

HARLEQUIN®
Makes any time special®

HARLEQUIN®
Presents®

Seduction and Passion Guaranteed!

Save $2.00 off the purchase of any 3 Harlequin Presents® titles.

$2.00 OFF!
any 3 Harlequin Presents® titles.

RETAILER: Harlequin Enterprises Ltd. will pay the face value of this coupon plus 8¢ if submitted by customer for this product only. Any other use constitutes fraud. Coupon is nonassignable. Void if taxed, prohibited or restricted by law. Consumer must pay any government taxes. For reimbursement submit coupons and proof of sales to: Harlequin Enterprises Ltd., P.O. Box 880478, El Paso, TX 88588-0478, U.S.A. Cash value 1/100¢. Valid in the U.S. only.

Coupon valid until June 30, 2002.
Redeemable at participating retail outlets in the U.S. only.
Limit one coupon per purchase.

108136

5 65373 00082 3   (8100)0 10813

HARLEQUIN®
Makes any time special®

HARLEQUIN®
Presents®

Seduction and Passion Guaranteed!

Save $2.00 off the purchase of any 3 Harlequin Presents® titles.

$2.00 OFF!

any 3 Harlequin Presents® titles.

5 2 6 0 4 1 8 2

HARLEQUIN®
Makes any time special®

HARLEQUIN® Blaze™

delivers Red-hot reads!

Save $1.00 off the purchase of any 2
Harlequin Blaze™ titles.

$1.00 OFF!
any 2 Harlequin Blaze™ titles.

RETAILER: Harlequin Enterprises Ltd. will pay the face value of this coupon plus 8¢ if
submitted by customer for this product only. Any other use constitutes fraud. Coupon
is nonassignable. Void if taxed, prohibited or restricted by law. Consumer must pay
any government taxes. For reimbursement submit coupons and proof of sales to:
Harlequin Enterprises Ltd., P.O. Box 880478, El Paso, TX 88588-0478, U.S.A. Cash
value 1/100¢. Valid in the U.S. only.

Coupon valid until June 30, 2002.
Redeemable at participating retail outlets in the U.S. only.
Limit one coupon per purchase.

108144

5 65373 00076 2 (8100) 0 10814

Visit Harlequin at www.eHarlequin.com
T5V6CHBUS
© 2001 Harlequin Enterprises Ltd.

HARLEQUIN®
Makes any time special ®

HARLEQUIN® *Blaze*™

delivers Red-hot reads!

Save $1.00 off the purchase of any 2
Harlequin Blaze™ titles.

$1.00 OFF!
any 2 Harlequin Blaze™ titles.

RETAILER: Harlequin Enterprises Ltd. will pay the face value of this coupon plus 10.25¢ if submitted by customer for this product only. Any other use constitutes fraud. Coupon is nonassignable. Void if taxed, prohibited or restricted by law. Consumer must pay any government taxes. Nielson Clearing House customers submit coupons and proof of sales to: Harlequin Enterprises Ltd., 661 Millidge Avenue, P.O. Box 639, Saint John, N.B. E2L 4A5. Non NCH retailer—for reimbursement submit coupons and proof of sales directly to: Harlequin Enterprises Ltd., Retail Marketing Department, 225 Duncan Mill Rd., Don Mills, Ontario M3B 3K9, Canada. Valid in Canada only.

Coupon valid until June 30, 2002.
Redeemable at participating retail outlets in Canada only.
Limit one coupon per purchase.

52604195

Visit Harlequin at www.eHarlequin.com
T5V6CHBCAN
© 2001 Harlequin Enterprises Ltd.

HARLEQUIN®
Makes any time special ®

Secret Passions

A spellbinding new duet
by

Miranda Lee

Desire changes everything!

Book One:

A SECRET VENGEANCE
March #2236
The price of passion is...revenge

Book Two:

THE SECRET LOVE-CHILD
April #2242
The price of passion is...a baby

HARLEQUIN®
Presents

The world's bestselling romance series.
Seduction and passion guaranteed!

*Available wherever
Harlequin books are sold.*

HARLEQUIN®
Makes any time special ®

Receive *The Art of Romance* absolutely free!

This wonderful collection of 30 romantic souvenir postcards will take you through a nostalgic journey of illustrative cover art, from charming Art Deco effects of the early 1900s to the crisper, more photographic style of today.

All you have to do is collect two proofs of purchase from any two TAKE 5 titles, send them in and you will receive *The Art of Romance* absolutely free! Harlequin will absorb all postage and handling costs.

Just complete the order form and send it, along with two (2) proofs of purchase from two (2) TAKE 5 volumes, to:

TAKE 5, P.O. Box 9057, Buffalo, NY 14269-9057 or
P.O. Box 622, Fort Erie, Ontario, L2A 5X3.

NAME

ADDRESS

CITY   STATE/PROV.   ZIP/POSTAL CODE

(Please allow 4-6 weeks for delivery. Offer expires June 30, 2002.)

PROOF OF PURCHASE

TAKE5

T5-POP

HARLEQUIN®
Makes any time special ®